D0443023

The Rogues' Game

THE ROGUES' GAME

MILTON T. BURTON

Thomas Dunne Books
St. Martin's Minotaur
New York

THOMAS DUNNE BOOKS.
An imprint of St. Martin's Press.

THE ROGUES' GAME. Copyright © 2005 by Milton T. Burton. All rights reserved.
Printed in the United States of America. No part of this book may be used or re-
produced in any manner whatsoever without written permission except in the
case of brief quotations embodied in critical articles or reviews. For information,
address St. Martin's Press, 175 Fifth Avenue, New York, N.Y. 10010.

www.minotaurbooks.com

ISBN 0-312-33681-0
EAN 978-0-312-33681-3

First Edition: July 2005

10 9 8 7 6 5 4 3 2 1

This book is dedicated to the memory of

my mother
Allyne Hocutt Burton
1917–2000

my son
George Walter Burton
1976–1987

my teacher and friend
George Nathan Oliver
1923–2002

THE ROGUES' GAME

ONE

It was a small city in Texas. The name doesn't matter. It's enough for you to know that it was west of the Brazos River and east of the Pecos, and if this description doesn't tell you anything, buy a map. The population hovered around fifty thousand for the first half of the century, but the war brought an airbase and the numbers soared while the local economy boomed. I'd been there for a week back in the fall of 1942 on assignment with the Office of Strategic Services, and I'd disliked the place enough that I intended to go back someday. There were complications for me when the war ended, and it was the spring of '47 before I could get my affairs in order and return. We traveled at night. It was late April, and already the thermometer was climbing into the high eighties in the daytime, but the nights were cool and the wind coming in through the open window of the car had a tart edge to it. Outside I could smell the mesquite and the sagebrush, and whenever we crossed one of the many little wet-weather creeks that cut up the land I caught the fine night odor of damp earth that means so much in that dry country.

About 10:00 P.M. I topped the last rise and saw the lights

of the city on the horizon. I glanced over at my companion. She was a weary-eyed, fine-bodied blonde named Della who stood a couple of inches over five feet and carried thirty-two years to my forty-three. We'd been together for the sixteen months that had passed since that cold, snowy night just before Christmas of 1945 when I first saw her sitting at the bar of the Mallard Room in the Peabody Hotel. Back in her younger days she'd been a Memphis debutante, but between then and now lay a failed marriage and a dead child. Not that I cared that much about her past since we each had what the other needed. What I got from the arrangement was frequent access to her lush little body and the unobtrusive companionship of an intelligent woman who loved long periods of silence. What she got from me was the willingness to get up and *move,* a willingness born of a restless energy that kept me from staying in any one place too long. This movement gave her a fragile sense of purpose and direction that had been absent from her life for a long time, and so far she'd been content to follow me wherever I led.

The evening we left Tennessee I paid for the car at a Nashville dealership. It was a 1947 Lincoln Continental convertible, painted a soft shade of cream with upholstery of dark tan leather. It was a fast, heavy machine with a twelve-cylinder engine that ran silky smooth as I glided away from the curb.

Originally my plans hadn't included Della, and there were a thousand things that could go wrong with my project in Texas and leave her stranded. Besides, the romance might sour on its own, and I have never wanted any woman I'm with to feel compelled to stay with me for lack of other options. These thoughts had hung heavily in my mind in the hours since we'd left Memphis. Finally I pulled over to the side of the street a mile from the Mississippi River bridge at Vicksburg. I took out my money clip, extracted five one-hundred dollar bills, then handed the money to Della and started to put the car in gear. She reached over and turned off the ignition. "What's this for?" she asked.

"Traveling money," I replied. "This time we're going to be a long way from home and I don't want you to feel trapped."

"I've got plenty of my own if I need to leave," she said with one of her rare smiles.

"Then spend it on yourself. Buy some new clothes."

She shook her head. "I've got enough for that, too." She reached over and put the five bills in my shirt pocket, kissed me lightly on the ear, then went back to the book she'd been reading in the dim glow of the car's map light. That's the kind of woman she was, and she'd grown on me fast.

The next evening in Texas when I came over the rise, I took her hand in mine and gently squeezed it until she woke up. "Hi," she said in a husky voice.

I pointed to the lights of the city in the distance.

"So that's it?" she asked.

I nodded and drove on without saying anything. The place had begun as a drab collection of huts and shanties that sprang up right before the Civil War on the east bank of the Rio Diablo—the Devil's River. Most of the year there was nothing about the Diablo to justify its name. It began as a thin trickle high up on the Llano Estacado and then flowed gently southward to join the Rio Grande many miles away. But with the spring rains it could swell from its banks in a matter of hours to fill its flood plain with a mad torrent that carried away everything in its path.

In the eighty-odd years since its founding, the town had grown until now it lay sprawled on both sides of the river, its two halves connected by a half dozen viaducts. The main drag was called Roosevelt Avenue. Before the war it was known as Texas Street, but the local boosters had rechristened it in a fit of gratitude to FDR for the airbase. Its eastern extremity had always been the saloon and red-light district. Called Buckshot Row after the favorite peacekeeping tool of a legendary frontier sheriff, it amounted to a handful of hot-pillow hotels and a dozen or so nightclubs. The clubs were gaudy, jerry-built places where soldiers and cowboys drank beer and danced and sometimes fought for the attentions of local girls and hookers alike. During the war when the base was swelled to capacity each of these dives had a back room where a couple of dice tables and a roulette wheel could be found. Back then the money was rolling in, and every street corner on the Row held a few whores and at least one skinny, rat-eyed pimp from Fort Worth or Dallas or Houston. Those days were long over now, and most of the joints were struggling to survive against rumors that the base wouldn't make the latest round of War Department budget cuts.

I drove on sedately through town. Traffic was light and the few cars abroad that time of night were clustered around a couple of cafés and the old Weilbach Hotel. The ancient, flickering streetlights had been erected when the first power plant was built not long after the turn of the century, and their feeble glow left the downtown shrouded in shadows. In the center of the city loomed the county courthouse, a grim neo-Gothic castle of native sandstone, complete with gargoyles, iron-barred windows and a roof of tarnished copper plating. Beyond the courthouse the business district soon gave way to eight or ten blocks of fine homes, most of them dating back to the late Victorian era when the place had been a prosperous shipping center for the cattle industry. The majority were in good repair, but several were beginning to show the effects of time and age and the town's ebbing fortunes. Surrounded by stunted oaks and cottonwoods, they still thrust their high-pitched roofs and prim cupolas into the inhospitable West Texas sky like a gaggle of old maids flaunting their outworn virginity.

I passed them with hardly a glance, then crossed the Roosevelt Avenue Viaduct that spanned the Diablo's floodplain. So far it had been a dry spring, and the river itself was but a narrow, placid ribbon shimmering in the moonlight. On the west side of town I stopped at a liquor store and bought two-fifths of White Horse scotch and several bottles of club soda. A mile farther on I found a tourist court that advertised water fans and free ice. It was a semicircle of small stucco cabins nestled in a grove of cottonwood trees, each with a carport and a covered portico.

"If the office is clean, the rooms will be too," Della said. She came in with me, looked carefully around, and then gave the place her nod of approval. When I paid for two weeks' lodging, the night clerk grabbed at the cash like a drowning man grabs a life preserver.

"No refunds," he said. "Please understand that. No refund if you leave early."

"Don't worry," I told him. "We may even be here longer than two weeks."

He went somewhere in the back and filled a thermos jug

with ice for me, then handed it over along with my key and receipt.

Besides a bathroom and a roomy bedroom with a sofa and an armchair, the cabin had a kitchenette off to one side in an alcove. I piled our luggage beside the bed and went to the sink and made us each a tall drink. I handed one to Della as she headed to the bathroom to soak, then stretched out on the sofa and took a long pull from the other, savoring the smoky taste of the whiskey.

I had no doubt that the payment of two weeks' rent would soon bring a visit from the cops. That's the way it worked back then in towns of that size. A man with a nice car and plenty of cash and a blonde with no wedding ring checked into a hotel or tourist court planning to be in town a while, and the clerk would call to report him as soon as he was out the office door. I didn't mind, though; I wanted a visit from the law because I knew just what kind of guy they'd send: the local bagman. But I was no stranger to dealing with crooked cops. Nor with criminals either, for that matter. After all, hadn't I come to town to meet a pair of old-time hoods named Icepick Willie and Chicken Little?

TWO

The knock came at nine-thirty the next morning. Della had just emerged from the bathroom wearing a black silk robe I'd bought her in Memphis the previous month. I opened the door and there he stood with ID already in his hand.

"Marne, Sheriff's Department," he said. "Mind if I come in?"

"Not at all," I said cheerfully. "I've been expecting you."

"Huh? Expecting me? I don't get it," he answered as he stepped into the room. He took the chair without being invited to sit, and I dropped down onto the sofa beside Della.

"Sure you do," I told him. "You've played out this scene before, and so have I."

A little lightbulb lit up somewhere inside Deputy Marne's head, and he nodded in understanding. He was a pudgy man of medium height, dressed in a tan suit with a red tie and a flat-brimmed western hat. His eyes were dark little marbles set in a round, doughy blob of a face that was as bland and free of guile as a baby's bottom.

"Then you won't mind showing some identification, will you?" he asked.

"Not at all," I said, and gave him my Texas driver's license. He studied it for a while, then handed it back.

"So what's your angle?" he asked.

"I'm looking for a poker game."

He threw his head back and laughed a braying little laugh. "No gambling here. Not in this town. It's against the law."

"I see," I replied, and nodded wisely. "Cleaned things up, have you? Reform administration and all that?"

"That's about the size of it, buddy." I said nothing. Instead I reached into my pants pocket and took out my money clip. Then I pulled off a nice crisp hundred like the ones I'd tried to give Della two days before and sat holding it in my hand, not offering it to him, but not saying anything either.

His eyes were on the bill. He licked his lips and started to speak, then snapped his mouth shut. He probably made one fifty a month, and back then you could buy a Ford or Chevy loaded with all the extras for fifteen hundred.

"Maybe the lady could take a walk," he finally said with a long look at Della.

I shook my head. I didn't like the idea of him coming in my place and telling me who went where. "I trust her with my life, so you'll just have to have a little faith in her too."

Della pulled her legs up under her, giving him a quick flash of soft, smooth inner thighs, a place he'd never be. Then she opened her book and began to read as though neither of us was in the room.

He nodded and returned his eyes to the bill. I placed it faceup on the coffee table and added another to it.

"You know, I could run you in for trying to bribe an officer," he said.

"That's right. You could. And you could also crack my head and keep the whole roll. Then a couple of days from now your boss might call you in his office and tell you that my father is a timber baron down East Texas who owns eleven sawmills and two banks, and that you don't have a job any longer."

"And none of it might be true," he said. "You might just be a tinhorn gambler with a flush roll and a big mouth."

"Right again," I said. "And that's the chance you have to take. But no matter what I am, if you run me in there won't be any more. At least not from me."

He nodded and licked his lips again. He stared at me in thought for a few seconds, then shot a quick glance at Della. She appeared lost in her book. After he zipped his eyes up and down her body a couple more times, he reached down with a short fat finger and a short fat thumb and picked up both bills. He folded them, and with a quick movement of his hand they disappeared into his inner coat pocket. "Okay. What's the story?" he asked.

"I wasn't entirely straight with you when I said I was looking for a game," I told him. "I already know where one is, and I want in it. I think you might just be the man to get me through the door."

"Which game?"

"The one that runs every weekend up in the Plainsman Suite of the Weilbach Hotel."

"Man, do you know how much money you're talking about? You'd need at least five thousand to even sit down at the table."

"I'm aware of that."

"You can front that kind of cash?"

"I don't have it on me, but I'm about to open a legitimate bank account and have some money moved here by draft."

He looked at me with a new respect. "Bank account, huh? Moving money by draft . . ."

"Can you get me in?" I asked.

"Yeah. It might take a few days. I'd have to see somebody that ain't always easy to see, but I could swing it."

"Good. Then here's what you do. Put that two hundred in your pocket and tell your boss the timber heir story. It'll pass. Tell him I'm a rich fool looking for ranch land to buy. Then I'll kick you an extra hundred every couple of weeks as long as I'm in the game."

There came a long pause during which he said nothing, but there was a greedy light in his eyes. The hundred every other week was what got him. He'd set the hook himself and all I had to do now was reel him in. "Is the story true?" he asked.

"What difference does it make if it's true or not? It'll pass if he checks on it. I guarantee that."

He looked at me dubiously. "I don't know . . . I really don't like screwing the sheriff out of his cut."

"Sure you do," I said cheerfully. "You're just worried about getting away with it."

"And all you want for the two hundred a month is just getting into the game and being left alone? Is that right?"

"For the most part. I might ask a few little favors along the way, but believe me when I say they'll be nothing you wouldn't do for a friend anyhow."

He thought for a moment more, and I could almost hear the wooden cogs turning over in his round ball of a head.

Then the ball bobbed up and down as he nodded. "Hand me that license again," he said.

I handed it over and he jotted down my name and number. "I'm going to check you out."

"Fine. I expected you to," I replied. I knew that when he called Austin he'd hear exactly what I wanted him to hear.

He rose from the chair and nodded at me. "Give me a couple of days. I'll come back when I have something for you."

At the door he turned, and asked me, "Say, you talk pretty smart, good grammar and all, like maybe you're a college guy. Are you?"

I nodded.

"I got a kid I'd like to be able to send to college. Where did you go?"

"Harvard," I told him. "Class of '25."

"Ahhh . . ." he said with another of his braying laughs. "Harvard my ass! You grifters crack me up."

I laughed with him and we had ourselves a grand old laugh. "But I went to law school here in Texas," I said.

"Law school!" he hooted. I thought he was going to choke to death. "That's too much. You ever considered trying to get on radio?"

I matched him hoot for hoot and gave him a brotherly slap on the back. He went through the door still cackling, convinced that I was nothing more than a roving gambler with a good line of con going for me. If it made him happy to believe it, I had no intention of wasting my breath trying to change his mind.

I closed and locked the door and turned to Della. "Let's go get some breakfast," I said.

When she stood, I gathered her into my arms and pulled her close. I stroked her hair softly for a minute and then gave her a light, delicate kiss on the lips.

"What's this for?" she asked.

"I just felt like holding you for a minute," I told her.

"You're always so gentle," she said and kissed me in return. "Maybe a little too gentle, sometimes."

"Get dressed," I said. "I've got to go make a phone call and tell Chicken Little the sky's falling."

THREE

Two days later Della and I met Icepick Willie and Chicken Little for breakfast in the coffee shop of the Weilbach Hotel. Little was a whip-thin man of almost seventy, about five nine, with cornflower blue eyes, pale skin and a fine-boned face. Dressed in a neat double-breasted suit and a dark fedora, he had a spare, self-contained quality about him, like a man who kept all his ducks in a row. His real name was Herbert Crosley Little, and his nickname had nothing to do with any lack of courage. As a point of fact, I never encountered anyone in my years of wartime service who had more nerve than he did, and I met Wild Bill Donovan several times. What had earned him the name Chicken was the fact that he was known all over the country as one of Oklahoma's premier breeders of gamecocks.

Little had been born in Oklahoma's Cookson Hills on a gully-washed fifty-acre farm that was almost too poor to grow weeds. As a child he watched his parents work themselves nearly to death trying to feed and clothe five children, all the while hewing dutifully to the letter of the law, both civil and scriptural. One evening when he was seventeen years old he lay exhausted in bed after twelve hours spent plowing knee-high cotton and contemplating a mule's ass from behind the handles of a Georgia stock. At that precise moment he decided that he would never again farm unless he was in the penitentiary and men were standing over him with guns. Having no education and no chance of acquiring any, he concluded quite coldly that his fortune would have to be made on the far side of the statute books. Soon he found a way to do it and still live with himself. Always an observant student of human nature, Little came to realize at an early age that some laws simply made no sense, going as they did against both the popular will and human nature. He believed that regardless of whatever ordinances well-meaning fools in Washington or Oklahoma City might choose to pass, one way or another men would contrive to enjoy the pleasures of whiskey, gambling and loose women. A southerner by both ancestry and temperament, he venerated women far too much to ever traffic in their flesh. Consequently, the only avenues left open to him were whiskey and gambling.

He had a few other interests as well, and a decade and a half earlier one of these interests had landed him in the Missouri State Penitentiary at Jefferson City for two years where he'd bunked three cells down from an intense young man named Charles Arthur Floyd. Before he left the pen, Chicken Little told Floyd that he should give up armed robbery, that it was a dead-end road, and he even went so far as to offer him a job. But Pretty Boy chose to disregard the advice, and within a few years he fell riddled with bullets from the guns of FBI agent Melvin Purvis and his posse.

Icepick Willie was Little's physical opposite—a big pink

blur of a man, soft and sloppy in a cheap gray suit and a dingy shirt whose cuffs were soiled and frayed where they protruded from beneath the sleeves of his coat. On his head he wore a threadbare tweed golfing cap pulled low over a pair of small, darting eyes the color of stagnant water. In his early fifties, he had a high, thin laugh that always seemed to have a hidden source, as though it sprang from some secret inner knowledge that he possessed and others didn't. I didn't know his real name and didn't know anyone who did. I'm sure it was on a police blotter somewhere, probably several somewheres, but I'd never bothered to try to find it. I'd been told that he was a peculiar individual, but the raw indifference with which he looked at Della almost made me shudder. This wasn't the reaction she usually drew from men, but she was of no more interest to Willie than a fireplug would have been. I'd never heard of him having anything to do with boys either, so I could only assume that whatever lighted his fires, it wasn't human. Which made no difference to me or my purposes. This was the first time I'd ever done business with him, and I intended for it to be the last as well.

When we finished breakfast, I gave Della the keys to the Lincoln and she headed off to find a bookstore. "Let's get some fresh air," I told the two men.

We strolled through the hotel lobby and out onto the street. "Classy place," Willie said. "Is this where the game's gonna be?"

"This is it," I replied with a nod.

The Weilbach had been built in the last decade of the nineteenth century by a cattle baron who wanted his town to have a first-class hostelry. It was fourteen stories tall, faced in sand-colored native rock with walls better than two feet thick. The lobby ceiling was a vast dome forty feet high, covered in Tiffany glass. The furniture throughout was heavy mahogany and walnut Victorian, upholstered in leather and velvet. Brass and marble were everywhere.

Its history had been spotty. The beef industry was just beginning to recover from the Great Blizzard and Die-Up of 1886 when a bad drought in the 1890s destroyed the cattle market once again. Thus the hotel opened in a grim economy and barely managed to limp along until World War I brought a munitions plant to town. It fared well in the false boom of the '20s, but fell on hard times after the Crash of 1929. For a few years during the Great Depression it was closed, its windows shuttered and its doors boarded up. With World War II came the airbase and rising beef prices. It reopened under new management, and once more its tile floors rang with the sound of boots and spurs. Generals and high-level Washington bureaucrats bellied up to the Longhorn Bar alongside defense contractors and prosperous ranchers. Loud talk and hard laughter were heard in the lobby, and every night the dining room was packed with successful, well-heeled men and their glittering women. Once the war ended, trade fell off and now it was struggling like the dives of Buckshot Row. I'd been told that the poker game upstairs was a steady source of welcome income for the hotel, with the management collecting a thousand dollars each weekend for the lease on the suite, a figure that didn't include drinks and food.

"When?" Willie asked once we were on the street.

"Probably four or five months," I told him.

"Shit," he replied. "Why wait that long?"

I threw a nickel on the counter of a sidewalk magazine stand and picked up a copy of the *Dallas Morning News*. Then I turned to face him, meeting his hard stare squarely. "Because I said so and I'm the one who's steering this deal. And because I know what I'm doing."

"Maybe you got cold feet and just want to put it off as long as you can," he said.

"Willie," Little said, his voice soft, "you don't want to talk like that to my friend. On that front he's paid his dues if anybody has."

Icepick Willie glanced at the smaller man. "I just don't see no reason to screw around for so long, Chicken Little," he said.

"Then you need to get out and let me find somebody else," Little said. "We're going to do it his way if it takes a year."

We walked on down the sidewalk. The day was bright and the smell of spring was in the air. There were new cars on the street, and the shop girls had abandoned their winter drab for the bright flowered prints that were fast becoming popular that year. A half block away the marquee of the Realto Theater advertised Humphrey Bogart and Lauren Bacall in *Dark Passage*.

"What's your hurry?" I asked Willie. "It's not going to cost you anything but a little waiting and a couple of trips down here from Little Rock. Other than that, you just go on about your business and we'll let you know in plenty of time when it's going to happen."

"I just like to move things along," Willie said belligerently. "And I don't see no need to wait no six months."

I stopped and turned to face him once more. "No, that's

not the problem. The problem is that you like to push and bully because it's your nature to do so. But you need to be aware from the beginning that it will not work with me."

"Better listen to what he's telling you, Willie," Little said.

Willie's face flushed. "Okay, hotshot," he said. "We'll do it your way, but just remember what the preacher says: payday someday."

"Yes, payday always comes, does it not?" I said with a lighter heart than I felt. By confronting the man so directly I had made an enemy of him. Afterward I would have to watch him. But for now I judged it better to have an enemy who would follow instructions than a friend who wouldn't.

"I'll be back down here in a couple of months," Little said. "I'm going to check into the hotel and spend some time there looking things over."

"Better not make it on a weekend," I told him. "There's no point in your being around when the game's going on."

"I know that," he said with a smile.

I looked at Willie and smiled and tried to make my voice as pleasant as possible. "You see, there's an ebb and flow to poker games like this one. A rhythm. Sometimes there's twice as much money on the table than there is at others. And then . . ." I shrugged. "Nobody knows why, but something happens, and for one magic moment they take on a life of their own, and then there's three, four, maybe five times as much. You just have to catch that rhythm. Besides, I'm the one who's going to be doing all the work."

By Willie's flat stare I could tell my little lecture had been lost on him. He wasn't interested in the poker game any longer. Nor did he care about the fine, sunny spring day or the pretty girls in their pretty print dresses. With him it was high noon on Testosterone Street, and he was the gun-slinger come to run the sheriff out of town.

"Need a ride back to your place?" Little asked me, break-ing the silence.

I shook my head. "I've got some things to do, then I'll catch a cab."

We shook hands in front of a Rexall drugstore a block down from the hotel. Willie smiled a beaming smile that was meant to look false and gazed at me with his muddy, lifeless eyes. "Payday someday," he whispered.

Needless complications. If they got too burdensome, I could make a call to Washington and Willie would be dealt out of the game.

"Take your time, son," Chicken Little told me in parting. "And let's do this thing right. Three months, six months. It's all the same to me."

I had no intention of waiting any longer than I had to, but our plans were soon sidetracked by something neither I nor anyone else could have foreseen that fine April morning. Even as we sat down to breakfast an old wildcatter named Coby Smith was drilling an oil well on a bleak, hardscrab-ble piece of land fifteen miles west of town. He'd bought the lease for fifty dollars and a 1935 Reo truck he traded to a nearly bankrupt rancher who hoped the ancient, wheezing vehicle would get him and his family to Texarkana, where he had the prospect of a job. Coby was in almost as bad a shape. He was dead broke and so overdrawn at the bank that he was ashamed to go to town where he might be seen. He had only enough diesel left to drill for two more days with a rig that was a piece of junk he'd cobbled together from smaller pieces of junk. His men hadn't been paid in a month, and one crew had quit him completely. Now he was re-duced to running two twelve-hour towers a day and work-ing as derrick man on the evening shift.

About the time I parted from Willie and Little the drill stem reached a depth of 4,162 feet in the Dalhart Sand For-mation, and its Hughes Tool Company bit broke through into a pool of oil slightly bigger than Manhattan Island. The well blew in, and in a matter of minutes high grade crude oil was spewing a hundred feet above the derrick top in one of the biggest gushers in West Texas history. Within hours the great Donner Basin Boom of 1947 was on and everybody, myself included, wanted a piece of the action.

FOUR

Della hadn't returned to the cabin when my cab pulled in at the tourist court. After I'd paid the driver, I unlocked the door and went on through the bedroom to the kitchenette, where I plugged in my traveling percolator. It had just quit bubbling when Deputy Marne knocked on the door. This time around things were a little more friendly between us, free of the tension that had marked our first meeting. And why not? I had him on the payroll now and we both knew it. "Coffee?" I asked after I'd ushered him into the room.

"Sure." He took it black and hot and unsweetened and drank it in quick little sips, his small eyes glowing with pleasure. "Say, how tall are you anyway?" he asked.

"Six four," I told him.

"Jeez!" he replied.

People often ask that question, and most of them are surprised that I'm not even taller. I think it may be because at 210 pounds I'm such a large-framed man. Or it may be because my hair has gone prematurely silver and they don't expect to see a thick pewter-colored mop on a man obviously in his forties. Or maybe they're just snoopy and it's one of those personal characteristics deemed socially accept-able to comment on. Who knows?

We both liked our coffee scalding hot, and we let the conversation lapse until our cups were empty.

"I think you're in," he said at last. "You just gotta go talk to one guy."

"Who?"

"The president of your bank, old man Rhodes. My con-tact fronts for him. That was a nice chunk of money you moved in here. My guy says as soon as the draft clears you'll be a pillar of the community in this town."

"Glad to hear it."

He gave me one of his quick, braying laughs. "At least you will be as long as your money lasts, anyway."

"Isn't that the way it works everywhere?" I asked.

"That's about the size of it, buddy. Now I gotta go." He hopped to his feet and went to the kitchenette where he rinsed his cup and put it in the sink. I started to like him a little then. It said something about the man that he didn't expect me to clean up after him.

"Hold it a minute," I said. "I need to ask a couple of those little favors I mentioned yesterday."

"Ahhh . . ." he said, his hard little eyes suddenly full of suspicion.

I shook my head and gave him an easy smile. "Calm down and don't worry. I told you I won't ask you to do any-thing you wouldn't do for a friend anyway."

"Okay, let's hear it."

"Della couldn't get a card at the public library because we don't have a permanent address yet. But they said if some solid citizen like yourself could call and vouch—"

"Say no more. It's done. I'll drop in on my way back to the office," he said, brightening a little. I guess he thought I was going to demand his boss's head in a bucket. That might come later, but by then he'd be ready to serve it up to me with trumpet flourishes.

"And she thinks maybe she needs glasses, so I hoped you might know a good eye doctor."

"Scopes," he said without even thinking. "Dr. Scopes. He's in the Wayland Building, downtown. My kid's near-sighted as hell and he's the doctor we use. Best in the city."

"And we want to get a house. Do you know a good realtor?"

I knew he would. Guys like him always know where to get it and who to get it from. He quickly pulled a notebook from his inner coat pocket and scribbled in it for a minute. "My brother-in-law," he said, as he tore off the page and gave it to me. "He's a straight-up guy. Deacon in his church and all. You thinking about buying?"

I shook my head. "I want to lease. Hopefully we can find something that's partly furnished."

He nodded. "He's the man to see. I'll call him and tell him to treat you right, deacon or no."

"Thanks." I followed him to the door.

"By the way," he said. "Did you hear what's happening out west of town?"

I shook my head.

"Word is some old guy brought in a big gusher. I thought I might drive out and take a look myself. Nobody ever heard of oil in this county till today."

"Gusher? When?" I asked with interest.

"Hell, right now. The thing blew in just a little while ago."

"Where is it exactly?"

"Just go west on Route Nine and you won't have any trouble finding it. Probably be a line of cars headed that way. One of the patrol guys said half the county is out there already."

I stuck out my hand and we shook for the first time. His grip was firm and dry. "Hey," he said, turning back just outside the threshold. "I told everybody down at the office that Harvard line of yours. Got a big laugh."

"I'm a clown, all right," I said with a big, sappy grin. "Say, did you ever hear the one about the traveling salesman and the two-headed farmer who had twin daughters?" I asked.

A few seconds later both of us were roaring with laughter. After I'd given him a parting slap on the back and watched him walk to his car, I glanced down at the piece of paper he'd given me. The realtor's name was just a name, but the sheet was personalized at the top. It read "Detective Ollie Marne" and gave a phone number. So his first name was Ollie. I liked that. It fit him. I folded the paper and put it in my wallet, then watched him climb behind the wheel and drive off. Something told me that Ollie Marne was going to be one of the best investments I'd ever made.

When he was gone, I went back in the cabin and unpacked and hung three suits I'd picked up at the freight office on my way home. I'd ordered them at a Memphis tailor's three weeks earlier—two dark blue of slightly different shades, one a charcoal gray, all three pinstriped, and all three made of summer-weight wool. I had to have my shoes custom made because my feet were size thirteen, D width. Since the first loafers hit the market, I hadn't touched a shoestring except on the rare occasions when I wore a tux.

I decided to get some fresh air. After pouring myself another cup of coffee, I took a Montecristo Corona from my travel humidor and went outside with my newspaper. To one side of our cabin sat a little patio with three wooden park benches arranged around a small concrete table. I lolled and smoked and read my paper, and my cigar was almost down to the end when I heard the crunch of tires on gravel. I looked up to see Della swing into the drive. The convertible top was down, and she was wearing a head scarf and dark sunglasses. I sat in silence and watched as she got out of the car and pulled off the scarf to give her hair a shake. It was parted on the left, and in the back and sides it fell to her shoulders in a golden waterfall that turned under at its end. That day she wore a pair of nicely fitted white slacks and a red silk blouse. I noted the graceful ease with which she moved, and as I watched her fine, firm bottom and full breasts I almost decided to cancel my trip out to the gusher. Almost, but not quite.

"Hey," I said. "You want to take a spin?"

"I've been spinning. Let's go get something to eat. I just had toast at breakfast, if you remember."

"We will, but there's an oil well I want to see first."

"Okay. Let me freshen up and get a drink."

"Bring me another cigar, please," I asked her.

When she returned a couple of minutes later, I opened the passengers' door and pointed to the wheel. "You drive,"

I said. "I like to look at a beautiful woman at the wheel of a fine car. It stirs me."

She handed me the cigar and cranked the engine. "So get stirred," she said, and slid her sunglasses on her face.

She was a good driver and a fast one, but soon we had to slow down to twenty miles an hour. The road was clogged with a steady caravan of cars going out toward the well. The last two miles we traveled took us thirty minutes to cover, but at last we came up to the edge of a low bluff that marked the beginning of the Donner Basin. From there we could see it, a mile away, blowing like mad. Some gushers and blowouts will crest and peak, then fall back to a trickle only to surge and blow once again as the pressure changes and shifts far beneath the earth's surface. But this one was pushing a steady stream of oil up out of the ground like an open faucet, and even from that distance the roar sounded like a hurricane.

She pulled over to the side and we stepped out of the car. "They're thrilling, aren't they?" she asked. "Gushers, I mean."

"You've seen one before?"

"Oh yes," she replied.

There's something dreadfully primitive about an oil well blowout, and I was hypnotized by its violence. We stood and watched the well for about five minutes until Della gave me a gentle poke in the ribs. "We've seen it. Now let's go do something about it," she said.

FIVE

We finally managed to get the car turned around, and when the traffic began to thin out halfway back to town Della started passing slow-moving vehicles on the right. And on the left. And a couple of times I thought she was simply going to plow the big Lincoln right through a snarl. I kept my mouth shut. In my view you don't tell somebody to drive and then complain about how they do it. Finally a couple of miles from town the traffic thinned out and the car surged ahead as she bore down on the accelerator.

"Your family has money, doesn't it?" she asked, the first words either of us had spoken since we left the well site.

"Some," I told her.

"Mine too. Do you have any of your own?"

I shook my head. "Just enough to live well from day to day and that's all."

"Same thing with me," she said.

She lapsed back into silence until we were almost to the city limits, then she turned her head and regarded me through the dark lenses of her sunglasses, the wind whipping her hair wildly about where it protruded from under the edges of her scarf. "Let's get rich," she said. "Let's start right now. Today. This very afternoon."

"I'd love to, but I don't know very much about the oil business."

"I do."

"Really?"

She nodded. "I grew up in the oil game. My dad was one of the pioneers in the El Dorado field up in Arkansas, and when I was in high school he was drilling in the Cherokee Outlet over in Oklahoma."

"I thought your father was a cotton broker."

She turned and looked at me for a moment, her eyes unreadable behind her dark glasses. "And I thought you knew that 'cotton broker' is a polite Memphis term for a damned old scoundrel who likes money and will take it anywhere he can get it."

I roared with laughter. She shook her head. "He's something, I tell you. Don't you ever play poker with him."

"Hey, I'm supposed to be sort of a pro at the card table," I said.

"You still better not play with him."

Without warning she pulled the car over to the shoulder of the road and skidded to a stop. Whipping off her sunglasses, she turned to stare directly into my face. "I want you to answer one question for me right this minute," she said. "You told that cop a few days back that you trust me with your life. Do you really?"

I looked into those deep blue eyes of hers and knew that this was one of those golden moments I'd remember until my last breath. Suddenly my senses were hyperacute. The very air itself seemed to hold an electrical charge, and the smells of the sagebrush and the soft new leather of the car seats baking in the noonday sun were sharp in my nostrils.

"Yes, Della, of course I do," I answered softly.

"Good," she said, and slipped her glasses back onto her face. "Now, which bank is the one where you deposited that draft?"

"Farmers and Merchants National. I'm supposed to talk to the president. He's a man named Rhodes."

She put the car in gear and roared back onto the highway with barely a glance at traffic.

It was an old-time bank, full of marble counters and bronze grillwork, the kind of institution where you might actually feel safe leaving your money. The place fell silent when we entered, and all eyes were on Della as she strode briskly through the lobby. "Go see your Mr. Rhodes," she told me. "I think I can get my business done out here."

Manlow Rhodes turned out to be a tall, slim man in his sixties, dressed in an elegant three-piece suit of dark blue wool that was ten years out of style. His hair was silver and sparse and his eyes were hard gray orbs set in a long, hard, gray face. A pair of rimless bifocals perched atop a thin, aristocratic nose that could no doubt smell bad credit and weak collateral as far away as a hound can smell pot liquor. His left lapel held a small diamond Shriners pin, and a Phi Beta Kappa key dangled from his watch chain. I had no doubt that in college he'd majored in accounting, and if I ever found out he wasn't a Presbyterian I'd lose my faith in the constancy of human nature.

His handshake was dry and bony, and when he waved me into the chair before his desk it was with the easy grace of a man who's been in charge of things for a long, long time. "Your draft cleared by wire yesterday," he said.

"Excellent. I didn't anticipate any trouble."

"So you like to gamble, is that right?"

"Yes sir, I do."

"Don't you ever lose?"

"Occasionally, yes. Everybody does."

He nodded. "I know, and that's why I never indulge in the vice. But I take it that you win more often than you lose."

"So far I have."

"The draft you left with us was much larger than I expected when Ollie Marne talked to my friend at the hotel. Thirty thousand dollars. For the time being at least, that makes you a substantial depositor in this institution. Therefore I feel obligated to tell you exactly what my interest in that poker game is."

"I couldn't help but wonder," I admitted.

"Who wouldn't?" he asked with a long sigh. "The simple fact is that the syndicate that owns the Weilbach has a large overdue note at this bank. That game has been going on up there for years, but a few months ago I learned that the hotel was only charging a hundred and fifty dollars a weekend for use of the Plainsman Suite where it's held. I forced them to go up to a thousand dollars. Many times that amount crosses the table up there each week, so why shouldn't the hotel profit some from the risk they are taking? Were it to be raided by the authorities the Weilbach's reputation would suffer, and the bank would suffer as well. That's also the reason that I demanded the power to veto any new players, and there have been a couple of real ringers who have tried to get in up there. I don't approve of the whole mess, to tell you the truth. But the game brings in a significant amount of cash, which has helped the hotel stay afloat. So, you can see why . . ." his voice dropped off.

"Yes sir, I can. But the question that's most important to me is, do I get to play?"

He gave me a nod that was a bare moving of his head. "I can't see any reason why not. Ollie Marne tells my friend that certain people down in Austin speak highly of you."

Before I could reply the door opened and Della swept into the room with Rhodes's secretary and a young lending officer trailing along in her wake like two rowboats behind a clipper ship. She strode up to the desk and laid a long, blue check in front of Rhodes. Then she put her hands possessively on my shoulders, and said, "I am trying to open an account here by transferring money from my bank back home. I told this young man that if he would call the Cotton Exchange Bank and Trust in Memphis, any of the officers there would guarantee any check I cared to write. But he insists that I will still have to wait until the check clears to draw on the account, and that just won't do."

Rhodes picked the check up and looked at it quickly. "Ten thousand dollars," he murmured.

He glanced back and forth for just a second between Della and me, then swiveled around and leaned across the desk holding the check out to the young man. "This gentleman here," he said, nodding his head toward me, "has more than adequate funds on deposit. He will be happy to guarantee the check for the young lady. Don't bother with disturbing anyone up in Memphis. Just open the account for her and give her access to the money immediately."

After the loan officer and the secretary left, I introduced Della to Rhodes. When she thanked him for honoring her check, he said, "Not at all, not at all. I just hope you enjoy banking with us."

"Oh, I'm sure I will," she said. "And now that you're my banker I would appreciate a word of advice, if you would be so kind?"

A soft murmur of assent came from the other side of the desk.

"Tell me, how many abstract companies are there in this town?"

"Just one. And it hasn't been very busy the last few years."

"It's not for sale, is it?" she asked.

"No, but I think it could be bought," he replied with a puzzled frown. "Why do you ask?"

"Oil."

"Oh yes, I had heard. Out west of town. I know very little of the oil business."

"Then you need to learn," Della informed him bluntly. "If I were you, I would go to Dallas or Tyler and hire some young banker who knows leases and royalties. When the East Texas field came in, the local bankers lost a lot of business because they didn't know enough about the oil game to appreciate its significance."

"Really?"

"Yes, and this strike is going to be big."

"You feel that strongly about it?" There was no sarcasm in his voice. It was an honest question from a man seeking information.

She nodded. "I was raised in the oil business. One more thing. I also need to know if there is a good surveyor, or a map company in town who will have plats of the area out around the Donner Basin?"

"Lipscomb and Associates Surveyors. They're on Roosevelt just three blocks past the courthouse."

"Thank you, and now I better go finish my business."

Rhodes got to his feet and walked her to the door and she quickly vanished back out into the lobby. After he'd resumed his seat behind the desk, he and I chatted for a few minutes, passing the time with meaningless pleasantries. Finally I rose and shook his hand once more. "If this is a good field the Weilbach should be in the black in no time," I told him. "It will certainly draw a lot of people to town."

"If it's a really big strike the problem with the hotel might not even matter anymore," he said. "You go on up there and play your cards anytime you want, young man. They'll be expecting you."

I hoped then that the strike would be big, and not just for Della and myself either. I had decided that I respected Manlow Rhodes the minute he committed me to guaranteeing the check for Della. He had strong-armed me a little there, and I couldn't help but admire him for having the guts to do it. It made me feel a deep sense of regret about what was going to happen in a few months.

SIX

I dropped Della off in front of the abstract company and drove on toward the surveyor's office with instructions to get plats and maps of everything surrounding the Coby Smith well site. I was back in an hour to find her hovering over a nervous-looking, dark-eyed young man in a brown suit who sat pounding away at a typewriter. Around them both orbited a fidgety older fellow in a tattered cardigan sweater and a printer's eyeshade.

"This is Mr. Wolfe," she said, pointing at the typing man. "And this other gentleman is Mr. Bobbet. And you and I are now in the abstract business."

"What?" I asked.

"We just bought Bobbet Abstract and Title Company. I think I'll change the name to Deltex Abstract. How does that sound to you?"

Before I could answer, she patted the typewriter man on the shoulder, and said, "We'll also need papers of incorporation for an outfit named Deltex Petroleum. But you can do those tonight."

He nodded and kept typing. She looked up at me. "Is

Deltex all right with you? We could put your name on it too, if you'd like."

"Oh, no you don't," I said. "What *is* he exactly?" I asked pointing to Wolfe. "And where did you find him?"

"He's an attorney, and I found him three doors down. He tells me he's a hungry attorney."

Wolfe looked up at me for the first time, his dark eyes sad. "Very hungry," he said. "I should never have come back here."

"Why not?" I blurted.

"Because this is a terrible town for Jews."

"I'm hiring his girlfriend," Della informed me. "She's a stenographer."

"She worked for me for a while but I had to let her go," Wolfe said over the mad clatter of his typewriter.

"I want you to examine this deed when he gets finished with it," Della told me.

I nodded dumbly. Bobbet looked dazed and I probably did too. When Wolfe finished the paper, he whipped it from the machine and handed it to me with a flourish. It was a simple warranty deed transferring to Della and me each a half interest in Bobbet Abstract Company. The building was not part of the deal. It was rented, so for the grand sum of four thousand dollars we were getting some decrepit office furniture and a room full of battered filing cabinets that contained summaries of the land records for the entire county. Bobbet was just signing his name when the front door opened and a tiny, dark-haired girl in a black dress entered, a notary seal in her hand.

"Mona, how kind of you to come here on such short notice," Wolfe said.

The deed was quickly notarized, Della gave Bobbet his check for four thousand dollars, and the place was ours. The young lawyer introduced Mona as his fiancée.

"Can you work late tonight?" Della asked her.

"Until I get some bills paid, I can work around the clock if that's what you need," the girl replied earnestly.

"How much do I owe you for the deed?" Della asked Wolfe.

"Is fifteen dollars too much?"

She produced her checkbook. "Not at all. And if I were to give you a retainer of a hundred dollars, would you promise that for the next few days you'll drop whatever you're doing and come running when I need you?"

Wolfe laughed and shrugged. "Drop what I'm doing? How can one drop nothing?"

"I take it that you mean yes?"

"You give me a hundred dollars and I will kill for you."

As soon as the young lawyer was paid and out the door, Della poked me gently in the ribs, and asked, "Would you please go get me a hamburger and then vanish?"

"Sure. Vanish till when?"

She shook her head. "I don't know. It may be late tonight so I'll just take a cab home. Get a burger for Mona too."

I went a few doors down to a hardware store and bought a coffeepot and a half dozen big mugs for the office. Stopping in at a grocery I picked up a carton of cold Cokes and a pound of coffee, then got them each a hamburger. I went back to the office, deposited it all on Della's desk and then left as she'd asked.

It was a little after nine that evening when I heard her key in the lock. She piled her purse and an armful of papers on the bed and stood facing me with one of her infrequent smiles on her face. "Did you know there's another well being drilled out there in the basin?" she asked.

"No, I had no idea."

"Look at this." She spread out a map and pointed with a pencil she pulled out from behind her ear. "It's a mile or more west of the Smith well. And look here."

She opened another map and pointed to where she'd shaded in several areas around the maiden well with a colored pencil. Just west of it lay a single large tract that hadn't been shaded.

"All this land that I've colored in is under lease," she said. "But this isn't," she said, pointing at the unshaded area. "It's the Havel farm. Almost nine hundred acres. Its east property line is only about a thousand yards west of the Smith gusher."

"And it's right between the two wells," I said.

"Yes, it is. And I want you to go out there early tomorrow morning and grab it."

"For how much?"

"Whatever it takes."

"Why is all this land around the Smith well already under lease?" I asked. "I thought nobody had ever believed that there was oil in this area."

"Oh, they think it's here, all right," she said. "But until today they thought it was too deep to drill for it at current prices. Humble Oil Company has been doodling around with the east end of the basin for years. Back in 1939 they drilled one well, and it turned out to be a dry hole. But it was out of the basin and a mile and a half east of Coby Smith's well."

"How did you find out all this stuff so quickly?" I asked.

"A lot of it is in the records, and I know who to ask."

"Well, how much an acre should I offer?" I asked.

"Humble got all this for ten an acre, but it's going to be higher since the strike came in. Start at twenty and give him a two-week draft. But get it no matter what you have to do."

One of the few things I knew about the oil business was that drafts were the normal way of paying for leases. By giving a draft rather than a check, the landman had ten days or two weeks to research the title and make sure it was good before the draft was paid by the bank. "What time do you want me to be out there tomorrow?" I asked.

"He's a farmer, so that means he's an early riser. Try six A.M."

"It can't be that early. I don't have any draft forms."

She gave me a quick smile. "I'm ahead of you," she said as she opened her purse. "I went by the bank. And I had Andy go ahead and draw up the lease. All you have to do is cut the deal and get him to sign."

"Andy who?"

"Andy Wolfe. The young attorney," she replied.

"Where in the world did you find that guy?"

"Like I said, three doors down. I just asked Mr. Bobbet where I could find the nearest lawyer."

"And you got a secretary thrown in on the deal." I laughed.

"Did I ever. And she's going to be worth her weight in gold. The girl has a natural instinct for running a chain of title."

"I wonder why she hasn't been working," I said.

"She was helping Andy for a while, but he couldn't pay her, and then she couldn't find another job. They've been desperately trying to get enough money together to get married."

"A marriage license is only a couple of bucks," I pointed out.

She looked at me like I'd grown a second head. "A girl her age wants a real wedding, silly. Especially in Jewish culture. It's all very traditional. I'm going to help her plan it."

I could have told her that her long-thwarted maternal instincts were obviously at work. I could have told her that, but wisely I didn't. "By the way," I said instead, "that was a slick move you pulled down at the bank today, putting me in a position where I'd have to guarantee your check."

She gave me a cold little laugh. "If you ever had notions of getting rid of me you should have made me take that mad money that night up in Vicksburg, because as it stands now you're stuck with me."

"How's that?" I asked.

"When that check clears I'll have less than a hundred dollars left in the bank in Memphis."

I shook my head in wonder. "When you plunge, you plunge deep, don't you?"

"Damn right I do. By the way, I went ahead and advanced Mona a hundred dollars against her salary. She works like a plow mule. I did myself a real favor when I hired her."

"Why tell me?" I asked.

"We're partners and I think you need to know what I'm doing. Now let's find someplace to have some dinner before this whole town closes up for the night, and then get to bed early. We've both got a big day tomorrow."

SEVEN

In retrospect it was one of the most important days of my life. I was getting sidetracked from my original purpose for being in town, but I reasoned that I would have plenty of time during the week to attend to my oil interests and still pursue the poker game on the weekends. After all, the poker game was intended to be a long-term project from the beginning. Besides, if a man isn't willing to get sidetracked long enough to get rich along the way, then he doesn't have much business being here in the first place.

Adolph Havel turned out to be an old Czech cotton farmer. He was about seventy and balding, with a thick, hard body, shaggy eyebrows and an iron ball of a head. Hospitable, he had a Mexican serving girl bring us coffee out on the porch of his house, a two-story sandstone structure with hand-hewn rafters and thick walls that must have dated back to frontier days. He also had an iron will to match his head.

"Already today has been one man out from the oil companies, but I won't deal with them," he said in a thick accent.

"Why not?" I asked.

"They vant to screw me."

"In what way?"

"They only offer to give me one-eighth of production royalty. I vant one-sixth and vill get it or vill never lease. In Loosanna dey give one-sixth."

"You've got it," I said firmly.

He eyed me suspiciously for a moment. "And a fifty-dollar-each-acre lease price, too."

I calculated quickly in my head. According to his deeds he had 887 acres. That came to almost $55,000. I only had $30,000, and none of it was mine. I closed my eyes for a few seconds and remembered that moment in the car the day before when I told Della I'd trust her with my life. I reached into my briefcase. "It will have to be a fourteen-day draft," I told him. "That's customary in the oil business."

Havel pounded his big fist down on the porch rail and said, "Vie haf deal. I vill get schnapps to toast. Or maybe you like beer?"

I should have taken beer. The schnapps was some kind of clear liquor that tasted like kerosene and kicked like a mule. I left Havel happy that day, but a week later he could have gotten ten times that amount. Yet I never heard a word of complaint from him. After the lease was drilled he realized so much from royalties that the original lease price seemed meaningless.

On the way back to town I passed the Smith well. Cars were still lined up along Route 9, but there wasn't much left to see. A half dozen trucks from a well service company out of Midland were clustered around a site, and the wellhead had been capped sometime during the night. Another company had brought in two truckloads of casing, and crews were standing by to cement the well in, all of it on the tab.

That was something I came to admire about oil people. The day before, Coby Smith didn't have enough credit to get an RC Cola and a Moon Pie at the little crossroads store a half mile from his drill site, but the minute the Midland company heard of the blowout they were on their way. They arrived about sunset and went to work capping the well without so much as a handshake. They knew better than anybody else that the strike might be a fluke, a small pocket of oil under great pressure that would play out in just a few days. But that's the way the oil business works. When a well is brought in, certain things have to be done *now,* things that won't wait until next week or next month after some gang of jokers has met and hashed it all out in a boardroom a thousand miles away.

I stopped for a late breakfast at a little café on the outskirts of the city. By the time I got to the office there were a half dozen landmen working away in the records room, and one guy stood pounding on the counter and yelling at Mona. He was having no more effect on her than the tide would have bursting against a granite cliff. She was utterly implacable. Maybe in a thousand years, but he wasn't moving this young woman today.

"Hey, fellow." I laughed, putting my hand on his shoulder. "Calm down."

He wheeled around and started to say something, then

noticed my size and bit it off. "What's the problem?" I asked.

"Do you know how much these people are charging to use their files?" he asked.

"No, I don't."

"Fifty bucks a day! Old man Bobbet used to get five dollars."

He was a soft-looking man, about five ten, dressed in a nice suit with a diamond tie pin and alligator loafers.

"Yes," Della said as she came out of the back. "And Mr. Bobbet wore moth-eaten sweaters and drove a beat-up old car. We bought this business to make money. So come up with the fifty dollars, or get out of here and quit wasting my stenographer's time."

He growled once more, hauled his wallet out of his pants and slammed a fifty down on the counter. "And I want a receipt," he said.

"Why certainly, sir," Mona said sweetly.

I followed Della into the back. "You've sure got things stirred up around here," I told her.

"You haven't seen anything yet. After this boom takes off I'll be getting fifty an hour, not a day."

"Della, for heaven's sake!"

"You keep quiet and let me handle this. Did you get the lease?"

I told her what I'd done and she looked at me in wonder. "But you don't have that much money, do you?" she asked.

"You said for me to lease it no matter what. I figure that if this turns out to be as good as you think, in a few days we'll be able to sell part of it for enough to cover the whole draft."

"But did you do that because . . ."

"I did it because when I said I trusted you, I meant it. All the way."

Her eyes got soft and misty. She turned away from me and dabbed at them with the sleeve of her blouse.

"Della," I said, putting her hand on her shoulder.

"Oh, hush!" she told me without turning around. "Go get me another hamburger."

We didn't have long to wait to find out the extent of the field. Three days later the second well came in and it was even bigger than the Coby Smith strike. The blowout completely destroyed the derrick and put one roughneck in the hospital with a broken back. Meanwhile a drill-stem test had been run on the Smith well, and it was flowing at the rate of more than three hundred barrels an hour through a three-inch choke valve. Had it been allowed to flow freely under its own pressure, it would have made more than twenty thousand barrels a day. The race was on.

EIGHT

"You don't know me very well," I told Manlow Rhodes.

"You're right about that, son," he replied. "In fact I don't know you at all."

It had been ten days since I'd given Adolph Havel the draft and I was in the Farmers and Merchants Bank trying to borrow money. I showed Rhodes my lease and my plats.

"Paying the draft is really not a problem," I told him. "I can get the money to do that on a few hours' notice. I've already had several offers from substantial men who want to front the money in exchange for a portion of the minerals I have here. But that's the best deal I can get so far."

"Then why do you come to the bank?" he asked.

"Because even if I sell . . . oh, let's say half interest in our holdings in the Havel tract for fifty-five thousand dollars, I still have to either sublease my remaining interest to another operator or pay part of the drilling costs to get it into production. And I can't afford to pay part of the drilling costs."

"I understand. What exactly are you proposing to me?"

"I want you to cover my draft and give me thirty days to

find a better offer. Hopefully, I can come up with an operator who will bail me out and cover the drilling costs for
half interest in the lease."

"Which would mean you want to borrow how much?"

"Twenty-five thousand dollars."

He nodded. "I see. Well, I took your friend's advice and
hired me a young petroleum man named Wallace Reed.
Let's let him take a look at this."

Reed was a brash, thirtyish fellow with crew-cut brown
hair and intelligent eyes. He examined the plat, then
skimmed over my lease, and muttered, "Damn!"

"Please, Wallace," Rhodes said with an indulgent smile.

"Do you know what this guy has here?" Reed asked.

"Of course not," Rhodes answered. "That's why I called
you in."

"Millions, that's what. This is the largest single tract anywhere around either one of those two wells that wasn't already under lease when this thing started. It's a gold mine.
And he wants to borrow how much against this?"

"Twenty-five thousand dollars," Rhodes said.

"If it's that good, then let me have thirty," I said.

"Why the extra?" Rhodes asked.

I grinned. "I haven't had time to get in the poker game
yet. I need a little money to play with."

"Poker," Rhodes said, and shook his head. He looked up
at Reed and raised his eyebrows. "So you recommend that
we lend him the money?"

"Of course we want to lend it to him," Reed replied.
"Ten times that if he needs it."

"No thank you," I said quickly.

"Very well," Rhodes said. "Draw up the papers and put

the funds in his account. Use the mineral rights as security."
He turned to me. "How long did you say you need the
money?" he asked.

"Thirty days."

"Give yourself three months," he cautioned.

"Just exactly what are you trying to do with this lease,
anyway?" Reed asked me.

"I want to find an operator who will pay off my note and
cover all the drilling costs for half of our interest in this
tract."

"I can help you there," Reed said. "Let me make a phone
call or two back to Tyler and I'll have somebody who'll do
all that in no time. Are you planning to lease any more
tracts out in the basin?"

"Della has picked up a few small parcels here and there.
Some of these speculators are running on such tight budgets
that they can't afford her fifty dollars an hour. So she lets
them use her records for a percentage."

"Della? . . ." Reed asked.

"She's the young lady who is doing so well with the old
abstract company," Rhodes said serenely. "She's been making some very nice deposits here lately."

"We're partners," I explained. "She was the one who sent
me out to Havel's to get this lease in the first place. I'm new
to the oil business."

"Mr. Rhodes, we need to talk about setting these people
up a line of credit," Reed said.

"We will, Wallace. We will." Rhodes looked across his
desk at me. "Are you a college man by any chance?" he
asked. "You sound educated."

"Yes sir, I am. Harvard, class of 1925."

Rhodes beamed. "I was Princeton, class of '03."

"I thought so," I replied with a smile.

"Thought what?"

"You're a Presbyterian."

"My goodness," he murmured. "Does it show that badly?"

Reed scooped the plat and my lease off Rhodes's desk. "I'm SMU business school on the GI bill and I don't know a damn thing about theology," he said. "So I'll go have one of the steno girls make up these papers."

"I like that young man," Rhodes remarked as Reed left the room. While we waited for my note to be drawn up, Rhodes and I had another nice visit. We talked about rowing and lacrosse and Harvard/Princeton games on snowy Saturday afternoons so far in the past that only an archeologist could have unearthed the records of them. His office was the perfect place for it—sedate and clubby with its walnut paneling and leather and brass. Who would have ever thought that in just a few days I'd be hauled in and manhandled by one of the most vicious sheriffs in Texas?

NINE

It's a source of amusement to me how religious bigotry goes by the wayside when a boom is on and there's money to be made. Before the Coby Smith well blew in, Andy Wolfe's prospects had been dim indeed. But now his proximity to the abstract company meant that his services were in constant demand by oilmen and speculators who were more interested in making fortunes than they were in snubbing an Israelite. He found himself called upon countless times each day to examine titles and help with tricky leases, and finally as a matter of convenience he moved his office next door. The landlord, who owned both buildings, agreed to build a passageway between the two. Workmen were sent over who cut through the plaster on both sides and then sledgehammered a crude opening through the brickwork. But such is the nature of an oil boom, and so great was the demand for carpenters and craftsmen by that time, that it was months before they came back to frame in the doorway and install a door. No one cared.

———

Within a few days of the second gusher Della was getting her fifty dollars an hour for use of the records, and the office was pandemonium from dawn to dusk. There were few complaints about the price. If a man was reluctant to pay, there were a dozen standing behind him who weren't. Besides, they always had the option of going to the courthouse to check their titles, and a few did. But this was a very time-consuming process. An abstract company has a listing of every transaction ever made on a piece of property going back to the earliest days of the Spanish land grants. These lists are either in card files or in large bound volumes, depending on the system that particular office uses. In this fashion a title can be run quickly, but at the courthouse it can only be followed by searching out each instrument, page by page.

But Della even dreamed up a way to make money off the public records in the courthouse. She identified five surveys in the basin where the leasing action was becoming the hottest, each of which was represented by one huge, thick volume in the record room of the county clerk's office. Then she made a phone call to a business college in Fort Worth. The next day she left the office under Mona's capable supervision and took the car and drove northward. I've always suspected that some money changed hands between her and the dean of the college, because three days later when the Texas & Pacific passenger train pulled into town, five of his most competent graduating stenographers stepped off the day coach. That night Della gave them detailed instructions, and the next morning they were waiting when the courthouse opened. Within minutes all five volumes were tied up for the day by a squad of brisk, no-nonsense young women who were preclearing titles. From that moment on practically every lease in the basin went through hands controlled by Della.

At first there was a great cry of misery from the assembled lease hounds. But since speed is everything in an oil boom, both they and the operators they worked for soon saw the wisdom of paying Della the premium price of several hundred dollars for a precleared and certified title rather than wasting valuable hours rooting it out of the records themselves. By then the irreplaceable Mona was making the queenly salary of three hundred dollars a month, and Andy was rolling in the money. It finally dawned on the two of them that their long-postponed marriage could take place, and Della and I attended their wedding at the synagogue in Odessa. Their honeymoon, a gift from us, was a three-day weekend in the Bridal Suite of the Weilbach. Monday morning they were both back at work.

Wallace Reed was as good as his word. Four days after I signed the note at the bank, he called the office to tell me that I needed to see an oilman named Layton Osborne from Tyler. Osborne and I met the next afternoon in the Weilbach's Longhorn Bar. He was a boisterous, heavy-bodied old wildcatter who had made untold millions in the great East Texas boom of 1930. He'd already been out to look over the lease and he liked it. After giving my papers a cursory examination, he took at face value Andy's written opinion that Havel's title to the place was sound.

"So what you want from me is drilling costs and fifty-five thousand to pay off your note, and for that I get an undivided half of all the royalties. . . . Is that right?"

"That's the deal."

He held out a thick, meaty hand that seemed as big as a

slab of bacon. "Have your lawyer draw up the papers. I'll be back in a couple of days."

"That's fine with me," I answered. "Where are you headed?"

"Hell, I'm going back to East Texas to find us a drilling rig. There aren't any available in this whole country out here. Don't you worry, though. We'll be making hole within a week." He quickly drained his beer. "Ain't this fun?" he asked, giving me a parting wink.

He was back in two days at the head of a convoy of trucks from Mustang Drilling Company out of Tyler. Before closing time that day our papers were signed and my note was paid off at the bank. Within twenty-four hours the rig was up and the well spudded in. It was a good well, and by the time it came in three weeks later the whole east end of the basin was leasing for a thousand dollars an acre. Frequently fistfights broke out in farmers' yards as lease hounds beat one another senseless over small tracts of land that a month before would have sold outright for twenty dollars an acre, mineral rights included.

Della got her library card, but she didn't have the time to read. She did manage to get by to see the eye doctor and he confirmed that she needed glasses. It took a week to get them from the optical lab in Dallas, but when they arrived I gave them my immediate stamp of approval. They were rimless with gold earpieces, and they looked especially fetching when she wore them and nothing else.

TEN

The weekend came and I made my first appearance at the Weilbach poker game. There had been a bit of lingering concern in the back of my mind that my newfound greed born of the oil boom was distracting me from my original purpose for being in town. Even though I wasn't facing a deadline, I had other people counting on me, people whose respect and goodwill I valued and did not want to lose. So it was with a special eagerness that I showered and shaved that Friday afternoon. After I'd toweled myself dry, I donned one of my new blue suits. It was double breasted, with wide, pointed lapels, and it fit perfectly; the tailor had done his work well. I picked a tie of dark maroon that matched the suit's pinstripe and knotted it around the collar of one of the stiffly starched cotton dress shirts I'd had custom made in a small shop in Manhattan. I folded back the French cuffs and selected a pair of gold-and-onyx cuff links out of the box on the dresser. With the addition of a matching tie pin and a fine Wimberly Panama hat, I looked like a prosperous executive. But I wasn't an executive; I was just a gambler who dressed like one because I've always believed that part of the psychology of winning at cards is rooted in looking better, smoother and fresher than your opponents.

Della had packed my overnight bag with a spare shirt, tie and underwear, along with my razor and a few necessary toiletries. About dawn Saturday I would catch a few hours' sleep, then shower, shave and change into the fresh clothes and be ready for another round at the table. Before we left the house, she made a couple of those minuscule adjustments to the knot of my tie that women always seem compelled to make, patted down my lapels, and I was ready to go. Fifteen minutes later she dropped me off in front of the hotel.

Except for the few years the Weilbach was boarded up during the Depression, the game had been held in the Plainsman Suite every weekend for over half a century. It had lasted through two world wars and a lot of history, and in that time it had acquired certain customs and conventions. It began at 6:00 P.M. each Friday afternoon and ended at precisely 6:00 A.M. the following Monday, or as soon after that time as the hand then in play was finished. Around nine on Friday night the porter called "Split the rent!" and the players who were present at that time were expected to divide the payment of the rent for the suite among themselves. It was then their responsibility to collect from later arrivals their share of the tab, though in recent months the game had run a surplus of several thousand dollars from which the rent was paid when the porter made the call. To try to shirk one's share of the rent was considered bad manners, and anyone who did it too often would be dropped from the game.

Each player who arrived was also asked to "feed the jenny" before he sat down at the game. This meant that he had to throw fifty or a hundred dollars into an ancient wooden cigar humidor called the jenny. This money went to pay the bill for food and drinks and to tip the personnel of the hotel for the service. The jenny also ran a surplus, and the service people were tipped generously.

The Plainsman Suite consisted of four bedrooms, a spacious living room, two bathrooms and a kitchen, all located on the top floor of the old hotel. The furniture was heavy and the carpets thick. Near one corner of the living room sat a round gaming table big enough for eight players. Its top was covered in green felt, and the chairs that ringed it were deep and comfortable. Nearby stood an elaborately carved rosewood sideboard that functioned as a bar. In the center of the room there was a long, deep sofa and a handful of plush armchairs. One of the Weilbach's waiters was assigned to the suite, and on weekends a cook was kept on duty around the clock in the kitchen.

The game itself was dealer's choice, but the types of poker permitted were limited to draw and five- and seven-card stud. Draw was rarely played anymore, and five-card stud was preferred by most of the players over the seven-card version, though perhaps every fifth or sixth hand was seven-card. It was a pot-limit affair, which meant that no bet could exceed the amount of money that was already in the pot. Theoretically it was a table-stakes game, meaning that no player could buy a pot by forcing a player out of the hand with a bet greater than the stake that player had before him at the time. However, this convention was a gentleman's accord rather than a fixed rule, and had been broken in the past, but only on the agreement of both players.

The regulars were a mixed lot. On that first visit the most interesting was a colorful fellow named Zip Zimmerman, a mining heir in his fifties who was chauffeured in each Friday from El Paso in a Cadillac limousine that was equipped with a bar and a leggy redhead. Zimmerman had been losing heavily for years, and it was said that the earnings from his gold and silver holdings piled up so fast that he had a hard time reinvesting it. He played a wild, swashbuckling and senseless game, sometimes plunging heavily when he held nothing and often folding when the odds were in his favor. He was there simply to have fun, and when he won an occasional big hand it was a matter of luck more than skill. He could well afford it, and the tension of the game never penetrated below his surface.

The rest of the men at the table were local businessmen and cattleman, and while some of them were at least fair hands at poker, only one of them was truly skilled. He was a quiet, courtly rancher named Wilburn Rasco, a smallish man in his late sixties, with a fine-boned face and weathered skin. A superb player, he was able to dissociate himself emotionally from the game, and when he dealt he handled the cards with a smooth precision. A gentleman to the core, he never crowed over his victories. When he lost he always smiled, but when he won his face remained blandly impassive.

I played on through the night and got a few hours' sleep Saturday afternoon in one of the bedrooms. Then I went back to the table until Sunday morning, when I decided to call it quits and phone for a cab. The cards never heated up and I won only eighteen hundred dollars that weekend. But that was fine. I wasn't there to get rich. Or to have fun either, for that matter, though I must admit I enjoyed the calm smile I got when I turned over the third of three tens against a pair of aces showing in a hand of five-card stud and raked in seven hundred dollars of Wilburn Rasco's money.

The only drawback had been that the man who was the object of my trip to town wasn't present at the table that weekend. But I wasn't worried; he was a regular and he'd eventually show up. Then the real game would begin.

ELEVEN

I'd been working with Ollie Marne's brother-in-law trying to find us a place to live, but there was nothing left to
lease in the whole town. So we bought. It was a nice three-
bedroom house of sand-colored brick, built back in the
1920s on one of the few shady streets in town. There was
nothing special about the house from an architectural stand-
point, but it had been centrally air-conditioned the year before, and this was its main selling point as far as we were
concerned. Della had left Mona in charge of the office that
day, and we were getting moved in on a Saturday morning
when Ollie Marne stopped by.

"My man treat you right?" he asked.

"You bet he did. We were lucky to find this place."

Della had bought three rooms of furniture in Midland the
day before, and the delivery men were there unloading it under her direction. I went inside and got Marne and me each
a cup of coffee and brought them out on the porch.

"You been playing poker?" he asked.

"Just once," I told him. "I've had my mind on other
things."

He glanced at Della, who'd just bounced out into the driveway in a pair of white tennis shorts and a sleeveless blouse. "Don't blame you," he said. He quickly drained the hot brew and looked around with the empty cup in his hand. "Want me to go put this in the sink?" he asked.

I shook my head. "Just set it on the floor. It might be best to stay out of Della's hair right now."

"Good thinking. So if you haven't been playing cards, what have you been up to?"

"Oh, buying a few leases here and there," I remarked casually.

"Buying oil leases, huh?" He shook his head sadly. "A little guy like me never can afford to get in on nothing like that."

He'd said it merely as a statement of fact, a bare reciting of what to him was an immutable law of nature, and his voice was free of the resentment such utterances usually carry coming from men of his class. I put my arm around his shoulders and walked him out into the street.

"Ollie, my good man, how would you like a chance to grab a piece of this oil boom?"

He looked up at me and then tilted his head a little to one side in thought. "You're not kidding, are you?"

I shook my head slowly. "No, I'm not. Tell me something. . . . Do you stay bought?" I asked.

"Usually. Why?"

"I want you to think for a while about where your loyalties *really* lie, and then we'll have another talk in a couple of days."

He turned to face me, his expression as free of deceit as it was of malice. "I can tell you right now," he said. "They're with my wife and my kid and my pocketbook. That may sound hard, but that's the way it is."

I shook my head. "Doesn't sound hard at all. A man's got to take care of his own. But what about your friends?"

He shrugged. "I got buddies. I don't know that I really have any *friends,* if you get right down to it."

We were at his car. "Ollie, it may be that you've been without a friend too long. I think things are going to be looking up for you from now on."

I opened the car door for him and patted him on the back. "You think about it and I'll see you in a few days."

As he drove away, I saw him look back in the mirror, staring at me as I stood in the middle of the hot, sunny street. A few weeks earlier I'd reeled him in. Now I was about to stuff him and hang him on my wall.

He was back the next Monday. Della was at the office, and I'd risen late and was in the middle of my morning coffee when the doorbell rang.

"I've decided that you're right," he said as soon as I closed the door behind him. "I need a friend."

"We all need friends," I replied sympathetically. I got him seated and poured him a cup of coffee.

"What exactly are we talking about?" he asked.

I brought out my briefcase and spread out the plat of the east end of the Donner Basin. "Right here," I said, pointing with my pencil. "This is the old Havel farm. Almost nine hundred acres. I've got it under lease, and we are just finishing the first well. What I'm going to do is give you two percent of the mineral rights on the lease."

He gazed at the plat for a moment, then looked up with a puzzled frown on his face. "I don't get it? Why me? What do I have to do for you on my end?"

I stared squarely into his dark little eyes. "Anything I ask you to do, Ollie. *Anything.* That's the price."

"What do you mean by that? What are you trying to get me into here?"

I shook my head. "Nothing you haven't already been doing for certain other people in this town, only now you'll be doing it for me, and you'll be getting paid decently for it."

He rubbed his face in thought. Then he reached into his inner pocket and pulled out a small flask. Quickly he poured a shot into his coffee and knocked it down in two fast swigs. He offered me the flask and I shook my head.

"How much money are we talking about?" he asked.

"The well came in over the weekend, and we've got three more planned. The geologists are saying now that the whole basin literally floats on a sea of oil. It'll take a few days to get the casing in this well, and then Brown and Root will take another three or four months to extend the pipeline down here from Odessa. After that the wells go online and you can expect a royalty check that will amount to between eight and twelve hundred dollars a month, every month, just like clockwork. And it will go up as new wells are drilled."

"Jesus Christ! For that kind of money—" He broke off and stared at me, his eyes big.

"I know," I said with a nod. "It's a brand-new Ford every six weeks, if that's what you want. Or a lot of other nice things for your family."

"How long will it last?"

"The geologists say twenty years, at least."

"My kid could go to a good college."

I had him and I knew it. I didn't need to say any more, but I'd been at this kind of thing so long that I had developed a longing for finesse, a desire to do things with a certain élan. An urge to gild the lily, some might say. So I asked about his child. "You keep talking about this kid of yours. . . . Do you have a picture of him?"

"Her," he corrected me, and pulled out his wallet. "My daughter." The photo he showed me was of a remarkably pretty little auburn-haired girl about ten years old whose good looks were marred only by the thick glasses she wore.

"She's a beauty," I told him honestly.

"Smart, too," he said, beaming at the compliment as he returned the photo to his wallet.

"So, do we have an agreement?" I asked.

"How do I know I'll really be getting what you say I'm getting?"

"We'll go to Dallas on your next day off, to one of the oldest law firms in the town. Fletcher and Reese. You check them out between now and the time we go. They'll sign a contract to represent you on this transaction, so they'll be your lawyers, not mine. Then they'll look over my paperwork. If it suits them, and it will, they'll draw up a deed and I'll sign it. The title to the mineral rights is guaranteed by a title insurance company here in town. You've got that and the reputation of the lawyers. So when do you want to go to Dallas?"

He didn't have to be told that we were going to use an out-of-town lawyer to keep our business private. "We're working ten days at a stretch with all this new stuff going on here in town," he said. "I'm not off till a week from tomorrow. How about then?"

"Fine," I said.

"But why me? What . . ." His voice trailed off.

"Why you in particular? Because you're a bagman for Will Scoggins and he's just about the most corrupt sheriff in West Texas. Which means you know where all the bodies are buried and who's sticking it to whom at any given time. Also, you can open certain doors for me quickly. To get the same level of services from somebody else I'd have to deal with either Scoggins or the chief of police. They would cost me more, and I couldn't trust them as much because they have their own rackets going, and they wouldn't need me nearly as badly as you do. And maybe it's also because I have a soft spot for pretty little girls with thick glasses whose daddies want enough money to send them to college."

I paused and let what I'd said sink in. "So are we on for the deal?" I finally asked.

He thought a few more seconds and then nodded with a shrug. "Sure. It's the only chance I'll ever get at a thing like this. But the one thing I don't understand is how you know I'll deliver my part."

"Ollie, I want you to look at me and think hard. This is very important, so take your time to decide. Do you *really* want to try to screw me?"

He stared at my eyes for so long I thought he'd gotten lost in them. Then he gave me a slow shake of his doughy head. "No," he said in a voice that was almost a whisper. "No, I don't want to do that, do I?"

I shook my head in time with his and we both sat shaking our heads wisely. We'd had a deep and profound meeting of the minds right then and there on that particular subject, and we were in firm and lasting agreement that Ollie Marne never wanted try to screw me on anything.

"I tell you what, Ollie," I said, breaking the silence. "You keep up your end and you're going to find out that Santa Claus really has come to town."

"You know, I can't figure you out," he said as he rose to his feet. "First it was poker, now it's oil. I wish to hell I knew what you really came to town for. You ain't here to kill nobody, are you?"

"That's it!" I said with a goofy grin. "You guessed it! You're on to me, Ollie. I'm here to shoot a pillar of the community."

"Huh?"

"Why sure! Killing upstanding citizens is a hobby of mine. I thought everybody knew that."

His face broke into a big smile and he gave me one of his braying laughs. "Move over, Jack Benny," he said. "You beat anything I ever heard."

It seemed like he always left laughing, so I laughed too and gave him the brotherly slap on the back that was getting to be like a lodge ritual. As I stood on the porch and watched him drive away, I reflected that sometimes the best way to lie to a man is to tell him the truth so unconvincingly that he just can't believe it.

Later that evening I sat reading a newspaper in the armchair in our bedroom. Della came out of the bathroom wearing the silk robe I'd given her, her hair wrapped in a towel. She stood at the foot of the bed with her back to me for a moment, then gave a little wriggle and let the robe fall to the ground, leaving herself naked. She treated me to the rear view of a long, luxurious stretch, then hopped onto the bed to lie facedown, her legs spread so that her ankles were a couple of feet apart. She raised herself on her elbows and looked back over her shoulder at me with an expression that was as old as Satan and as deadly as sin itself. "I thought the sight of my lovely bare carcass might give you some ideas," she said. "But it looks like you're going to read that paper all night, so I guess I'll just go to sleep."

I threw the newspaper aside and walked over to the bed. Shucking off my bathrobe, I stepped out of my pajama bottoms and reached down and grabbed her feet. I flipped her over on her back and crawled up on the bed to loom over her. "Oh, I've got all sorts of ideas," I said. "I just don't know if a little girl like you is up to them."

"Try me. . . ."

We did not go gentle into that good night.

TWELVE

Problems. The next morning I got a call from Icepick Willie. He was in town and wanted to see me at the hotel. I refused, but agreed to meet him at a truck stop café I knew a couple of miles north of the city limits. I found him there in the rear booth. He was dressed much the same as he had been at our first meeting, with cuffs that were still dirty and frayed and a tie that was a road map of stains from past meals. A large platter of sausage and eggs sat before him, and he was shoveling it down like there would be no tomorrow.

"I need some dough," he looked up and said before I had a chance to speak.

"Then go earn some," I said as I eased into the booth opposite him. "I'm not your fairy godmother."

He shook his head and forked a big piece of sausage into his mouth. "Can't do it. Things are tough up in Little Rock right now. We need to get rolling on this job here."

"No," I said emphatically. "I told you you're not going to hurry me."

"How about an advance, then? Call it a loan against

future proceeds. Chicken Little will tell you I'm good for it."

I regarded him coldly for a few moments, then asked, "Do you really need money or are you just playing games?"

"Hell yes, I need the money. What do you think? That I got time to come down here just to fool around?"

"Okay," I said. "I'll go for it." I pulled my roll from my pocket and peeled off a thousand under the table. I slipped the money beneath the edge of his plate and then got to my feet.

"Thanks," he said, putting the bills into his pocket.

"Just one thing," I told him. "Don't show up in this town again until we're ready. Not for any reason. And don't you ever contact me again. If you need something, then you get in touch with Little."

He stared up at me with his flat, unreadable eyes. "Don't tell me what to do," he whispered.

I put my hands on either side of his plate and leaned down so that our faces were only a few inches apart. "Understand me, Willie. This isn't some childish face-off between the two of us like we were kids on a school playground. This is for real, and there are forces involved here that you can't even begin to imagine. Forces that could sweep both of us away like a pair of tumbleweeds. Now you cut out the foolishness and stick with the plan or something's going to happen that you won't like. And don't ever call me again. Understand?"

We stared eyeball to eyeball for a long time until finally he gave me an almost imperceptible nod.

"Good," I said, and turned and walked away.

On Tuesday I saw Chicken Little in the hotel lobby. He looked as grim as an undertaker in his dark suit and gray fedora, and we passed one another with barely a nod. I wanted to tell him about Willie and his recent trip to town, but I knew it was a bad idea for us to be seen together at the hotel. Soon, I realized, I'd need to take a trip up to Tulsa to visit the old man.

I went out lease hunting the next day and returned in midmorning with the paperwork on a small twenty-five-acre tract that lay five and a half miles west of the second well. I didn't know it at the time, but it turned out to be one of our best investments, lying close to the center of the field where the pool was only thirty-three hundred feet below the surface.

I'd just handed the lease to Mona when I heard a commotion in the outer office. A few seconds later Sheriff Will Scoggins and one of his deputies pushed their way into Della's private cubbyhole at the rear of the building.

Scoggins was a tall wide-bodied man of about sixty, fat but with plenty of gristle under it. He wore a loose, floppy suit of dark brown summer-weight wool and a wide-brimmed cowboy hat with a rattlesnake hatband. He had mousy gray hair and a mean, sagging, jowly face with two bright little eyes set closely together over a great looming beak of a nose. A long-barreled Smith & Wesson Triple Lock .44 in a western style holster rode near his right hand.

I knew his record and it was a sorry one. As a young man he'd started his career as a city cop in El Paso, but was fired when caught forcing a burglar's wife to sleep with him in return for not arresting her husband. After that he drifted around the oil boom towns of West and Central

Texas for a few years, working variously as a constable and city marshal, taking his rake-off from the gambling and prostitution that always sprang up like mushroom growths in the wake of each new strike. Along the way he came up with the idea of returning home and running for sheriff. He won the election with the help of several well-heeled citizens who expected little in return from him beyond subservience and a willingness to look the other way. Now in his twenty-second year in office, he was overbearing and steeped in corruption.

After he'd taken Mona's arm and steered her from the room, he shut the door soundly behind her and then leaned against it. He ignored Della and gave me a long stare that was meant to be intimidating but wasn't.

"Can we help you?" I finally asked.

"I've got something on my mind that we need to talk about," he said in a thick, gravely voice.

"So let's talk," I told him.

"We've had some complaints about you two."

"What sort of complaints?" Della asked, casually pushing her work aside.

"A lot of people don't like the way you're gouging folks with this fifty-dollars-an-hour business."

"Oh, I see," she said, her voice tart and self-assured. "Well, I don't care what people don't like. I'm not running a charity here."

"You might not be running anything much longer if you take that attitude."

"We're busy," I told him. "We don't have time for this."

"Then you can just damn well take time. Do you know who I am?"

"No," I said. "But whoever you are, you could certainly use a better tailor."

"Wha—" he began, reflexively glancing down at his pants. Then he stared up at me with a sour expression. "I'm the sheriff of this county."

"Congratulations."

He wanted to shoot me at that point. Men like him are always enormously impressed with themselves, and disappointed to no end when others don't share their estimate.

"Sheriff, the abstract business is an unregulated industry," Della said. "I can charge a thousand dollars an hour if I want, and no one can do anything about it. You should know that."

"He hasn't gotten any complaints," I told her. "This is a shakedown, pure and simple."

"You need to watch your mouth, city boy," Scoggins said. He pulled a plug of tobacco from his pocket and gnawed off a chew. "And I better not have to tell you again or I'll haul you in for a little private session at the jail."

"What do you really want?" Della asked.

"Like I told you, a lot of folks are upset over this. You're violating the law, and it's something we need to talk about."

"Violating the law?" Della asked. "You must be crazy."

"Show me which law you're talking about," I said. "Let's go next door to my lawyer's office and look it up in the state statute books."

"It's a local ordinance," he said. "It ain't got nothing to do with the state."

"Ahh, I see," I said. "But if you wanted to you could probably put in a good word and get it suspended by the city council or the county commissioners court or whatever. Right?"

"I might," he replied. "But what you need to understand is that this is a tight community. You people come in here and you suck up all that money. Then you'll be gone when this oil deal is done, and the money will be gone with you. Folks resent that. That's the kind of thing our little ordinance is designed to prevent."

"And when was it passed?" I asked. "Last week?"

"It don't make no difference when it was passed. It's on the books."

"Then let me tell you something that's been on the books longer than your ordinance. *Freemantle Vs. Portland,* Maine, 1847. Winning brief argued by Rufus Choate before the U.S. Supreme Court. Other than Sunday blue laws and liquor laws, counties and municipalities can act in restraint of retail trade only in times of declared emergency, insurrection, and martial law, and then only with the consent of the state."

"You talk like a lawyer," he said.

"I *am* a lawyer."

"Then why aren't you practicing law?"

"You're a man. Why aren't you acting like one?"

His face turned red. "Are you trying to talk yourself into jail?" he growled.

"No," I answered. "If I wanted to land in jail I'd try to file a complaint against one of your pimp buddies like that boy did who got beaten to death in your lockup back during the war."

"All right, Mr. Big Mouth. Lawyer or not, you're coming with us. Grab him, Joe."

The deputy took me roughly by the arm. Della rose to her feet and started to say something but I cut her off.

"Don't worry. He just wants to scare us into coming across."

They cuffed me and hustled me out to a black four-door Ford patrol car and pushed me into the backseat. Neither of them said a word on the way to the county jail. I hadn't expected them to. The silent treatment is intended to unnerve the subject and increase his anxiety about his fate. It didn't bother me. I'm naturally quiet anyway.

It was a rambling trip that took about twenty minutes. We went out Roosevelt Boulevard to Buckshot Row, where the deputy went into two of the dives. He was back in a couple of minutes each time. Obviously they'd arrested me in the middle of a collection run. It surprised me that Scoggins would be running his own bag, especially with a witness present. I decided that he was even more foolish and arrogant than I'd been told. Finally my silence got the better of him. "You don't say much," he remarked.

I only grunted in reply.

The jail was a three-story sandstone dungeon that looked like it had been built in the Middle Ages. Scoggins's office was a pine-paneled chamber on the first floor, its walls full of guns and wanted posters. The desk was a big oak affair with a deep, high-backed executive's chair behind it. A pair of mounted steer horns hung behind the desk, and a framed blowup of John Wayne in *Tall in the Saddle* graced one end of the room.

The deputy unlocked the cuffs and slammed me down into a chair facing the sheriff's throne. Or at least he slammed me as hard as you can slam a man six inches taller

than you who isn't fully cooperating in the slamming.
Scoggins motioned him out of the room and he left, closing
the door behind him. The sheriff then took his place behind
the desk and regarded me like an Oriental potentate sur-
veying his domain.

"You got that wrong," I told him and pointed to the picture of John Wayne.

"Huh? . . . What do you mean?"

"Wayne always plays the honest lawman."

He was fast for a man his size. Like lightning he reached
across the desk and slapped me on the left side of my head.
I saw it coming and rolled with it, but his hand was thick
and hard and the blow landed solidly enough to leave my
ear ringing and my face numb. "You need to remember
who you're dealing with," he said.

"I always know who I'm dealing with. Are you sure you
do?"

He wrinkled his brow in thought and played around with
a pencil for a few seconds, rolling it about on his desktop
with his palm. "I was going to go about this by closing you
down for a couple of days," he said.

"What would that have gained you?" I asked.

"It would let you two steam a little and give you enough
time to think things over. But Ollie Marne told me that
might not be a good idea since old Colonel Garrison said
you're a straight guy. That made me think. Do you really
know Garrison?"

He was talking about Homer Garrison, head of the
Highway Patrol and the Texas Rangers. He was a capable
and honest man, and I knew that he despised Scoggins.
The attorney general and the Rangers had investigated

Scoggins twice, but they had come just short of enough evidence for an indictment both times.

"Why don't you call Austin and ask him?"

"I'm asking you."

"I met him a time or two back during the war," I said without interest.

I suppose he expected me to claim we were blood brothers. The fact that I wasn't particularly impressed by my own credentials seemed to puzzle him. "I don't get it. What in hell are you, anyway? An undercover Ranger?"

"You better hope not," I told him.

"Huh? Why's that?"

"When's the last time you heard about somebody slapping a Texas Ranger without finding himself in a world of misery afterward?"

That troubled him. Another frown furrowed his brow. "Somebody told me you worked for some government outfit back during the war," he said. "Is that the straight goods?"

I laughed. I couldn't help it.

He reddened. "What's so damn funny, hotshot?"

"You."

"Wha—?"

"You take a man who for all appearances is perfectly respectable, and who's been vouched for by the head of the state police, a man you think might have even been an agent of the U.S. government at one time. Then you try to shake him down in his place of business, and finally you wind up hauling him off to jail and slapping him around. Pardon me for asking, but don't you think a lawman who behaves that way is pretty stupid?"

He reddened even more deeply and was about to slap me

again when I stopped him with a word. "No," I said calmly. "Don't do that. Right now you have nothing to do with the reason I'm in town, but that could change, and you wouldn't like it."

He stopped and thought for a minute. While he was thinking, I took a Montecristo from my coat pocket and stripped it of its wrapper. He watched me as I put it in my mouth and lighted up. My absence of fear had thrown him. He was a bully, a man accustomed to having all the advantages in situations on his own ground where people cowered before him. Back in those days in Texas a county sheriff could get away with slapping just about anybody by claiming that the person in question had attacked or insulted him, but we both knew his efforts to intimidate me couldn't go far beyond that. Something told him that he was on thin ice in some way he didn't understand, so we just sat and stared at each other while I smoked my cigar.

Finally he spoke. "You know, a guy that talks the way you do could piss somebody off enough that you might have some real trouble."

I sighed and shook my head. "Sheriff, this is all pointless. We're going to keep operating the abstract company the way we want to and you know it. And we're not paying you any shakedown money, either. If you close us down, I'll just go get an injunction against you. Why don't you stick to leaning on your whores and your bartenders and leave legitimate people alone, and then we can all prosper and be happy."

"This is my town and I run it my way."

I laughed again. "You don't run this town any more than I do, and we both know it. That's not the way it works in this country. It's never one man. It's always a group, a power structure, and you're not really part of it. You may haul water for them and keep the sewers clean, but you don't run anything."

He leaned back in his chair and tried to understand it all. But before he could get it ciphered out, a deputy I hadn't seen before opened the door, and said, "Boss, I hate to bother you, but some lawyer's out here and he's got Manlow—"

He was interrupted as Andy Wolfe pushed around him and stepped into the room. "I want to know what you have my client charged with," he said.

"Nothing," Scoggins blurted in surprise. "I ain't charged him with nothing."

"Then what did you arrest him for?"

"I don't know that you could say that I actually arrested him. I just wanted to ask him a few questions."

"Then you better release him to me right now or I'm going to federal court in El Paso and get a writ of habeas corpus and serve it on your ass before you can sneeze."

"Why, you arrogant little shit," Scoggins growled.

I thought Andy had overdone it. The sheriff was rising out of his chair, probably with the intent of dismembering the skinny young lawyer, when Manlow Rhodes appeared in the doorway and stood there silently, his hard gray Presbyterian eyes pinning Scoggins back in his chair like a bug on a board. A long hush fell over the room.

"I was trying to tell you that he had Mr. Rhodes with him," the deputy said, breaking the silence.

"You *are* through with this man, aren't you, Sheriff?" Rhodes asked.

"Sure, Mr. Rhodes. We were just having a chat. All very friendly."

"Then you won't mind if he comes along with us, will you? We're all late for a luncheon date out at the country club."

Rhodes knew exactly how to rub salt in the wounds. Cottonwood Country Club was one of the most exclusive clubs in West Texas, and I doubt that Will Scoggins had ever been through the door. The idea of a scruffy drifter like myself and a brash young Jewish lawyer sitting down to a fancy meal within its sacred precincts probably enraged him more than anything that had happened that whole morning.

"Be my guest," Scoggins said, throwing up his hands in surrender.

As we went through the outer office, the clerks stopped typing to ogle us. A fat, tobacco-chewing deputy who sat in a chair tilted back against the wall froze with his spit can halfway to his mouth, his small, suet-ringed eyes contemplating us suspiciously. I'm sure that we made an odd trio to them, and I wondered how often they'd gotten to see a man who'd been brought to their jail in irons escorted back out fifteen minutes later by the town's leading banker.

Few things ever feel quite as good as getting sprung from the clutches of the law. I had been hauled in a couple of times back during the war as a part of my work with the government, and I had felt the same sense of elation each time I stepped back out into the sunlight. We quickly climbed into Rhodes's car, a 1939 Packard Club Coupe that had been so well maintained that it looked as though it had just rolled out of the factory.

"My thanks to both of you," I told them as we pulled away from the jail.

"Will Scoggins is trash," Rhodes said bitterly. "Someday he's going to overreach himself and I hope I live long enough to see it."

"Andy, it was certainly smart of you to go get Mr. Rhodes," I said.

"It wasn't me that thought of it."

"Who—?" I began.

"Your friend Della," Rhodes said. "A remarkable young woman. She sent Andy to the bank and then called me herself."

"What surprises me," Andy said, "is that he pulled this in front of witnesses."

"One witness," I told him. "He was careful to push Mona out of the room so there were just the two of us and the two of them. And they were cops."

"It's an old story in this town." Rhodes said. "Now let's go have that lunch."

THIRTEEN

On our way we swung by the office so I could assure Della that I hadn't been murdered. Andy begged off lunch, claiming he had too much work to do. The Cottonwood Country Club turned out to be a sprawling building of tan brick surrounded by several hundred acres of golf course just south of the city limits. The big Packard whisked quietly up the curving drive to the front portico and stopped. Rhodes turned the car over to a liveried Mexican attendant, and soon we were seated in the dining room. It was regal, with brocade-covered walls, stiff white linen and sparkling crystal.

My host asked for a weak bourbon and water and I took a strong scotch and soda. We both ordered prime rib with asparagus and a garden salad.

"I wish Andy could have come with us," Rhodes said.

"I do too," I agreed. "I liked him from the first time I met him, but he certainly earned himself a lasting place in my heart today. It looked for a minute there as though he was going to fight Will Scoggins right in his own office. And I must admit that you're quickly becoming one of my favorite people too," I finished with a grin.

"Think nothing of it," he replied. "And you're right about one thing. . . . Andy might well have fought Scoggins. That young man is the real thing. Tough as a boot."

"What's the story on him?"

"He's a local boy, and his father ran a hardware store here in town. Andy went to the University of Texas and was almost through law school when Pearl Harbor was bombed. He joined up, fought in Europe, and had an impressive combat record. After the war, he finished his education, passed the bar, and then his father died. He had to come back home and take care of his mother. It's that simple. He could be very successful in Dallas or Houston or even Tyler, but the poor old woman is a semi-invalid and she refuses to leave town. All her friends are here, so I suppose I understand."

"How about Mona?" I asked.

"Basically the same story. Her parents were also merchants, but they both died when she was in high school and she couldn't afford college. So she went to stenography school over in Fort Worth."

"Are there many Jews here in town?"

He shook his head. "Only a half dozen or so families. And there is considerable prejudice against them. Years ago I proposed Andy's father for membership in this club, but he received eight blackballs. Yet some of those very same men socialized with him at the Masonic Lodge. Aren't people fools sometimes?"

"Indeed they are," I agreed.

The waitress was back with our drinks. "Well, you've certainly had an interesting morning," my host said when she'd left the table.

"Yes, and I really do apologize for bothering you about this business."

"Think nothing of it," he said with a tight smile. "It was the right thing to do."

"Why do the people here tolerate a brute like Scoggins?" I asked.

"It's a complicated matter."

"I'm a good listener."

He sighed and took a long breath. "There are two factions in this city. I represent one. It's the older and I think the more decent of the two, if I may be so foolish as to use such a word. I represent the faction that would like to see this town run as fairly as possible. My friends and I are willing to tolerate the dives and the prostitutes and the gambling dens because that's how people choose to amuse themselves, however regrettable it might be. But we don't want them to be the sort of places where working men and soldiers are skinned at crooked tables or rolled by pimps, and then beaten senseless and thrown in jail by crooked cops who are hand-in-glove with the hoods. That is exactly the state of affairs we have now, and there is a substantial cadre of influential people here in town who're content with the situation. But what the idiots don't understand is that they are terribly shortsighted. However, they contribute generously to Scoggins campaign, and he makes it a policy never to agitate those who support him."

"Shortsighted? In what way?" I asked.

"Take the airbase, for example. If it's closed, the reason will have less to do with War Department cuts than the way the base personnel have been treated in the dens and whorehouses over the years. Did you know that two young airmen died in the jail under questionable circumstances back during the war?"

"I had heard about one of them, but I'm not surprised there were more."

"And it's happened with civilians too. But this stunt to-day was a new low, even for Scoggins. It's the first time he's ever tried to shake down a legitimate business so openly. The way his mind works he just couldn't stand to see two outsiders doing as well as you two are."

"Do many of the businesses in town pay him off?" I asked.

"A few. But until now it's always been more a matter of goodwill than outright extortion."

"Do you think I have anything to worry about from him tomorrow or next week or next month?" I asked.

He shook his head and smiled. "Let me tell you a little story about Will Scoggins. About twenty years ago he got into an altercation with a young man one night out at the county fair. It was sordid thing, really. Scoggins had been trying for some time to seduce a young woman who'd been working down at Wilson's Ice Cream Parlor on the square. He was married at the time, of course, but back in those days he had the reputation of pursuing every unattached female who appealed to him. This young woman would have nothing to do with him, and eventually she began dating a fellow from out south of town, the son of an Irish immigrant who had become prosperous as a sheep rancher. At any rate, Scoggins jumped this boy one night at the fair, and Scoggins wasn't wearing his gun. It was a personal thing that had nothing to do with his capacity as a lawman, and the long and short of it was that the young Irishman beat him to a pulp in front of at least a hundred people. To add insult to injury, the boy was about four inches shorter than Scoggins and probably fifty pounds lighter in weight. But the point of my story is that at the time I didn't know Scoggins as well as I do now, and I wouldn't have given ten cents for that young man's life. In fact, a friend and I tried to get him to leave town, but he refused."

"What happened to him?" I asked.

"Nothing. Nothing at all. I felt sure that Scoggins would exact some kind of horrible retribution, perhaps even murder him, but he never lifted a finger against the kid. A few months later the young man married the girl from the ice cream parlor, and he still runs the family ranch. So my answer to your question is no. You have nothing to worry about from Will Scoggins unless I do too. My feeling is that now that he's aware that you are an associate of mine he won't bother you anymore."

"I hope not. This is not what I had in mind when I moved here. It's a nuisance."

"Not the sort of thing you studied for at Harvard, eh?" he laughed. "By the way, have you met Clifton Robillard yet?"

Suddenly I was very alert. "No, but I've heard that he's a regular player at the Weilbach game. I've also heard that he gambles heavily on sporting events of all kinds."

"He does, and he's lucky. He's also one of the powers behind Will Scoggins."

"You don't say. . . ."

"Indeed," Rhodes said. "You see, he's the major stockholder in the other bank in town, Mercantile State. But beyond that, he's the chief landlord down on Buckshot Row.

It's a matter of public record that he owns several of the buildings where the dives and whorehouses are located, but the rumor is that he has interests in the businesses themselves as well."

"Fascinating. I'm looking forward to meeting him. What's he like personally?"

"He has decent enough manners, though he doesn't always use them," Rhodes said. "And he's quite a womanizer."

"What do you know about Ollie Marne?" I asked, changing the subject.

He looked at me slyly. "What's your interest in Ollie?"

"Oh, I've met him a couple of times and I was just wondering."

"Ollie rides the fence between the two factions. That's about all a man in his position can do. Have you and Ollie become friends by any chance?"

"Something like that."

"And does Ollie see your friendship as a positive asset to him?"

"Very much so," I answered.

"Then I believe you can trust him. I truly think that Ollie would like to be a better man than his job and the circumstances in this town will allow him to be. And he's really an excellent peace officer in some ways."

"Really?" I asked, somewhat surprised.

He nodded. "He's a good investigator, and he's not lacking in physical courage. The opposite is true of Scoggins. He's a braggart and a damned coward."

Our food came and we lapsed into pleasantries. At the end of the meal Rhodes leaned back in his chair and gave me a thoughtful stare. "All this business may change. This oil boom is going to bring a new class of men to this town, men who won't stand still for Scoggins and his shake-downs." I nodded.

"You're right, Mr. Rhodes, and I'm one of them. That's why I asked if you thought he would be any further threat to me. I have ways to protect myself from a man like him."

"I don't doubt that you do," he said with a knowing smile. "Scoggins is going to have to adjust to changing con-ditions. We all are."

We finished our coffee and Rhodes drove me back to the office. I thanked him once again for bailing me out of trou-ble. "Think nothing of it," he told me. "The next time we go to lunch I'll bring my wife and we can make it a foursome with your lady friend."

"I gave Mona another raise," Della told me that night. I'd just come out of the bathroom. She was bundled up under the covers with only her head and one book-laden hand sticking out.

"Details," I said with a long sigh. "What is it with you women and details?"

"You own half the business and I like to include you in decisions."

"Okay, so I am now officially included. If you think she needs a raise, it's fine with me."

"It's not a matter of her needing it. It's that she deserves it. I'd be lost without her. By the way, don't you know how to play bridge?"

"Sure. I'm only so-so at it, though."

"Me too, but Mona tells me that she and Andy love it

and don't really have anybody to play with. I thought about having them over some evening for a few rubbers. Is that too much card playing for you?"

I shook my head. "Not at all. I can relax playing bridge. Poker's fun, but it's work too."

"Then I'll invite them soon. I'd really like to get to know them better."

"I like them too, and I think we ought to do something else as soon as possible."

"What?" she asked.

"You're getting slow in your old age," I told her as I flopped down on the bed and slipped my hand under the covers. "What are you wearing under there?"

"Nothing," she said, and stuck out her tongue at me. "And you're the one that's slow. I've been buck naked for the last thirty minutes and you never noticed."

"How would I notice? You're all covered up."

"That's certainly not my fault."

FOURTEEN

Unless you've lived through an oil boom you can't begin to appreciate either the swiftness with which it unfolds or the speed at which fortunes are made. When the Daisy Bradford Number 3 well in Rusk County ushered in the great East Texas Field in October of 1930, the population of the village of Kilgore shot up from seven hundred to ten thousand in just two weeks. The Donner Basin discovery wasn't far behind it in drawing people to town. In the weeks after the Smith strike every train that pulled into the depot carried roughnecks and roustabouts and their families. They also came in cars and trucks and by wagon, and a few even came on foot. Tent cities sprang up overnight at the edges of town, and the dives of Buckshot Row began to thrive once again as legions of whores and pimps and gamblers swept in behind the workmen and promoters. The rumble of engines was constant as trucks hauling drilling rigs and equipment rattled through the streets at all hours of the day and night.

There was money to be made everywhere. A hamburger that brought a quarter the day Della and I hit town now went for a buck, and a five-dollar room in a cheap tourist court rented for fifty if you were lucky enough to find one. The Weilbach was booked solid by oilmen who paid by the month and paid ahead of time. One wealthy operator named Simon Van Horn hauled out his checkbook and leased the Presidential Suite for a year in advance, and a couple of other men made similar arrangements for smaller suites. An enterprising young capitalist bought five acres of mesquite jungle on the south edge of town, bulldozed away the undergrowth and installed thirty-five shabby, road-worn travel trailers which he advertised to let at fifty dollars a week. They were all rented by nightfall of the day he put up his sign.

The municipal utilities couldn't keep pace with the influx of people, and twice the city reservoir ran completely dry. Drinking water had to be trucked in from Midland and Odessa, and at the worst of the shortage a gallon of distilled water sold for five dollars. I bought a half dozen five-gallon jerry cans, and several times had to buy water at two dollars a gallon from a sharp old farmer south of town who had a natural artesian spring on his property. During the worst of the shortage Della and I had to make do with spit baths for a week, and I was grateful that our house had air conditioning or we wouldn't have been able to stand our own stench. Membership in the YMCA skyrocketed as droves of people joined so they could use the pool to bathe under the pretext of swimming. The city hired a civil engineer to deal with the problems, and after a week of calculations he told the council that at the rate the population was growing they would need five new deep wells if the town was to survive.

Crime rates soared. Knifings and shootings became an everyday occurrence. A second red-light and honky-tonk district sprang up, this one outside the city limit on the west side of town. It was thrown together in less than a month with sheet iron and green pine lumber in a ten-acre dry wash where an old Basque herdsman had once kept livestock. Soon it became known as Nanny Goat Gully, and for a while it had the highest crime rate of any area its size in the country. But few people really cared because the money was rolling it. At last the disorder reached such a point that Manlow Rhodes led a delegation of concerned citizens to Austin to ask the governor for help. Specifically, they wanted a declaration of martial law. There was ample precedent for such an action. In 1922 Gov. Pat Neff had imposed martial law in Sweetwater when an earlier oil boom destroyed civil order in that town. Similarly, Gov. Ross Sterling had sent the National Guard into the East Texas Field in 1932. But unfortunately the present governor was neither Neff nor Sterling. Instead he was a plump, handsome glad-hander named Buford Halbert Jester. Called Beautiful Buford with the Marcelled Hair, he was an intelligent but weak man who wanted nothing more than to attend testimonial dinners and bask in the love of the people while he bedded every young Capitol secretary who could be wheedled out of her panties by his golden-throated voice. When the delegation arrived at his office, he listened patiently to their complaints, all the while nodding in sympathy, his noble brow creased in a frown of manly concern. Afterward, he read a lengthy prepared statement to them and the assembled press. When its convoluted syntax was unraveled, it was found to contain little more than the assurance that the governor was in favor of virtue and against sin. Martial law was not forthcoming.

A week later Col. Homer Garrison sent Bob Crowder and ten other Texas Rangers into town on his own initiative. They arrived just after sunset one hot evening on the Texas & Pacific Thunderbolt, their rifles on their shoulders and their horses in a special car attached to the rear of the train. Within an hour they were patrolling Buckshot Row and Nanny Goat Gully. Their methods were often ruthless, but as Crowder later told the press, they hadn't been sent to town to organize a debating society. Crime rates fell as the worst of the hoods and thugs who'd seeped into the community fled before they had occasion to clash with Crowder and his men. Still, in the first two weeks they arrested more than sixty individuals who were wanted in Texas and other states for serious felonies, and that number included a handful of murderers. The Rangers' efforts were hampered by the fact that without a declaration of martial law they had to cooperate with local law enforcement, and local law enforcement meant a sheriff's department headed by Will Scoggins, a man fully as corrupt as the elements he was paid to control. But I was not without a friend even in that savage land, and that friend was named Ollie Marne.

I played again at the Weilbach that weekend, but the man I'd come to town to see wasn't there that time either. Near midnight Saturday evening I felt that I had come to know Wilburn Rasco well enough to make a friendly inquiry. "Say, what about this Robillard that people keep telling me about?" I asked.

He gave me a sharp glance. "Do you know Clifton?"

I shook my head. "No, but I've heard around town that he's one of the big players in this game."

"Aren't you taking enough off me to satisfy you?"

"Hah!" I answered with a rueful smile. "I seem to be down about a thousand to you right now. Actually, I'd hoped that Robillard might prove to be easier pickings. I've been told that he's quite a gambler."

"He is, and he's a fair hand at the poker table. But I think his business dealings have kept him busy the last few weeks."

"Really?"

"Yeah. He teamed up with a fellow from Fillmore, and the two of them have been wheeling and dealing in oil leases since this strike began."

"Is that so?" I asked. "And just who is this gentleman from Fillmore?"

"Name's Simon Van Horn. Ever heard of him?"

I shook my head and changed the subject. I'd told the truth; I'd never heard of Van Horn, but I planned to find out about him as soon as I could.

Wednesday came and I took Marne to Dallas and gave him a look into a whole new world. After my run-in with Scoggins, I thought it better that we not be seen openly together in town, so we arranged to meet early that morning at a crossroads store on the north side of the county. Marne left his car there and we drove the rest of the way in my Lincoln. A wave of postwar idealism had swept through the country, and Dallas was in the middle of one of its periodic reform binges. The previous year a young combat veteran named Steve Guthrie had been elected sheriff on a platform that pledged to run all the hoods out of town. He was doing a fair job of living up to that promise. The Italian crime syndicates had never really gotten a strong foothold in Texas because the powers that be, who never wanted them here in the first place, allowed the local law enforcement and the Texas Rangers free rein when dealing with out-of-state thugs. Their efforts were matched by the ferocity with which such homegrown mobsters as Herbert Noble and Benny Benion defended their territories. These two men had been at war with each other over the control of organized gambling in Dallas since 1938, but now Guthrie was putting considerable pressure on both operations. Illegal casinos had been raided and closed, and the state's liquor laws were being rigidly enforced. But Dallas is Dallas, and I gave the reformers about eighteen more months before the citizenry grew weary of this overabundance of virtue and returned things to normal.

We pulled into town at lunchtime, and soon we were feasting on rare prime beef in the dining room of the Adolphus Hotel. After our meal I took him to the offices of Fletcher & Reese on the twelfth floor of the Magnolia Building. I could tell it was his first visit to a premier big-city law firm. I watched his eyes run over the polished mahogany walls and the rich Oriental carpets, and before long an exquisitely clad secretary ushered us into the office of one of the senior partners, Elwood Fletcher himself. Fletcher had done some work for Bill Donovan during the war, and he and I were well acquainted. A little taller and heavier that Manlow Rhodes, he was cut from the same Calvinist cloth and projected the same air of fastidious competence.

"Mr. Marne," he said to Ollie, "as you've been told, we will sign a contract to represent you in this matter. And even though this gentleman here is paying our fee, we will be your attorneys of record for this transaction. Would that be acceptable?"

That's when Ollie Marne impressed me the second time with his common sense and instinctive good manners. He shook his head. "If it's all the same to you Mr. Fletcher, I'd just as soon not put you to the trouble of making out no contract. If you say you're lookin' out for my interests that's all I need."

"Very good," Fletcher said, obviously pleased. "The matter is in order. It's that simple. The title is as sound as any title can be."

He went on to explain to Ollie what exactly he would be getting for his "ten dollars and other good and valuable consideration," as the deed read.

"What does this 'ten dollars' business mean?" he asked.

"This transaction is being handled as a sale. That way all parties can avoid the problem of a gift tax."

Ollie Marne understood avoiding both problems and taxes. He quickly skimmed over the mineral deed, then reached for his wallet. "Then I guess I owe this guy ten bucks, don't I?" he asked with a grin.

I signed the instrument as agent for Deltex Petroleum and took Ollie's ten with a wink. When we left the attorney's office I drove one street over and a few blocks down and pulled up in front of Neiman Marcus. "Come on," I said to Ollie.

"What are we doing here?" he asked as I steered him through the front door.

"Your wife didn't get to come today, so you're going to buy her something nice," I told him.

Loyal this man might be, but smart he was not. "Hey, that's a good idea," he replied and headed toward the women's hats.

I grabbed him by the arm and pushed him into the lingerie department. "Buy her something really fine," I said. "If you're short on cash, I'll lend you whatever you need."

I figured that he must have had trouble stopping once he got started, because he reappeared thirty minutes later laden with boxes. We stopped at a bookstore a few doors down and I bought his little girl a dozen Nancy Drew books. "You're sure she's never read any Nancy Drew?" I asked.

"Hey, I know what my kid reads!"

We whisked along in silence until we were several miles out of Dallas. Then Marne said, "Listen, I really feel bad about that run-in you had with the sheriff. I hope you don't think I had anything to do with it."

"I know you didn't, Ollie. Forget about it."

We fell back into silence. A few miles down the road he pulled his wallet from his pocket and extracted a photograph. "My wife, Dixie," he said, handing me the photo.

Much to my surprise she was a fine-looking auburn-haired woman dressed in a halter top and a pair of white shorts. She had a sweet face, long dancer's legs and a full figure. I gave the photo a careful examination and then handed it back. "Ollie, my good man . . . you did well for yourself," I said.

"I bet you never expected to see a lug like me with a woman like her, did you?"

"No, to be perfectly honest, I didn't."

"I'm going to tell you something that don't nobody in town but me and Dixie and Will Scoggins know. Dixie was a hooker when I first met her."

I shrugged. "We've all got skeletons in our closets, Ollie."

"She was twenty-two years old and working in that house down at La Grange. She wanted to get out of that kind of life real bad, and I was crazy about her. She didn't love me at the time and I knew it, but I think she does now. Our little girl was born three years later, and nobody could have been a better momma to a kid than Dixie has been to her. She's a fool about that child, and I guess I am too. Dixie's a good woman, but the fact remains that she was a whore, and Will Scoggins won't never let me forget it."

"It sounds to me like she just had a wild youth," I said with a dismissive wave of the hand. "It happens to a lot of girls. Scoggins is the real whore. He's dropped his pants time and again to hold on to his office, and you and I both know it."

"Thanks for saying that," he replied. "I guess you're a pretty good guy after all."

"Yes, I am," I replied. "But I'm no saint, and I'm buying insurance with you today. You need to remember that."

He nodded, his head bobbing up and down like a fishing cork. "I know, and when the time comes I plan to do my best to come through for you."

I reached over and clasped him on the shoulder. "Ollie, the other day Manlow Rhodes said something nice about you. He told me that you are as decent a man as circumstances in town will let you be."

"Really?" he asked in a surprised voice.

"Yes, and coming from him it's quite a compliment."

"Yeah, I guess it is."

"Don't worry. We're the good guys this time around. Maybe not always, but this time we are. I promise you that."

"Oh no," he said. "The good guys are just clowns and I want to go out a winner." I glanced over and there was a look of mild sadness in his hard little eyes. "I may not be very smart," he said, "but I've seen enough to know that."

FIFTEEN

That Friday when Della paid her staff we suddenly found ourselves in a position familiar to many Texas oil people: we were rich and broke at the same time. The abstract company had brought in over a quarter of a million dollars since we'd acquired it, and except for a small fund set aside to cover overhead we'd used every dime of the money to buy leases. It hadn't occurred to us to pay ourselves any kind of salary, and now both our personal checking account and the pantry at home were empty and the electric bill was overdue. I gave Della $200 out of the now-replenished poker account so she could eat while I played, and she dropped me off in front of the Weilbach at a few minutes before six that evening.

The complexion of the game upstairs was changing. Pots were getting bigger and more money was flowing across the table each weekend. A couple of the regular players had found that it was becoming too rich for their blood and dropped out, only to be replaced by oilmen who had come to town with the boom. The tension was also greater, and the talk around the table was becoming more barbed, a violation of another of the game's unspoken conventions. While card-playing buddies may needle one another in a friendly fashion at their regular Friday night game, this type of behavior has always been frowned upon at serious poker matches. The excuse is that poker is a gentleman's pastime, and that gentlemen don't act in such a fashion. The truth is that dedicated players really don't like to say any more than they have to for fear of revealing patterns about their play.

Zip Zimmerman was there that Friday, losing as always, and Wilbur Rasco was present and playing his usual cool, deadly game. One of the newcomers to the table was Simon Van Horn, the man Rasco had identified as Clifton Robillard's partner in the oil business. He was a tall, slim man in his early fifties, and in the past week I'd learned from my contacts that he was probably the wealthiest of all the new arrivals in town, a man with a national reputation who had served on President Roosevelt's Petroleum Allocation Board back during the war. At the poker table he was a competent player whose game was weakened by his habit of putting his ego on the table along with his money, a quirk that was to prove very profitable to me in the weeks to come.

The other oilman present that evening was Howard Northcutt, an enormous, shambling hulk of a man who was given to backslapping and loud laughter. He was also one of the boldest and most aggressive poker players I'd ever seen. Then there was Clifton Robillard. A man of medium height, he had a trim, compact body, long arms, and long tapering fingers. His face was long too, with a finely sculptured nose over a neatly trimmed silver mustache and a wide, full mouth. Something of a dandy, he always dressed carefully in sparkling white dress shirts and custom-tailored suits of the most recent style and fashionable cut. That evening it was an elegant slate gray with a fine gold pinstripe.

I knew that he'd inherited some money from his father, who'd been a land speculator and cattle trader back in the nineteenth century. Right before the First World War the family had founded the Mercantile State Bank, which was Manlow Rhodes's only competitor in town. Robillard himself had prospered through some unspecified involvement with the local munitions factory during the first war, but he'd lost heavily in the Crash of 1929, and for a time it looked as though he would go under. He made a comeback in the late '30s, and since then his fortune had multiplied several-fold. He was politically connected as well. During the second war he'd served in the state senate, where he was noted for his loyal support of Governor Coke Stevenson's conservative policies. Over the years he'd earned such a reputation for ruthlessness in business that his name was even feared in some quarters. Now in his midsixties and basking in his own mystique, he was rich, licentious, and doomed. He was the reason I had come to town.

"Oh yes," Robillard said ten minutes later as we were taking our places at the table. "I've heard about you. I thought somebody said that you went to Yale University."

"Harvard," I replied.

"Harvard, no less." He gave me a firm handshake and an affable pat on the back, but his eyes were cold and unfriendly and his voice was a soft, throaty purr that reminded me of a diesel truck idling; it gave the hint of power rarely used but always there in reserve.

The game heated up quickly that evening. I'd only been at the table about an hour when Zip Zimmerman's oddball luck hit and he took a pot with more than $4,000 in it, several hundred of it mine. About nine o'clock I won a $2,700 pot, then just before midnight I went head-to-head against Clifton Robillard for the first time in a hand of five-card stud. On the first deal I had a king showing against his eight. I bet a $100 and he called it and dropped a $500 bill on the table. I matched him and everybody but Zimmerman folded. On the next round I drew an ace and Robillard paired his eights. The ace did me no good at all, but I had a second king in the hole to go with the one showing. Zimmerman wisely dropped out when the trey he drew didn't improve the nothing he already had.

I have one fixed policy. I never look twice at a hole card no matter what. If you can't look at your card one time and remember it for the few minutes it takes to play a hand of poker, then you have no business at the table. Still, many people, and even some fairly good gamblers, will take a second and sometimes a third look. Often a player will remember the denomination of the card, but not the suit and will have to look again if, for example, he winds up with three diamonds showing and only remembers that the hole card was red.

On the next card I drew a third king while Robillard drew a jack and immediately took another quick peek at his hole card. I knew at that point I was about to get some indication of how good a gambler he was. Twice before he had looked quickly at his hole card in the same quick, furtive fashion, and both times it was when he had paired. I knew it because I'd paid to find out, staying in with losing hands just to see his hole card. His peeking could be a tell, which is any physical mannerism or habit that, when repeated in the same circumstances, gives away a person's game. And if his peeking *was* a tell, it was a blatant and obvious one and it meant that he was a mediocre gambler. If not, he'd been intentionally running a false tell on me earlier, and now I had no idea what his hole card was. If the latter was true, it meant that he was a more sophisticated player, and I wanted to know which.

"Pair of kings bets," the dealer called.

I checked to him just as I would if I was a timid player who held a pair of kings and nothing else, and was concerned that the jack had given him two pair. He bet $200 with $2,300 on the table, bringing the pot up to a total of $2,500. It was a bet designed to keep me in the game.

"Raise," I said. I threw the $200 onto the table, then followed it with three $500 bills. "Fifteen hundred to you, Mr. Robillard."

He appeared surprised, but it could easily have been false surprise. "Well, well," he murmured. "The college boy thinks he has a good hand, it seems."

I had decided earlier that I would be the very soul of courtesy in dealing with him regardless of how snide he became. "Yes sir, that's what I think," I replied. "And it will cost you fifteen hundred dollars to see it."

"I don't believe you've got that third king," he said with

a smile. "A man with that third king in the hole would have looked at it at least once, just to make sure it hadn't changed spots since the first time he saw it."

I said nothing, and he met the $1,500, and then threw another $1,500 in on top of it.

I called his raise and tapped the table for cards. He drew a six and my card came up a five. He was beaten, though he didn't know it yet.

He looked over at my stake. "You're in this hand pretty deep for a fellow who came in the door so light, aren't you?" he asked. "What have you got left over there? About four thousand?"

"Pair of kings still bets," the dealer said.

Robillard's eyes were a pale, icy blue, and I looked right into them for perhaps ten seconds and said, "Pair of kings checks."

He glanced over at my stake again, and said, "You know, college boy, I could buy this hand right now. I think that little stack of bills in front of you is about all you have."

"But you don't know how much I have in my pocket, Mr. Robillard," I answered politely.

"I know how much I've got," Wilburn Rasco said, and reached into his coat. He pulled out a long, thick wallet that bulged with currency and threw it over on top of my stake. "There's about ten thousand dollars there, son. And you can owe me. You just use as much of that as you need to."

Robillard turned his head to regard Rasco. "What do you think you're doing, Wilburn?" he asked.

"It's been done here before, and you know it."

"Is that right?"

"Yes, that's right," Rasco replied. "But I'll tell you what

ain't been done. Nobody buys pots at this table. This may be a no-limit game, but the understood rule has always been that you don't go over a man's table stake unless he's agreeable to the bet. And then you take a marker for the difference if you win. That, by God, is the way we've always done it, and I've been playing in this game for twenty-five years."

Rasco's voice held a cold fury. Whether his anger came from some old insult he'd suffered at Robillard's hands or whether it sprang from the bad manners the man currently concealed beneath his velvety demeanor I had no idea.

"Thank you, sir," I told him, and looked across the table at my opponent. "Now, Mr. Robillard . . . one way or another, I'm going to get to see that jack you have in the hole," I told him politely. "So you need to either bet or check. Unless, of course, you want to fold."

"I wasn't going to try to buy it," Robillard said smoothly as he counted out $2,500 and carefully dropped it on the table. "I was just commenting on the possibilities."

I thought about raising him by throwing Rasco's whole wallet onto the table, but there was some chance he might fold. And at that point it was worth more to me to see his hole card. I handed Rasco's wallet back and pushed my own money into the pot. "Even call," I said.

The room was silent. Robillard made no move to touch his cards. "I believe I'm the one who called," I reminded him.

His eyes never left my face as he reached down and slowly turned over the jack of hearts.

"Not quite good enough," I said as I flipped over my third king.

He smiled when he saw the card, but his eyes said that the loss had pricked his ego badly. Excellent. That had been my intention.

The hand we'd just played told me that he was a mediocre gambler. Unless, of course, the whole thing was contrived with the eye to bigger takings down the road. And that could well be the case. I know because I'd done things equally complicated myself. Even when the table is straight and free of cheating, poker is a game of chicanery and deceit. The basic mechanics and rules can be learned by an intelligent child in an afternoon or less, but a lifetime is not enough to master it in the heart where it's really played.

Several years earlier I'd been trapped on a long train trip with nothing to do, and I'd fallen into a card game with four older men. One of them was a sixty-year-old preacher who refused to play for money. We managed to round up about a thousand matches and divided them up four ways. And for the life of me I couldn't beat that old preacher at five-card stud. I won a few hands, but after about four hours of steady playing he finally cleaned me and his two friends out. Besides being a superb player, he was as good a card mechanic as I ever met. He rightly concluded that even in a friendly game where no money was at risk, I wouldn't let him get away with cheating me directly when he had the deal. So several times he stacked the cards to let one of the other players beat me, then siphoned the stakes away from them with his superior playing skill. It had been an amusing experience that cost me nothing and taught me something about human nature.

I'd paid no attention to his name when he first introduced himself, and following the lead of the other two I'd simply called him Reverend. As I rose from the table he reached over and clasped my shoulder in a fatherly grip. "Young man," he asked, "did you ever hear of a fellow called Cornbread Broussard?"

"Sure," I answered. "He was from south Louisiana, and he got that name because he didn't like light bread and wouldn't eat it. Back about thirty years ago he was considered the king of the stud poker players here in the South."

He pulled a business card out of his pocket and handed it to me. It read "Reverend Victor Broussard, Thibodeaux, Louisiana."

"That was me," he said, "in the days before I accepted the Lord Jesus Christ as my personal savior." He gave my shoulder another fatherly squeeze, and said, "You ought to quit this game boy. It'll kill a man."

Broussard might have gotten religion, but it hadn't rid him of the killer instinct a good poker player needs. I doubt that he ever worked harder for any of the fortunes he'd won and lost in any of the plush New Orleans gaming rooms where he once played nightly than he did for those worthless matches that night on the train. He lusted after victory regardless of the stakes, and to him the matches were little more than a means of keeping score.

SIXTEEN

The tension in the room was broken, and everyone but Zimmerman and Northcutt rose from the table for a break. I poured a cup of coffee from the pot at the bar and made myself a sandwich at the buffet table. One of my other rules is that I never drink when I gamble. Not even so much as a bottle of beer or a single glass of wine. Nor do I smoke, though I will occasionally chew on a cigar.

I'd just taken the first bite of my sandwich when I felt a hand on my shoulder. I turned to see Wilburn Rasco smiling at me. "That was good playing," he said with a broad smile.

"Thank you. And that was a very generous move you made. If he'd overbet me I would have been sunk. I didn't have the money to meet him."

"I knew you didn't."

"But why did you do it?" I asked. "Not that I'm ungrateful, but I am curious."

"For one reason, Clifton can be a real horse's ass sometimes, and I wanted to set him back on his haunches. Besides that, Manlow Rhodes asked me to look after you up here."

"He did?" I asked, surprised.

Rasco nodded, a broad smile on his face. "Yeah, he said you couldn't stay out of trouble, gettin' thrown in jail and whatnot."

"He told you about that, did he?" I asked, and felt my face stretch into a grin in spite of myself.

"Hell, everybody knows by now. But don't worry. To most of the decent folks in this town, getting crossways with Will Scoggins is a badge of honor."

"You and Mr. Rhodes are friends, I take it."

"For fifty years. There's not a better man in this county, even if he is awful stiff-necked about what he considers sin."

"And what's that?" I asked.

"Why, just damn near everything that's any fun," he answered with a laugh. He shook my hand and drifted over to the bar, leaving me pondering the hand I had just won. Some time back I saw a movie in which two supposedly top-notch poker players went head-to-head. At the climax of the game one spotted the other's tell. It was the man's habit to eat cookies as he played. At last the hero noticed that his opponent ate his cookie in a certain fashion whenever he was bluffing. I had to laugh. To me it didn't even make good theater because no truly competent gambler has a tell that obvious, and if you spot one that's so blatant in a player of high reputation, then the behavior is intentional and you are being set up. Real tells are subtle and usually involve tiny mannerisms and expressions that are not even under the conscious control of the player. I wondered if the whole thing tonight with Robillard had been calculated to give me a false tell. I hoped so. Considering what I knew of his past, I'd expected better from him than I'd seen that evening.

A few minutes later the game resumed. I stayed with it until about four the next morning, then grabbed a few hours' sleep in one of the bedrooms. The play slowed down during the day Saturday though I was able to slowly increase my stake to something over ten thousand dollars. At six that evening I excused myself and met Della for dinner in the hotel restaurant.

"Having fun?" she asked.

I smiled across the table at her. "To tell you the truth, I'm having the time of my life."

"Winning?"

"I've doubled what I brought in here. How about you? How's your weekend going?"

"I've been reading."

"You mean you actually took the day off?" I asked. I was surprised that she hadn't been to work. Since the boom began she had kept the office open on Saturdays because of the demand.

"Yes. I think it's okay to relax a little now. We've made it."

"Made what?" I asked.

"Our fortune. We are now financially secure. We wouldn't even have to wait for the pipeline if we didn't want to. We could sell out now for enough to live good for the rest of our lives."

"Is that what you want to do?"

She shook her head and looked across at me quizzically. "Do you have any idea what we're going to be worth when the leases we hold now all get drilled and into production?"

"I have no idea," I said honestly.

"Then I think I'll keep it to myself. If you knew, you might decide to take your half and leave me for some wild woman."

"Della, what would you say if I told you that you're the only wild woman I'm ever going to need?"

I played the rest of the evening Saturday but was unable to engage Robillard again. Howard Northcutt and I went head-on in a couple of good hands, and I won about $1,500 from Zip Zimmerman in the wee hours of the morning.

It had become the custom of late for some of the players to bring call girls into the suite, and the bedrooms were often in use. It was obvious that the security on the game was getting more lax as time went by and new players were admitted to the table. From the time the oilmen began to arrive in town there were always a few sexy women lounging around the suite, though I could rarely tell who they were with. Late that Saturday night Clifton Robillard brought up a lush-bodied brunette. As soon as we'd all had time to admire her and envy him, he took her into one of the bedrooms. I was to learn in the coming months that he consumed women at an impressive rate for a man his age.

About five that morning I excused myself from the game and left. It had been a profitable weekend, both financially and in terms of my ultimate objective. For a while I'd felt a sense of residual guilt that I was letting myself get side-tracked with the oil business. I had other people counting on me who had financed my trip to town and who had an interest in my eventual success.

I was also pleased to see the women coming to the suite; their presence fit into my plans quite nicely. The only thing left to do in the weeks ahead was to play my usual game and bide my time until the moment was right.

SEVENTEEN

That Monday morning I ran into my first real snag in the oil business. The week before I'd made a verbal agreement to lease 217 acres that lay about five miles from what oilmen call the fairway, by which they mean the centerline of the field where the oil is most abundant. The tract was something of a long shot, but the geologist's report indicated that the extremity of the field was probably at least a mile beyond the place I was interested in.

I'd made an offer of three hundred an acre as a lease bonus, and it was quickly snapped up by the owner, a small, prim, retired bookkeeper from Odessa named Meese. The previous year he'd inherited the land from his wife, who in turn had inherited it from her grandfather. The only problem was that Meese wouldn't take either a draft or a personal check. I promised him that if the title checked out I'd bring him a certified check Monday.

I went back into town where Della had one of her assistants do a quick emergency search on the title. Then I took her findings to Andy and prevailed upon him to give me a fast opinion. He pronounced Meese's title good. I was at the bank when it opened Monday to get the check, then I hurried out to Meese's house, a small, prim structure that matched its owner perfectly. As I pulled into his driveway I almost hit a big blue Cadillac that was swinging out onto the highway. As the car flashed past me I saw that Simon Van Horn was at the wheel with Clifton Robillard beside him. They nodded at me, then looked at one another and broke out into laughter.

"Top of the morning to you, too," I muttered and gave them an offhand wave.

Meese came out on his front porch at the sound of my arrival. "I don't believe we can do any business today," he said as I approached his porch.

"Why not?" I asked.

"Well . . ." he hedged. "Things have changed a little since you were here."

He took a seat in a big hickory rocking chair. I came up on the porch but he didn't ask me to sit. "They offered you a better deal, didn't they?" I asked.

"Who offered me a better deal?"

"Those two birds in that Cadillac," I replied with a jerk of my thumb back toward the road. "What did they give you? Twenty bucks more an acre? Fifty?"

"Now, you listen here, young fellow . . . a man has to look out for himself in this old world."

"My father always taught me that a man has to keep his commitments," I said.

"You need to remember that we didn't have anything on paper," he said, shaking his finger at me like a schoolmarm. "And you know that as well as I do. Just show me anything we had on paper, and I'll rip up the other man's check."

I stared at him silently until he began to squirm just a little. "Three fifty," he finally said. "I got three fifty."

"Did you bother to mention that you and I already had a deal?"

"Sure I did! How else do you think I got them to bid up that high? Of course, if you really want this lease bad enough, then you ought to be able to beat three fifty. . . ." His voice died in the sound of my laughter. "What's so funny?" he asked.

"You've already proven yourself to be a lying scoundrel," I said. "So why would I want to do any more business with you? Do you really expect me to offer four hundred, shake hands again and then come out here in the morning and find out that they've gone four fifty? How foolish do you think I am?"

I walked down the steps and was almost to my car when he called after me, "Even the Good Book says the Lord helps those that help themselves."

I turned and went back up on the porch. Putting my hands on the arms of his rocking chair, I leaned my six-foot-four-inch frame down until I loomed over him with our faces only a few inches apart. He cringed away, his eyes wide with fear. "No it doesn't," I said with a big happy grin. "That's not in the Bible at all. But I'll tell you what is. . . . 'The Lord God of Hosts shall cast down all those who worketh iniquity, and great shall be their lamentations on the day of Judgment. . . .'"

A half hour later I was back in the office. "No lease?" Della asked. "What happened?"

"Van Horn and Robillard," I said. "They slid in under us."

"How did they know we were after that tract?"

"They may not have," I said. "It could have been just a little unethical business competition, or it could have been Robillard trying to get even for the poker game this past weekend."

"What happened at the poker game?" she asked.

"Just what I came here to make happen," I said. "I humiliated him good."

"So you think? . . ."

"Who knows. But please stress to the girls that they need to keep quiet about what goes on here. . . . Okay?"

"I'll do more than that," she said. "I'll have Mona start keeping an eye on them."

Two mornings later I was just about to leave the house when the phone rang. When I lifted the receiver I heard Col. Homer Garrison's deep voice rumbling ponderously across the miles between me and Austin. "How's things going out there?" he asked.

"Well, there's a lot of oil coming out of the ground these days," I replied.

"So they tell me. Say, son . . . Are you still hooked up with the New-nited States gumment?"

I paused before answering, my senses suddenly alert. "I've maintained a few contacts in the government, if that's what you're asking," I finally replied.

"Hmmmm . . ." he mused. "I sure do wish I could get a straight answer these days. I'm sort of a yes-or-no kind of man, you understand. Older generation and all that."

I couldn't help but grin. "Oh, come on, Colonel. You've

dealt with the state legislature enough to know sometimes a man just isn't in a position to give you a yes-or-no answer. That doesn't stop his heart from being in the right place."

"No, I guess it don't. And as far as I know yours always has been."

"Colonel Garrison, what's on your mind?"

I heard a deep sigh. "Well, I've got a little inside information for you."

"Information? About what?"

"Clifton Robillard."

I was instantly wary. "Why would I care about Robillard, Colonel?"

"Don't you try to shit me, boy," he said cheerfully. "Do you remember that story in the papers about General MacArthur asking me to come over to Japan to run the MP's for the occupation gumment and set up a civilian police force for the Japanese?"

"Yes sir, I remember it," I replied.

"Good. My point being that there are some people in high places who occasionally value my ideas, however ignorant and countrified they might seem to you younger folks."

"Your point is well taken, Colonel," I said dryly. "Now, what about Robillard?"

"It all started with a young banking examiner," he began, his voice now shorn of its bumpkin inflections. "It seems that he got his tail in a crack with some gambling debts, then he went to . . ."

After he'd finished ten minutes later, I asked, "How long can you hold off on this?"

"How long do you need?"

"Late November?" I asked hopefully, my fingers crossed.

I could almost hear the tiny little gears spinning in his great dome of a head as he quickly considered. "I don't see why not," he finally said. "The charges haven't even been filed, but the bank examiner has already made a deal for five years probated. I don't figure Robillard is going anywhere."

"Thank you, sir," I said with relief. "But will the bank examiner keep quiet?"

"Son, there's no limit to what this young fellow will do to keep out of the pen. He's heard some stories about this state's correctional facilities, and he didn't like 'em."

"Thank you once again, Colonel," I said.

"Don't mention it," he replied. "As you probably know, my main interest in this matter is Robillard's close relationship with Will Scoggins. That man is a disgrace to law enforcement. But people like them eventually outsmart themselves, don't they?"

"Indeed they do," I replied.

"You take care now, you hear?" he said, all hayseed once again. "Keep ol' Bob Crowder honest for me."

I hung up the phone and sat there on the sofa with my mind racing. I must have stared out the window for ten minutes before I finally made up my mind and reached for the telephone again. It seemed as though it took me forever to get through to Chicken Little. "We need some more men," I said as soon as I had him on the phone. "Not for our project, but for something else I've got in mind that same night."

"Lord help my time, boy. . . . What kind of fellows are you talking about?"

I told him.

EIGHTEEN

Little had to come down to southern Oklahoma for business that week. We agreed to meet Wednesday at a little bootleg beer joint on the Red River north of Bonham in Fannin County. "I talked to a couple of boys in Kansas City," he said. "But the deal is going to have to look pretty sweet to get them involved. I mean, there are jobs everywhere they could do, but . . ."

"How does about two hundred thousand sound?" I asked, grinning. "That's a conservative figure."

"Shitfire!" he said. "In a town that size? I don't see how that's possible."

"The oil boom, Little. Plus Christmas."

"But how do you know?"

"You've heard me mention my friend Ollie Marne? Well, Ollie talks a lot."

"Hell, Marne ought to know if anybody knows," he said, and drained his beer.

"That's right," I agreed. "Cops know those things. And before I forget, there's one other change in plans I need to mention."

"Yeah?"

I told him and he shrugged as though he could care less. "This way will be a lot easier on you," I said. "And safer. Like this, Robillard stays around to reap the fruits of his labor, so to speak. And you don't have to . . ."

He shook his head and waved his hand in dismissal. "That don't make any difference. I can do it one way or the other. It's your decision, but don't modify this thing on my account."

"I know that without being told, Little," I said softly. "So do you think these guys will go for it?"

"Hell, I feel pretty sure they will. When do we do it?"

"The same night as the poker game. I can come up with a couple of moves to make it easier. But what's to stop them from doing it on their own time and cutting us out once they find out where it is? That worries me."

He looked at me for a moment, his pale blue eyes cold and remote under the brim of his fedora. "They know better than to fool with me that way. There ain't no profit in that for nobody."

"Okay. I'll take your word for it."

"How does the split go?" he asked.

I shook my head. "You can get whatever you want out for your trouble, but as far as I'm concerned they can have the rest."

He leaned back in the ratty little booth and laughed like I'd never seen him laugh before.

"What's the matter?" I asked. "Did I say something funny?"

He finally got control of himself and pulled out his handkerchief. "That's going to be a new one on them," he said, wiping the tears from his eyes. "They'll be flat bumfuzzled. They've never done a job with a man who worked for free."

I grinned. "Just tell them that steering jobs is a hobby of mine."

That set him off again. "Boy, you are a sight!" he finally managed. "When this is all over I got to tell Annie that one."

"And you say these men are good at what they do?" I asked.

"Hell, this one fellow I talked to is maybe the best in the country."

A few minutes later we parted. "Hobby," he muttered, still laughing as he climbed into his car.

NINETEEN

The next week I suffered anther annoying setback. In the early days of the oil boom the leasing activity and drilling had spread westward across the Donner Basin from the site of the original Coby Smith strike. At Della's insistence I had leased 260 acres three miles down the basin from the maiden well that was owned by a crippled cotton farmer named Elijah Kraft. I'd paid a hundred dollars an acre for the lease, but now land surrounding Kraft's was going for five times that. I'd had more than one opportunity to sell or sublet the lease at a tidy profit, but I'd held on to it, convinced that oil would eventually be found under the whole basin. Then, in the middle of an otherwise fine week, Della got a call from Manlow Rhodes asking me and Andy to both come to his office at the bank. The young lawyer beat me there, and when I walked in his dark eyes were burning and his face was a mask of pure rage. "You're not going to believe it," he said as soon as I walked in the room.

"What?" I asked.

"This," Manlow Rhodes said, and pushed a piece of paper across the desk toward me. I picked it up and gazed at it in disbelief. It was a certified check from Elijah Kraft for something more than $24,000.

"I don't understand," I finally said.

"Maybe this will help," Rhodes said with a grim smile, and handed me another piece of paper. "It's photostatic copy of a deed of trust for the tract of land you leased that was executed by Mr. Kraft three years ago in behalf of Clifton Robillard as trustee for the Mercantile State Bank. It appears that Mr. Kraft borrowed five thousand dollars against his farm at that time, and that about a year ago he fell delinquent in his payments. Which makes sense, considering that he broke his back eighteen months ago. As I'm sure you know, when one borrows against real property in this state one signs a deed of trust that is held in abeyance and only executed in the event that the conditions of the loan agreement are not met."

"Of course," I said. "It's basic real-estate law."

"Correct. And this other photostat I have here is the notice of foreclosure that was filed with the county clerk's office about a week before your lease was signed."

"I get it now. . . ." I began.

"Not completely, you don't," Andy said, pulling a red leather-bound ledger from his briefcase. "I checked that particular title twice. You see, I keep a journal of everything I do to clear each title. The last thing on my checklist is 'Recent Filings.' That means I look through all the instruments that have come into the clerk's office but which have not yet been recorded in the official public record. See this?" he asked, pointing at an entry with a date and time beside it. "At that time *nothing* was present in the clerk's office to indicate that foreclosure was in progress on this tract."

"I don't doubt you, Andy. But what happened?" I asked.

"I spoke with Robillard on the phone yesterday," Rhodes said. "He claims that Andy merely neglected to check the unrecorded instruments, but I don't believe it for a minute."

"Damn right," Andy said.

"Shortly after I talked to Robillard," Rhodes continued, "I had Wallace Reed look into the matter. It appears that once Mercantile Bank had secured title to the Kraft farm, Robillard worked out an arrangement whereby a gentleman named Simon Van Horn would purchase the mineral rights from the bank for a sum sufficient to pay off Kraft's original loan and let the farm itself revert to Kraft and his family."

"And that amount was?" I asked.

"Around three thousand dollars."

"But why in the world didn't Kraft pay off the note at the bank with some of the money I gave him for the lease?"

"He claims that he did, and I don't doubt him. He deposited the draft, and as soon as it had cleared, he mailed a check to the bank along with a letter asking for a release, which never came to him."

"Mail?" I asked.

Rhodes shook his head sadly. "A lot of these old farmers operate that way. I've lent money by mail any number of times."

"But what happened to his check?" I asked.

"Hell, they sat on it to see what was going to happen with the field," Andy said. "Then when it got good they tore up the check and bribed some sorry son-of-a-bitch in the county clerk's office to backdate the filing of the foreclosure notice."

I looked at Rhodes. He gave me a slight nod. "I imagine that's about how it happened."

"But why did they even bother to let him have the farm back?" I asked.

"Goodwill," Rhodes answered. "They were betting that if the old man got his surface rights back he wouldn't mount any sort of legal challenge to the foreclosure. Besides, that farm's not worth more than twenty dollars an acre without the minerals, but it will grow a little cotton and that's about all poor Kraft understands anyway."

"So they swindled the old fellow out of thousands of dollars' worth of minerals for a pittance," I said.

"Yes," Rhodes replied. "That's exactly what they did. And to me the proof that Kraft is telling the truth about mailing them the payment is the fact that he sent his daughter in here yesterday with the remainder of your money in this certified check. If he'd been dishonest, he could have simply spent it all, and your only practical recourse to recover it would have been a civil suit. Besides, he says that he wants to pay you back the two thousand that he spent."

"That'll be the day," I said. "No way I'm going to take that old man's money. But above and beyond the loss of a valuable lease, I just hate for him to get treated like this."

"So do we all," Andy said. "But I don't see a thing we can do about it."

I didn't say so at the time, but there was something I could do about it. There are two ways to hustle a man, whether it's at poker or pool or anything else. You can play poorly and let him beat you and thereby convince him that he's the better player. All the while, of course, you're setting him up for the one big hand or game where you skin him alive. This is the obvious way, and seasoned players have learned it and are duly skeptical of losers who keep wanting to up the stakes. There's a second technique. It's much harder to pull off, and it can only work on a certain type of individual. But it is the way of the true artist. You beat him more times than he beats you. You don't beat him really badly in most cases, but you stay ahead. Yet you do it in such a way as to convince him it's luck and not skill. And while you're doing it, you crow just a little about your success, you take on an arrogant demeanor that's aimed at his testicles, and you make it a contest of manhood. If he's the right sort of man, and if you do your work properly, when the time comes you won't have to set him up; he'll do it for you and beg you to give him a trimming.

Like his friend Simon Van Horn, Robillard was a man who laid his ego on the table every time he placed a bet. And while the amounts we gambled for meant little to either of us, the act of losing diminished his manhood in his own eyes. Consequently, he was prime meat, and though he didn't know it yet, he was one hog I was going to scald very thoroughly before it was time to scrape him.

TWENTY

A record drought began in the middle of June. For weeks on end the sun bore down while farmers scanned the skies for signs of rain with dwindling hopes. The land baked. Crops withered in the fields and cattle ate the grasslands down to the roots. Those ranchers who could afford it leased pasture in the less arid eastern part of the state where there was still grass to be found. Those who couldn't were faced with the grim prospect of having to sell off parts of their herds in a plunging market. Two cattlemen committed suicide that summer, and each time I went by the bank the lobby was full of ranchers and cotton farmers waiting to see Manlow Rhodes. He helped those he could help; the others he could only turn away, knowing full well that in some cases his refusal amounted to a death sentence. The bank's reserves hovered just above the legally required minimum for months on end, and as the oil money came in as deposits he sent it back out as loans. Through it all he remained steady and silent.

The air itself became dirty as the trucks that rumbled incessantly through the county kept the roads churned into a cloud of dust that settled over everything. A shirt collar was filthy by noon. Laundry that was hung on clotheslines to dry came back into the house as dirty as it had gone into the washtub. Women ceased going out in their best clothes, and white dresses and blouses were no longer seen on the streets. I cleaned the filters on the air conditioners every day and Della bought the most powerful vacuum cleaner she could find and used it almost continuously, yet the dust still crept in and settled everywhere.

I played at the Weilbach nearly every weekend, and soon came to be accepted as a regular. I clashed a few more times with Clifton Robillard in those weeks, and I was beginning to wear on his nerves. I never mentioned the Meese or Kraft leases, and neither did he. Finally, during the second weekend in August my chance came and I bore down on him hard. With a little help from the cards I managed to trim him of $17,000 between Friday night and the wee hours of Sunday morning. Several thousand of it was a result of the natural attrition that occurs when an inferior player confronts a superior one. He lost a number of small pots simply because I knew the odds better than he did and outplayed him. Then an opportunity came and I hit him hard. It was a hand of five-card stud, and I would like to be able to say that I won it because the gods favored me. But the gods had nothing to do with it since I'd dealt it to myself some twelve hours earlier on my own coffee table at home.

Every week a bonded courier delivered fifty new decks of playing cards to the hotel from a novelty company in Dallas. Half of these decks had blue backs while the other half were red. Whenever a player called for new cards, a deck of the color opposite the one then in play would be handed over by the porter whose responsibility it then was to count the cards in the discarded deck. Once he was satisfied that no one had held any cards out to run into the game later, he tore the discarded deck in two and threw it away. The previous weekend I'd simply pocketed one of the red decks when the porter was distracted.

It's easy enough to run in a cold deck when you're the dealer, but it's also dangerous to win a big hand by doing so. It is somewhat more difficult to cold deck a game when it is another player's turn to deal, but it can be done; every stage magician pulls off more difficult illusions every time he performs. The only practical time is when it's your turn to cut the cards. For my plan to work, it also depended on a certain number of players in the game. If there was one too many or one too few at the table, the order of the cards would be thrown off and the hand would be useless. I also wanted as few players as possible in the game at the time I sprang my trap. The more players at the table the more chance that someone would stay for a round or two with a poor hand and throw the order of the cards off. I chose five players as the average number at the table in the early hours of the morning, and fate gave me the extra bonus of Zip Zimmerman's absence. Zip had been my real worry because he was the one player likely to stay in the hand for a round or two while holding junk in the face of good cards. About 1:00 A.M. everything fell into place and I slipped the cold deck into the game on the cut.

After the first two cards were dealt, Robillard had the ace of diamonds showing, and I knew he had a second ace in the hole. I held the jack of hearts on top, and he bet a modest $500. The other three players folded, and I pretended to deliberate for a few moments, then called him. On the next round he drew the queen of spades and I drew the eight of hearts. He bet $1,000 and I raised him a $1,000. Surprise showed on his face, but he met the raise and tapped the table for cards.

His next card was the queen of clubs. Mine was the seven of hearts. The dealer called my possible flush and Robillard's pair of queens. Robillard checked, no doubt hoping to sucker me into betting since he had the ace of spades in the hole, which gave him two pair. I tried to feign relief as I also checked. On the final card he drew his third ace and I drew the ten of hearts. The dealer called his two pair and my possible flush.

My opponent took another quick peek at his hole card, then looked across the table at me and smiled. "I'm willing to believe you have that flush, my friend," he said. "So I believe I'll just check."

He hoped I had the flush, he should have said. And he was sandbagging me in hopes that I'd bet heavily so he could raise me. I wasn't hesitant in satisfying him on that score. There was a total of $6,000 in the pot, and I matched it. Robillard leaned back in his chair thinking he had me beaten since his third ace gave him a full house, and he wanted to savor the moment. When I dealt the hand that afternoon at home I had intentionally added a pair of queens to go with the aces rather than a pair of numbered cards. Against a flush they didn't make the hand any stronger than a pair of deuces would have, but such is human nature that face cards always seem bigger and inspire confidence, especially when paired with aces. And I wanted him just as confident as possible. "That's a nice strong bet," he said. "But I believe I'm going to have to raise it."

He only had about $5,000 left in front of him and he pushed it into the pot. I tried to look surprised as though I had been expecting him to fold against a bluff.

"I'd even like to go a little heavier than that if you were interested in taking my marker," he said.

"I would be more than willing to take your marker, sir," I said, trying to put a worried frown on my face. "But I've always thought it unlucky to exceed table stakes. It's a superstition of mine."

"Oh, I see," he replied with a patronizing smile. "Well, then . . . Are you going to call the bet?"

"Give me just a moment to think, please," I said.

"Take all the time you want."

He sat back comfortably in his chair, the very picture of confidence. I took at least a minute, time he would know had been spent for my own sadistic amusement the moment I turned over my hole card. I fingered my money dubiously, then finally nodded and met his raise. "Even call," I said.

This time around he didn't have to be reminded that it was up to him to show his hole card first. He reached down with a carefully manicured hand and slowly turned over his third ace. "I guess that says it all, doesn't it?" he asked.

"Not quite," I replied. With the most casual, offhand motion I could summon, a motion no more studied than turning the page of a dull novel, I flipped over that glorious, magic nine of hearts that gave me a straight flush. He froze for a moment in disbelief, then lunged to his feet, his breath coming in short gasps.

"I don't complain about getting beat," he finally managed

to say. "I don't like it, but I can stand it. But what I want to know is why you took so damn long to call that last raise? What have I ever done to make you treat me like that?"

It was my turn to have a self-satisfied smile on my face, one that I hoped he found truly hateful. "That's just the way I like to play the game of poker, Mr. Robillard."

He quickly got control of himself once more. "I see," he said, nodding solemnly. "Well, you did pretty good this time. But I once heard about a smart man who said that in the long run God's with the big battalions."

"He had it wrong," I said, my voice as cheerful as his was cold. "In the long run we'll all be dead."

TWENTY-ONE

I went home and slept through most of that Sunday, then rose early Monday morning. Della had left early to go to the office. Just as I finished my morning coffee the phone rang. "Can you come to the office?" I heard Della ask.

It only took me ten minutes to pull myself together and drive downtown. I found Della and Mona closeted in Della's inner sanctum with one the stenographers we'd hired from Fort Worth. She was siting in a straight-backed chair in front of the desk crying her eyes out while Della and Mona loomed over her like a pair of angry hawks. I'd noticed the girl before. She was a short, curvy brunette with a wide red slash of a mouth and a provocative manner. The office chatterbox, at lunch she either had her nose in one of the collection of movie magazines she kept in the drawer of her desk or else she was regaling the other girls with vivid stories of her love life.

"Meet Lisa the leak," Della said.

The girl wailed louder. "I didn't do nothing," she objected. "I swear."

"Hush," Della told her. "Be quiet or I'll call the police right now."

The girl managed to throttle it back to a tolerable level. "Go ahead and tell him, Mona," Della instructed.

"I should have seen it before I did," Mona began. "Lisa ran the title on the Meese tract and on the Kraft lease too. None of the other girls had a hand in either, and none of them knew a thing about them. Then there have been at least three other tracts that have been grabbed out from under us that you never knew about. . . ."

"Three?" I asked. "But why didn't you tell me about them?" I asked.

"I didn't realize what had happened until this morning when I looked to see who had run the chain of title in each case. Lisa checked and passed on every title where the company failed to get the tract we were planning to lease. And who do you think got the leases in every case?"

I nodded. "Van Horn and Robillard . . ."

"Right," Della said.

"I want to leave," Lisa sniveled. "You can't keep me here. It's kidnapping."

"Swell," Della said. She grabbed the phone and slammed it down in front of the girl. "Just go ahead and call the cops," she said. "They'll be glad to come get you."

The wails began once again.

"And you remember that partition deal with Ned Roberts that fell through a few weeks ago?" Mona asked above the din.

"Sure," I said.

She pointed at Lisa. "There's the reason right there.

What tipped me off was seeing her with the two of them Friday night."

"Two of who?" I asked. "You mean Robillard and Van Horn?"

She nodded. "Andy and I were both just too beat to drive up to Odessa for synagogue, and I didn't even feel like cooking us any supper. About eight o'clock we decided to go to that little barbecue place down past the Row. That's when we saw Miss Priss here coming out of the Roundup Club with Van Horn and that other guy. Then I realized what had to be happening."

"Now that I think about it," I said, "both of them were late getting to the poker game at the Weilbach last Friday. They didn't come in until around midnight."

"They were with her," Mona said. "So the first thing I did when I got to work this morning was start checking the records."

"How do you know she was the one who ran the titles?" I asked.

"Because I make each girl sign off on every bit of work she does," she replied. "That way if any sloppy work starts showing up I know who's doing it."

Della took a step closer to Lisa. "Which one of them are you sleeping with?" she asked her. "Van Horn or Robillard? Or are you servicing them both?"

"How can you say that?" Lisa shrieked. "That's so awful!!"

"Which one is it?" Della demanded. She and Mona began to close in on the hapless girl like two young lionesses after an exhausted gazelle. "Was it Clifton Robillard? Don't you know that man's old enough to be your grandfather?" Della asked.

"That's disgusting!" Mona spat.

"I never did it with him! I swear."

"Then it was Van Horn," Della said.

"Just a few times," Lisa said, her tears running like Niagara. "I mean, he's young . . . Sorta."

"He's in his late forties, and you're not but twenty-two," Della said. "Besides, he's married."

"Yeah, but he's got a real bad marriage—"

"Oh, for heaven's sake!" Della said in exasperation. "Don't tell me. . . . His wife doesn't understand him. Right?"

"Yeahhh? . . ."

"What did he do?" Mona asked. "Promise to introduce you to somebody out in Hollywood?"

"How did you know that?" the girl gasped.

Della and Mona both rolled their eyes. "And your father's a minister," Mona said. "I've heard you mention that. What would he think about you sleeping with a married man?"

"Your dad's a preacher?" I asked. "What kind?"

"B-B-Baptist . . ."

"Then you ought to know you could go to hell for what you've been doing," Della said coldly.

At that the girl's wails rose to an unearthly crescendo.

Della looked at me, and asked, "What do you want to do?"

I considered. I could strong-arm the girl into feeding false information from me to Robillard and Van Horn. But to what purpose? The Meese affair hadn't really been directed at me financially; it was intended simply as an annoyance because that was the kind of man Robillard was. It would be nice if I could get him and Van Horn to waste a pile of money leasing useless land. But they had access to the same geology reports I had, and there was little chance they would fall for a completely bogus tract. Van Horn especially; he was far more knowledgeable as an oilman than I was. Then there was the fact that Lisa was probably too stupid to play a double role with any conviction. We would simply be better off without her. "Get her out of here," I finally replied.

Mona opened the door. Lisa gazed up at me uncertainly. "Go," I said. "And don't ever come back."

Mona stood back from the doorway. After casting her eyes wildly around for a few seconds, the girl lunged to her feet and bolted from the room like an unbroke filly. Mona pushed the door shut behind her.

"That poor fool has no more brains than a gnat," Della said, and dropped wearily into the chair behind her desk.

"She has enough sense to know she ought to be loyal to people who're paying her a generous salary," Mona countered.

"You're right," Della admitted.

Mona heaved a deep sigh and looked at us with a stricken expression on her pretty face. "It was all my fault," she said. "I'm the office manager and I should have caught it before I did. I'll be happy to resign if you want me to."

"Oh, for God's sake, Mona . . ." Della began.

"No, really . . . I feel so responsible. . . ."

"Just hush," Della said.

"The losses were minimal, Mona," I said. "But what

gets me is the idea that they would do something like that."

"But isn't there any legal recourse?" she asked.

"I don't know," I said. "There are some federal laws that cover industrial espionage, but I don't know if they apply to oil production. I don't think they do, and the charges would be next to impossible to prove anyway. That fool girl would be useless as a witness. A good defense attorney would shred her to rags."

"I guess we've put a stop to that business," Della said that night as we climbed into bed. "Are you going to mention it to them?"

"You mean Robillard and Van Horn? I don't think so."

"Why not?" she asked.

"I've been boring in pretty heavily on Robillard ever since I started playing poker at the hotel. It was reasonable to expect a man like him to retaliate."

"Do you think it really was retaliation? Or just normal business skulduggery?"

"Maybe some of both. But Mona needs to keep a close eye on those other girls up there."

"Oh, she already is. She called the whole staff together today and read them the riot act. I don't think there will be any more problems."

"Just please promise me one thing, Della," I said with a grin.

"What?"

"If you and Mona ever get it in for me, just go ahead and shoot me. I'd prefer it to the way you two skinned that poor girl alive today."

"Nope. No promises. If you've got it coming, then . . ." She fell silent and raised her eyebrows.

"Ahhh . . . Cruel, wanton woman . . ."

"If you'll shut up, I'll show you how wanton I can be."

TWENTY-TWO

The next morning I arose at four and got an early start to Tulsa. The previous Friday a small box that bore a Virginia postmark had come in the mail. Inside the box were three keys and a stiff note card that contained a carefully typed address and nothing else. I knew then that it was time for another talk with Chicken Little.

The week before we'd decided that sharing one car was becoming too much of a burden. Della frequently drove out to the basin to check leases on her own, and I often found myself desperately needing transportation when she was gone in the Lincoln. We went shopping for her for a vehicle, and a few hours later she drove away from the local Ford agency with a new woody wagon whose metal was painted a deep maroon.

"It goes good with your convertible," she said.

As I watched her swing out into the street in her new car that day I could only laugh inwardly. Not that long ago I'd been a lone eagle, answering to no one besides myself and responsible for nothing beyond my car and several suitcases of clothing. Now I'd not only acquired a woman eleven years my junior but a house and a station wagon as well. The previous fall I'd had a modest income from a trust, and now I was well on my way to becoming an oil baron. Things had certainly moved fast since I met that girl; I was on the verge of becoming domesticated, and much to my surprise I didn't find the prospect all that unpleasant.

It was a long drive. Around noon I made a quick stop for a light lunch at a little roadside café about fifty miles north of the Red River, and then pushed on until I finally pulled into Little's yard not long before suppertime. I'd known the old man ever since I was a kid. My father was a bred-in-the-bone Cajun from a little town a few miles outside Lafayette, Louisiana. He'd come to East Texas not long after the turn of the century and gone into the timber business. Dad was a ruthless but likable man, and in a few years he had established a sizable fortune that included a controlling interest in a thriving bank in Lufkin. But like many Cajuns, he was addicted to gambling in general and cockfighting in particular. Though my devout Presbyterian mother finally succeeded in getting him weaned off gambling, he never gave up his love of cocking. In his later life he watched avidly even though he no longer bet. He and Chicken Little were lifelong friends, and some of my finest memories were of the many summer weekends I'd spent at Little's place during my youth.

The house was a sprawling structure of whitewashed clapboard with a tin roof that stood on a wooded bluff overlooking a wide bend in the Cimarron River a few miles out from town. The old man occupied one of a pair of deep hickory rocking chairs that sat on the front veranda. He wore khaki pants, a much-washed and much-darned white dress shirt and a weathered fedora. A stoneware demijohn with a cob stopper sat on a small table beside his chair, alongside a sugar bowl, a saucer of lemon halves, and a pair of heavy mugs.

"Come on up here and set a spell," he said as I climbed the steps. "I was just fixing to make a hot toddy. Have one with me."

I took the other chair and shook his thin, bony hand. "I'll have a drink, but not a toddy. Haven't you got any ice?"

"Ice," he grumbled, getting to his feet. "A grown man that don't know how to drink whiskey."

He disappeared into the bowels of the house and returned in a couple of minutes with a steaming kettle and a mug of cracked ice. I pulled the cob from the demijohn and poured a good dram over the ice. The liquor was almost clear, with only the barest trace of amber coloring. Little put two spoonfuls of sugar into one of the other mugs, then squeezed in half a lemon. He partially filled the mug with hot water and gave it a stir with the spoon. When the sugar had dissolved, he topped it off from the whiskey jug. I took a pull of my own drink and gasped.

Little grinned. "Pure corn. It'll do the job, won't it?"

"Yes," I answered once I'd gotten my breath. "But there are easier ways to get it done."

He laughed. "I'm running three stills right now near Waverly over in the Cookson Hills," he said. "Big stills. Got men hired to tend 'em for me."

"What in the world do you do with that much corn whiskey?" I asked.

"Take it over to Little Rock and sell it for five dollars

a gallon. The man that buys it from me cuts it, doctors it up and flavors it, and then sells it to bars for two and a half a fifth. Then they sell it by the drink for bonded stuff. They say this fellow can make green corn whiskey taste like eight-year-old bourbon. It more than doubles a bar owner's profit on a bottle."

"Why don't you flavor the whiskey up yourself and get all the profit? Just run it straight from Cookson down to Hot Springs."

"I hear what you're saying," he replied, nodding slowly and raising his head to gaze off at the horizon, a faraway look in his eyes. Chicken Little had numerous theories about life, some of them deeply theological, and I sensed that he was about to expound on one of them.

"I could do that," he said thoughtfully. "But it might take some killin' to get things set up right, and that kind of behavior is liable to lead to hurt feelings. Besides, I've always had this notion that the Good Lord wants each man to make his living in certain ways that he laid out for him in the days of his youth. I believe that if a man strays into other fields he's asking for trouble from Above. That's why I didn't want to buy into none of that oil business when you mentioned it, even though I did appreciate the offer. The only time in my life I ever went to the pen was because I strayed from my appointed course and got into some activities the Lord had reserved for other folks."

"I saw you down at the Weilbach," I said, changing the subject. "How do things look?"

"Good. I don't believe it's going to be any problem at all. That stairway being so close to the door helps. And the deputies they got hired to guard the thing are awful careless."

I nodded. "Yeah, they've gotten even more so since the oil boom blew in. So are we on?"

He laughed his ready laugh, his pale blue eyes dancing. "Why, hell yes, we're on. I told you that when you first come up here last year."

"I know that's what you said then, but you hadn't had a chance to look the situation over at that time. I don't mean to ask a friend to commit suicide for me."

"Ain't no suicide to it, so you stop talking that way. That kind of talk's bad luck. Don't you worry. I know what I'm doing."

"How about the other crew?" I asked. "Are they in?"

"I think so. The main man is a fellow named Tobe Perkins. I've known him forever, and I guarantee that he's one of the best. But he wants to meet you."

I considered for a moment. "Sure, why not?"

"Good," he said with satisfaction. "I'll set it up. He says that he wants to meet the man who's steering the deal. It's a prudent move on his part, and I don't blame him."

"Me either," I said.

We fell silent and stared off to the west where the setting sun was a blood red half circle in the hills beyond the broad silver band of the Cimarron River. I could smell the rich odor of the river bottom in the distance, and somewhere nearby a dove called to its mate. A soft breeze had been blowing, rippling the grass and fluttering the leaves of the blackjack trees that surrounded the house. Suddenly the wind lay and a hush fell on the world. I reached for the jug and poured another dram of moonshine over my ice. Down in the river bottom an owl hooted twice, and from somewhere behind the house came the muted clang of a cowbell. It ceased and the silence reigned once again. Finally Chicken Little spoke. "Willie has been crabbing about the long wait."

"What's wrong now?" I asked with a sigh.

"He claims he's short of money and he needs to get something going pretty soon. Says he's had bad luck here lately in other ventures and needs a little money to live on."

"Is there any truth in that?"

Chicken Little shrugged. "I wouldn't be surprised. You see, Willie's got some very odd tastes and they can get expensive."

"You realize that he's already been down to Texas bothering me about money, don't you?" I asked.

"No, I didn't know that. . . ."

I nodded. "I gave him a thousand that time. What would it take this time?"

"I think a couple of thousand would shut him up till Christmastime, at least. It's come to the point that we're going to have to either do something or cut loose from him. And if we do, we'll need to find somebody else."

"No, we don't want that," I said, shaking my head. "I suppose it's reasonable since it's taking so much longer than we thought. We can't expect anybody to thrive on air and goodwill."

Little nodded. "I believe it's a wise move. And fair. He claims that keepin' himself free to jump on this deal when the time comes has caused him to miss some opportunities, and I don't doubt it. I'll be glad to front the money, if you want me to. That's no problem. I would have went ahead and give it to him already, but I didn't want to make no kind of move without checking with you first."

I pulled out my money clip and stripped off the two thousand. "Just make sure he knows the wait is going to be worth it. That game is getting hotter and richer all the time."

Chicken Little nodded again and took the money.

"Willie ain't really a close friend of mine," he said with a sigh. "And I regret the trouble he's caused you. I wouldn't have picked him in the first place except that I didn't have much to choose from. Most of my old cohorts have fallen by the wayside."

"You're the last of a vanishing breed, Little," I told him seriously.

He nodded sadly. "I guess so. Besides, Willie will be rock steady when the time comes, and that's worth some aggravation. He won't talk, and he won't never rat out his partners. That you can count on. The Little Rock police beat him half to death a few years back over a chickenshit burglary, and they never got a damn thing out of him."

We lapsed back into silence once more and sat watching the growing dusk. From somewhere behind the house a dinner bell clanged loudly and I heard a woman's voice call us to supper. I'd started to rise from my chair when I felt Little's hand on my arm. "Sit back down a minute," he said softly. "There's one more thing you need to know."

"What's that?" I asked.

He sighed. "Your friend's coming up here for the cockfight tomorrow night."

"Which friend?" I asked.

"Clifton Robillard."

TWENTY-THREE

Little was a country man and his house was a country house. It had that clean, spare feeling that only sparsely furnished farmhouses seem to have, with their high ceilings and waxed pine floors and interior walls of painted planking. The dining room held a heavy oval table of golden oak that was covered with a cloth of white damask and laden with a great platter of fried chicken and bowls of country vegetables. The room was cool and filled with the odor of freshly baked cornbread, and over our heads a ceiling fan turned languidly in the soft evening air. Two people, a man and a woman, were already seated at the table. Little introduced the man as Tom Moore, a huge, silent Cherokee of about thirty years who conditioned and pitted the gamecocks. Moore's wife was a tiny, intense young Indian girl named Lacy who had a pretty face and a shy smile.

My host removed his hat and hung it on a hall tree that stood near the door. He took his place at the head of the table and a moment later his wife, Annie, came into the room carrying a steaming bowl of cream gravy. She was a small woman near his age, still lovely despite her years, with a calm face and a pair of liquid brown eyes a man could get lost in. As soon as she set the gravy on the table, I scooped her up in a big hug and swung her around, her feet off the floor.

"Put me down, you big ox," she said with a laugh.

A few moments later we were seated at the table. We all waited with our hands in our laps while Annie said a long blessing, then we dug in. When the meal was finished, Little and I rose from the table. I went over to where Annie sat, and leaned down to give her another kiss on the cheek. Poking me gently in the ribs, she looked up, and said, "Don't be gone so long the next time, stranger."

She'd been one of my favorite people as long as I could remember. Like many young mountain girls, she'd come down out of the Ozarks not long after the turn of the century with stars in her eyes and dreams in her heart. Landing in Hot Springs, she got a job as a waitress in one of the resort hotels where she soon fell under the thrall of a gambler named Spunk Morgan, a surly, ill-tempered man from Kansas who used her hard and often beat her unmercifully. Somewhere along the way she encountered Chicken Little and true love blossomed. Not long after they met, Spunk Morgan suffered a belated attack of good manners and vanished, never to be heard from again, and the happy couple quickly wed. Less than a decade later they moved to the farm near Tulsa where they raised three children—two boys and a girl. The girl and the older boy were both college graduates, but their youngest son was in the Oklahoma State Penitentiary at McAlester doing ten years for manslaughter. "There's wild blood coming from both sides in them kids of mine," Little once said to me sadly. "And blood will tell whether it's in people or fighting cocks."

One time several years earlier over a bottle of good scotch that loosened his tongue, he'd told me of a trip he and Annie made back to the Ozarks in the early days of their marriage. They stripped and swam naked in a wide, gravel-bottomed pool where Licking Creek meets the White River, and then spread out an old quilt on a bed of honeysuckle and made love in a shaded glade where all around them the green-clad mountains rose high into the sky.

"Annie's a Baptist now," he said once he and I were reinstalled on the veranda. "She got religion a few years back, but I don't begrudge it. My momma, God bless her poor old soul, was a Holiness, and I reckon that she got slain in the Spirit at least a dozen times."

"Slain in the Spirit?" I asked, puzzled.

"That's when the Spirit of the Lord descends on you and knocks you out cold. Usually you come up talking in tongues. I've seen it myself on occasion, though it has never happened to me. But as for Annie being a Baptist, it hasn't made her any less lively where it matters. However, I've told her several times that she could stand to pay more attention to that verse in the Bible where it says a Christian woman should bridle her tongue."

I laughed. "I don't think there is any such verse, Little."

"Well if there ain't, they ought to be."

Before he had a chance to explore other deficiencies in the Holy Scriptures, I brought the conversation around to our business. "Here," I said, reaching in my pants pocket for the keys that had come in the mail the previous Friday. "It's a garage," I told him. "A good, sturdy building, with meshed windows and strong doors."

"Have the windows been painted up on the inside?" he asked.

"No, but that's a good idea. I'll take care of having them blacked out as soon as I get back home."

"It won't hurt a thing to be safe," he said. "We don't want nobody looking in there and remembering that car. You got the address?"

From my wallet I took the card that had come with the keys and gave it to him. Without looking at it he dropped it into his shirt pocket where he'd put the $2,000 I'd given him earlier.

"Who rented the garage?" he asked. "We need to make sure the rent is kept current."

I grinned but he couldn't see it in the darkness. "Nobody rented it," I said. "It was bought by a moving company up in Cicero, Illinois, that's really just a post office box."

"Is that a fact?" he asked casually. I could hear the smile in his voice.

"Yeah, and the car's a dark gray '41 Pontiac four-door with a rebuilt motor. It's registered to the moving company."

"When's it going to be put into the garage?" Little asked.

"A couple of days beforehand. It's got a brand-new battery and runs like a dream, so you shouldn't have any trouble with it."

"Sounds good to me."

"Now, what about Clifton Robillard?" I asked. "Do you know why he's going to be up here tomorrow night? I don't like coincidences. They spook me."

"Ain't no coincidence to it that I can see. I've been told that he's been making the cockfights around Tulsa for years, and since this is the big fight of the year it makes sense that he'd be here. It's been advertised in cocking newspapers all over the country, and I imagine there will be a whole slew of folks from down in Texas."

"How did you find out he was coming?"

"A fellow I know just happened to mention his name and I perked up my ears. This man talked to him on the phone last week, and Robillard said he'd be looking for some heavy betting action."

"You don't know him, do you?" I asked.

"Not by name or I would have mentioned it when you first come up here and told me about him. I may have seen him around, but I ain't never met him that I can recall. I just figured you'd want to know."

I thought for a long while. The only risk I ran was that it was not wise to have Robillard see me and Chicken Little together. But that was a very minor risk. If everything went right, he'd hardly be in a position to tell anyone. On the positive side, running into him at the chicken fight would give me the pleasure of popping up where I wasn't supposed to be and perhaps irritating him even more than I already had.

"I probably should play it safe and go home in the morning, but I think I'll stay an extra day and try to get under the man's skin," I finally said.

"That's fine with me, boy. It's your call."

"Can you put me up another night? I hate to be an inconvenience to you."

"Oh, hush. You're always welcome here and you know it."

"I'll need to phone Della and let her know I'm staying over."

He nodded. "It might be best not to call from here at the house, though."

I quickly agreed. In those days a long-distance call was made by first dialing the operator, who then called your party for you. When the call was completed, she made a separate receipt for it, then the carbon of the receipt was included when the bill came. Which meant that the phone company kept a paper record of all long distance calls. And the cops knew it.

"We'll take Annie into Tulsa tomorrow for lunch at the Mayo Hotel," Little said. "She'll like that and you can make your call from a pay phone."

TWENTY-FOUR

The next day we drove into Tulsa where I made my phone call, then we went to the Mayo for lunch. It was the town's premier hotel, patterned on the Plaza in New York, and its dining room was regal.

After our meal Little checked in at his two bookmaking parlors, while Annie was off at Metzinger's Department Store with a handful of cash he'd given her. Then we came back downtown and I parked across from Metzinger's where we could sit and talk until Anne appeared.

"How's the booking going?" I asked. "Do you do pretty good with it?"

"I clear about five hundred a week out of the pair, and nearly that much from the whiskey. Of course, I could squeeze more out of both of them, but I like to spread it around. I never was a hog about money, and it all works better if you give everybody a nice cut. You know what the Bible says about not binding the mouths of the asses that thrash the grain. And I have to kick a part of the gambling money up to the outfit up in Kansas City, and that cuts down my net. But it's always been that way."

"Do they get a piece of the moonshine too?"

He shook his head. "Otis Shamblin put a stop to that back in 1934. Did you ever know Otis?"

"No, but I've heard my dad talk about him."

"See, I inherited my whiskey business from Otis. He had a bunch of stills over there in the Cookson Hills back during Prohibition, and all I had to do with the moonshine operation in them days was trucking the liquor up to Kansas City for him, though I brought up several loads of import stuff of my own that came in at night along the Texas coast. Back then the Italians up there were buying all the corn whiskey they could get from us and not crabbing about the price, neither. I figured that after the repeal come in, the bootlegging business was just about done for, but Otis had talked to a fellow up in Kentucky who told him all about flavoring it up and selling it for bonded whiskey. Otis is the one that got that business started here in Oklahoma, and he come to me to help him get sugar. I had a contact down in Texas where I could get the stuff by the truckload, so me and Otis went into business. Well, it didn't take the boys up in Kansas City long to hear about it, and they decided they were due a piece of the action. Four of them come down one Saturday in a big fancy Packard looking for Otis, and they just vanished, Packard and all. Then a few days later another carload come looking for the first bunch, and they up and disappeared too. No one seemed to know where they had went. It was all a great mystery."

"No kidding?" I laughed.

"It's mercy's own truth if I've ever told it. From what I heard, they kinda regrouped up there to figure out how to deal with the situation. They hadn't never had two whole carloads of folks just evaporate away like that, and it was a new experience for them."

"What did they finally do?" I asked.

"They decided to leave Otis Shamblin alone, that's what they did. There just wasn't enough profit in the operation to fight a war from two hundred miles away and come out ahead. And hell, everybody up there in the hills knowed what had happened to those fellows. But there was one funny little follow-up to the story. Otis had a backhoe he'd used for this and that, a wheezy, wore-out old thing that popped and snorted something awful. You could hear it five miles away. Now, Otis's oldest son was a churchgoing family man, and one night the preacher was at this boy's house having supper when Otis cranked up that old backhoe to scrape out a ditch out behind his barn. When them folks sitting around the table down there heard it, one of the kids jumped up, and said, 'Hot damn!! Granddaddy done kilt himself another carload of them Eye-talians! I wanna go see!' "

By the time he finished the story I was doubled over in laughter. Little shook his head. "Otis Shamblin was the tush hog of the Cookson Hills, and didn't nobody but God Almighty ever get the best of him. He died about five years later and I took over the business."

That evening about six, Little came into the kitchen where Annie and I sat drinking coffee. He was wearing a stiffly starched white shirt with French cuffs. His wide flowered tie was of mottled blues and golds, and I noticed that his cuff links were gold rooster heads set in onyx ovals. Under his left armpit rode a black shoulder holster that carried his old Colt Pocket Auto. He had a dark blue pinstriped suit coat slung over his shoulder, and on his head sat a new fedora of dark gray felt. "You about ready?" he asked me, the unlighted Camel bobbing in his lips as he spoke.

I got my own coat from the back of my chair, and Annie made adjustments to both our ties. Little kissed her goodbye and minutes later we were on the road.

TWENTY-FIVE

The pit was a large warehouselike building in a creek bottom several miles north of Tulsa. The place was surrounded with cars and trucks that ranged from fancy convertibles and limousines all the way down to ancient Model T Ford junkers and worse. To one side of the parking lot lay a roped-off area reserved for fighters and their vehicles. Little motioned for me to swing into this part of the yard. An off-duty deputy sheriff was guarding the entry to keep out non-fighters, and he waved us through as soon as he recognized my companion.

"What kind of fight is this, exactly?" I asked.

"It's a derby. It'll go on two days and the prize money goes to the last three cockers still in the game after the last fight. But I'm not in it. What I'm here for is a five-cock grudge match between me and a man named Bo Thompson from up at South Bend, Indiana. Bo's got a breed he calls Thompson's White Hackles and they are good chickens. He's also a son-of-a-bitch, but he comes by it naturally so I don't hold it against him."

"Who's going to win?" I asked.

He shrugged. "He has some fine birds. Overall I've got the best flock, and in a year's time I'll get maybe five percent more wins than he does from the same number of fights, but his best cocks are hell on wheels. If you want to bet on something where the odds are just about as even as a damn coin toss, then put some money on either one of us here tonight because I figure that's just about the call. I sent seventeen birds up with Tom earlier today and I imagine Bo will have at least twenty."

"Why did you bring so many if you're only going to fight five?"

"To match weights at weigh-in. We have to come within two ounces of one another's birds, so it may take that many to find five pairs that match up. And we may have to trim feathers to get that. But I leave all that business to Tom these days. I trained him good and he's got a head full of sense that he come into the world with, so I don't worry about it."

We climbed from the car and headed toward the pit. Near the door we ran into a pair of men I'd known for years but hadn't seen in almost a decade. Jack Amber and Little Tommy Trehan had been partners since they met in an Allied convalescent center in France after both had been wounded in the First World War. Amber was a tall, courtly individual who originally came from a crossroads village not far from my own hometown down in deep East Texas. Trehan, an ex-jockey, was a tiny man who'd been born to an unmarried slattern in London's notorious East End in the waning years of the last century. When the First World War broke out, he saw military service as a way out of a dead-end life in the slums. Initially rejected because of his height, he persisted in his efforts to enlist, and was successful after the Somme Campaign when the thinning British ranks made recruiters less fastidious of the printed rules concerning the minimum size for soldiers.

After the Armistice, the little Englishman accompanied Amber back home to Texas, and during Prohibition they became the society bootleggers in Houston. They also had a small bookmaking operation, and in those days Trehan could often be found at the Maceo brothers' Turf Athletic Club on Galveston Island where he was the odds maker for local sporting events.

Both wore suits and ties that night, though Amber had removed his coat against the heat. When I introduced them to Little, the old moonshiner peered at the larger man quizzically for a few moments, then said, "I know Jack Amber. Me and him did some whiskey business back years ago."

"I remember it well," Amber said, shaking Little's hand.

"What brings you two up here?" I asked.

"We kept getting customers who wanted to place bets on this grudge match," Amber said. "We got the odds out of Hot Springs, and then booked the action, but we decided to drive up and see what all the excitement was about."

"Well, I'm the man with the Tulsa Grays," Little told them. "How are the odds running on my match?"

"Eight to seven in your favor," Trehan said.

"Shit," Little said in disgust. "I wonder what genius thought that up. I wouldn't give myself better than even money here tonight."

"Whatever you say, mate," Trehan agreed with a quick nod.

Little shrugged. "Well, I guess maybe them boys down in Hot Springs think they know more about cocking than I do. Let's go inside."

The pit was pandemonium. At least five hundred people were crammed into the building, most of them sitting on rude bleachers that rose on all four sides to near the ceiling. The air was thick with tobacco smoke, and the odor of sweat mixed with strong drink was almost overpowering. The pit itself was a square enclosure surrounded by a board wall about three feet high. A fight had just finished and the pitters were taking their birds from the pit. Both cocks appeared dead.

When Chicken Little entered the building, a great cheer went up from the crowd. It was obvious that he was the hometown favorite, but he took the acclaim in stride. He gave a quick wave to the spectators, then turned back to shake hands once again with Amber and Trehan. "My regards in case I don't see you again," he said. "I need to go tend to business."

All around us bets were being settled and new ones made. Across the way a couple of men who were dressed like Manlow Rhodes stood talking and backslapping with three bleached-out Okies who looked too tired and defeated to have even considered going west with the Dust Bowl migration, while nearby a sweet-faced thirtyish woman in a sequined cocktail dress counted out a lost wager to a smiling old Negro who wore the most ragged pair of overalls I've ever seen on a man in public. And in front of them all, in the middle of the first row of spectators, sat Clifton Robillard and Simon Van Horn.

Van Horn saw me about the same time I noticed them.

He poked Robillard in the ribs and pointed my way. Robillard swung around and recognized me immediately. He motioned for me to come over, but I gave him a friendly wave and turned to Trehan and asked him a question. It got the voluble Cockney started talking, and I watched Robillard out the corner of my eye while the small man prattled on. Soon Robillard rose to his feet and started walking toward us, followed by Simon Van Horn and two younger men.

"Bad pennies just turn up everywhere," he said as soon as he was close enough for his silky voice to be heard over the din of the crowd.

I swung around and stuck out my hand. "I was just thinking the same thing."

As usual, Robillard looked like he'd just stepped out of an ad in *Esquire*. He wore a three-piece suit of cream-colored linen, a red tie and a wide-brimmed Panama hat. Van Horn wore blue seersucker and was hatless. The two men with them were younger and looked like professional strong-arm, and not particularly bright strong-arm, either. The larger of the pair was a bulky, tough-looking guy in his late twenties who had a headful of long, oily hair and a sullen expression. The other was a smaller man with a crew cut and a surly, pinched face that could have fit on a B movie villain. Both were decked out in what was called the California style back then, which meant they were dressed badly. Their version of bad meant light-colored suits worn over two-toned knitted polo shirts with matching brown-and-white shoes.

I shook hands with all four men. The larger goon hesitated for a moment before extending his paw while he looked me over with a scowl that was meant to be intimidating. "Dewey Sipes," he said.

I treated him to the same goofy grin that I'd given Ollie Marne at our first meeting, and asked him if he'd heard the one about the two-headed farmer. This earned me nothing beyond a deepening of his scowl. I quickly forgot about him and turned my attention to Robillard.

"I'm surprised to see you here," I said. "I had no idea you were an enthusiast of this sort of sport."

"Well, I could say the same thing about you," Robillard answered.

"I'm not, actually."

"Oh, I see. Then you don't bet on the contests?"

"I hadn't planned to," I replied.

"That's a shame. Earlier in the evening I tried to get a little action going with your friends here," he said, indicating Amber and Trehan. "But they didn't want any part of it."

"I only wager on things I understand," Trehan remarked pleasantly.

"You mentioned that before," Dewey Sipes growled.

"That's right, I did," the tiny Englishman answered belligerently. "And I'll bloody well say it again as often as I bloody well like."

Sipes opened his mouth to speak, but Robillard gave him a glare and he snapped it shut.

"Well, I thought I might find some real gambling men up here with this big grudge match and all the advertising that's been done," Robillard said. "But it looks like it's all tinhorn stuff."

"I would have thought you get enough action back at the Weilbach," I told him.

"Oh, I take it wherever I can get it. I love to gamble. Sometimes I go as far north as Saratoga for the horse races."

"I see. Just exactly what did you have in mind?" I asked.

"I thought maybe somebody might like to go four or five thousand on this grudge match tonight. That's what I offered your friends, but they weren't interested."

"Tell me about that five-thousand-dollar bet," I said.

"I like the Thompson's Whites," he replied. "I hear they're giving the Grays eight to seven odds over at the Springs, but I got enough confidence in the Thompson birds to offer even odds. Think you might be interested?"

"I've only got about a thousand on me," I said.

"That's all right. I'll take your marker when I win."

Why I plunged in, I don't know to this day. I was as ignorant of cockfighting as it was possible for a man to be, and even Chicken Little didn't give himself better than even odds. But I had come to Texas in the first place to confront Clifton Robillard, and fate seemed to be handing me an opportunity to do it away from the poker table. Besides, it was really a win/win situation for me since I now had the extra money to play with. If he lost, I had just burrowed myself that much further under his skin; if I lost it would only serve to make him more arrogant and reckless at the Weilbach game, something that would make his inevitable fall just that much sweeter when it came. So I pretended to deliberate for a minute, rubbing my chin thoughtfully. "I've got a better offer," I told him. "How about twenty-five and I give you Hot Springs odds."

"What? Just twenty-five hundred? But I wanted to go at least five—"

I interrupted him. "No sir. Twenty-five thousand. And

I'll give you Hot Springs odds and take *your* marker when *I* win."

Such a bet was unheard of in cocking circles in those days, and he looked at me in disbelief. Then, for just an instant, I was able to enjoy the expression of pure, vertigolike fear that swept through his cold blue eyes, and I honestly believe that at that precise moment he began to suspect that I was something more than I appeared to be. No matter what the outcome that evening, I'd unnerved him. Of course, he was worth many times that sum, but some things I'd heard around town had led me to suspect that he was cash poor at the moment. If that was true and he lost, he might be hard-pressed to come up with the money on a few days' notice.

It was Trehan who broke the silence. "Well, mate, you said you wanted to find a real gambling man, and it appears to me that you are bloody well looking at one right now."

"What's it going to be, Mr. Robillard?" I asked. "You were looking for some action and here it is."

Robillard glanced at Simon Van Horn.

"Don't try to pull me into this mess," Van Horn said, holding up his hands. "I think you're both crazy to even think about betting money on damn chickens in the first place."

Robillard regained his composure. "Your man's birds are favored," he finally said.

"That's right, they are. But Mr. Little himself says that he doesn't give his own cocks better than an even chance to win. If you lose, you only owe me around twenty-two thousand, but if I lose I'll owe you the whole twenty-five. If it was pot odds in a poker game it would be the time for you to call rather than fold."

He had very little choice after the way he had talked. And like all plunging gamblers, he was more inclined to dwell on the joys of winning than on the possibility of defeat. He finally nodded and extended his hand. "All right, it's a bet."

We shook hands once more, then stood around for a while talking about not much of anything. After a time he and Van Horn and the two young toughs drifted away.

"Let's go out to our car and have a drink," Amber said, taking my arm and steering me toward the door.

A few minutes later we were taking pulls out of a bottle of Johnny Walker when Trehan asked, "Bad blood between the two of you, mate?"

"A little. And it looks like there's going to be more, doesn't it?" I answered with a grin.

"What's his gripe?"

"I've hit him pretty heavily here lately at the poker table, and he doesn't like to lose."

"Who does?" Trehan asked.

"I think this is one for the record books," Amber said.

He was right. The grudge match started a half hour later, and after ten minutes the first two Tulsa Grays were stone dead and it looked like I was going to be paying off the largest single loss of my life outside the poker table.

TWENTY-SIX

I saw a mild ray of hope when the third of Little's cocks won handily after forty minutes in the pit. The referee gave the crowd a ten-minute break while the vendors worked the crowd selling soft drinks and peanuts and cotton candy. There were whole families present that night, many of them clans of rough Okie and Arkie hill people, but there were others who were soundly middle class. I noticed two young couples, high school boys and their bobby-soxer girlfriends. One of the girls was pale and looked as though she was on the verge of fainting, but the other had a ruddy blush to her cheeks and a gleam in her eye that was almost sexual. During the last fight her gaze had been fixed on the pit, and her breath was coming in short, breast-heaving little gasps. Unless I missed my guess, a violent and atavistic sport had made another convert.

Then the fourth fight began. In cockfighting the roosters have their spurs clipped off and long blades known as gaffs are attached to their legs. These gaffs are razor sharp and make the whole affair quite bloody. The fight starts after the handlers have gone through a preliminary ritual called billing that consists of holding the cocks face-to-face where they can only peck at one another. This is supposed to raise their rage to a murderous pitch and it usually does. The fight begins when the referee calls out, "Pit your cocks!" and the handlers turn the animals loose with their right hands. There's a whole set of rules that circumscribe the posture and behavior of the handlers, rules so elaborate and arcane that I'm convinced anyone who can master them would also be capable of becoming a nuclear physicist.

The fourth fight lasted about fifteen minutes and ended when the Thompson bird let out one long, bloodcurdling squawk and then fell over dead. The referee called another break before the final fight. The tension in the room was palpable enough that it could have been boxed and sold at the concessions. During the lull in the action a couple of fistfights broke out, only to be quickly broken up by the off-duty cops who were on hand. I felt the tension myself even though it was a no-lose situation for me. But I'm naturally competitive, and I didn't want to win by losing; I wanted to win by winning.

Soon the handlers were in the pit billing the cocks. When the referee called for them to loose the birds, the two roosters came together and flew at least four feet up in the air. When they separated I thought I'd lost. Little's Tulsa Gray fell to the ground on its back, utterly motionless, both feet in the air and its head to one side, its tongue hanging out. The referee was about to call the fight when it came alive and jumped to its feet. It shook itself off, and then tore into the other bird like the Twentieth Century Limited passing a freight train.

It was the bloodiest fight of the evening. Three times the

birds got their gaffs tangled and had to be separated by the handlers. Both were exhausted by the time it ended. At the last scratch the birds wobbled toward each other from opposite sides of the pit and struck, flying only a little more than a foot into the air this time. When they came down the Tulsa Gray was again on its back, but it was clearly alive and its right gaff was sunk in the Thompson bird's brain. After a few quivering death throes, it was all over, and Little's bird even managed to get to its feet. With the last of its energy it climbed atop the other rooster and crowed once before it fell to the side, spent but still alive. I was $22,000 to the better, and it gave me as much satisfaction as any wager I ever won.

The famed Bo Thompson was a tall, thin, bent man who looked like a human question mark with a sour face. The referee brought him and Little face-to-face in the center of the pit and they shook hands to the roar of the crowd.

"Time to settle all wagers," the referee called out. Thompson dug his wallet from the depths of his coat and pulled out a single one-dollar bill, which he then handed to Little. The old man held the bill high above his head and the hometown crowd went wild. When the cheers died down, he stepped out of the pit, and said to me, "I need to go check on Tom and the gamecocks. I'll be just a minute."

I nodded and told him to take his time. What I had witnessed that night had hardly been a Harvard/Yale game, but winning $22,000 from Clifton Robillard had given it a certain rough charm of its own.

And that was that. I waved to Robillard and tried to get away without talking to him, but he motioned for me to wait. I went around the pit, threading my way through the crowd, and met him halfway. Van Horn stayed in his seat and the two young toughs were nowhere to be seen, though I thought nothing of it at the time. Robillard stuck out his hand. His face held a forced smile, and the fear I'd seen earlier was gone from his eyes. "I'll have your money next week," he purred. "Is poker night okay, or do you need it before then?"

"No hurry," I told him.

"Would you like to have a drink?" he asked. "I know a good night spot."

I shook my head. "Thank you anyway, but I'm tired and I know Mr. Little wants to get back home."

"Then I will see you Friday night at the Weilbach."

Chicken Little soon returned and we left the building. The parking lot was lighted by three large lamps hung high on electrical poles, but our car was in its darkest corner. To get to where I'd parked the Lincoln in the last row of the contestants' section, we had to walk between two large trucks—a one-ton Chevy panel job and a Dodge stake bed. Little was a few feet ahead of me and to my right. The Chevy was to my left. The old man had just reached the back of the Dodge and turned to say something when I saw an arm go around his neck. The arm was wearing a light-colored coat sleeve and my mind also registered the toe of a two-toned shoe when a blur came out from behind the Chevy. I saw Chicken Little pull his knees up into a standing fetal position and slide from the man's grasp, leaving the attacker with an armful of fedora and air. But by then I had problems of my own to contend with.

The blur in front of me had a club that was about the length of a cop's nightstick. If he'd tried for a hard poke in my solar plexus, he might have incapacitated me, but like most amateurs he was overeager for a knockout. Instead, he made a great roundhouse swing at my skull that gave me time to react. I lowered my head and raised my shoulder, pivoting my upper body toward rather than away from him as he had expected. Not only did this surprise him, but it had the effect of making him overswing and hit my shoulder with his arm rather than the club. I landed one good, stiff punch to his left kidney and reached up to grab two handfuls of oily hair. Then using every ounce of my strength, I slammed him face-first into the side of the Chevy panel truck. The impact stunned him and brought him to his knees. This gave me a couple of seconds to get an even better grip on his head, and as soon as I had his greasy mop woven into my fingers, I pounded his face into the truck's fender three more times as hard as I could. Bones snapped and teeth flew. I stepped back to see Dewey Sipes on his hands and knees, his face a broken, pulpy mass of blood and snot, his eyes gazing out at nothing with an expression of complete amazement. Then I kicked him in the belly as hard as I could, and heard him retching soundly as I turned to Chicken Little. He didn't need any help. He and his attacker were both on their hands and knees. The goon was trying desperately to crawl away while Little slashed and hacked at the backs of his legs with what I knew was the razor-sharp old German-made switchblade he'd carried for years. By this time the man was screeching at the top of his lungs and imploring any number of deities for relief. Finally, he managed to lunge to his feet and bolt away, and even in the dim light I could see the backs of his pants shiny with the blood that was now streaming from numerous cuts and slashes.

I pulled Little to his feet and he reached down to get his now-mashed fedora. We sprinted the last few yards to my car and we were soon on our way out of the parking lot. I pulled my handkerchief from my pocket and tossed it to the old man. He wiped the blood from his hand and knife, and then looked at his hat sadly. "That damn hat was brand-new," he said in disgust. "And I think I got blood on the sleeve of my coat, too. Well, I guess I asked for it. I was hacking at his shins by the time I hit the ground. Maybe I ought to have pulled my gun and shot him, but I didn't."

"They were with Robillard earlier tonight," I said.

"I saw them."

"The other fellow was a friend of his named Simon Van Horn."

"Well, if they were with your buddy Robillard, then he set 'em on us for sure. The question is why."

"You didn't hear?"

"Hear what?"

"I won a heavy bet off him tonight by backing your Tulsa Grays."

"Really? How heavy?"

"Twenty-five thousand dollars."

"God Almighty, boy . . . I think you *are* crazy!"

"Me crazy? And you won what tonight?" I asked. "A dollar? All this trouble for a dollar? And you call me crazy?"

As I swung the car out into the highway, I heard his high, reedy laughter ringing out against the darkness of the Oklahoma night.

TWENTY-SEVEN

I was packed and ready for the road early the next morning. I kissed Annie good-bye at the breakfast table, and Little and I shook hands on his front porch.

"Well, when do you want to do it?" he asked.

"It's got to be late November. There are some other considerations that make that the prime time."

"That's good enough. Being able to wear an overcoat is always an advantage on a deal like this. And I'll set up a meeting with Tobe Perkins and call you in a few days."

"Little, is Perkins really solid?" I asked. "I mean will he stool?"

"I'd bet my life that he won't. He never has, and he's sure had the opportunity. I've known him for forty years."

"How old is he?" I asked.

"Tobe's in his late fifties, but he's in real good shape. You see, he's been clean as a whistle for better than ten years. Except for a little moonshining, that is. And hell, that ain't even hardly a crime. I know he'd like to make one more good heist to get his hands on a little something to put aside for his old age."

"Okay. Here's what you do. Tell him about me and my background—"

"Except the things I ain't supposed to know," he said with a grin.

"Right," I said, grinning right back at him. "Convince him that I'll do what I say I'll do, and tell him that if this deal blows up in our faces I'll see to it that he has the best lawyers money can buy, and that I might even be able to pull some strings with the government."

He appeared puzzled. "Okay, but there really ain't no need for all that. . . ."

"Yes, there is," I said with a fiendish smile. "I've had another idea."

He reached up and pushed his fedora to one side to scratch his head above his left ear. "I sure wish you'd quit having them ideas, boy. I just want to sit on my front porch from here on out and watch the sun go down."

"Bull," I said with a laugh. "You're having fun and you know it. And if that two thousand doesn't hold Willie until time to move, you just let me know. Or go ahead and give him another thousand and I'll pay you back later."

"Okay. I hate that all this business with Willie has happened. He's gone downhill here lately. Did you notice how grimy he was when we first came down to see the hotel? He didn't used to go around that way. He's never been the sharpest dresser on earth, but at least he stayed clean." He shook his head and sighed. "Willie's the only thing about this whole deal that frets me, and if he keeps on aggravating me I may just pull his plug and find somebody else."

"It's your call, Little," I said. "Do what you think is best."

As I drove off I looked back in the mirror and saw the old man standing on the porch, a worried frown on his face.

I got tangled up in a long, southward-bound military convoy about a hundred miles out of Tulsa, and it took me better than eight hours to get to Dallas. Listening to Tommy Dorsey on the car's radio as I drove made me realize that Della and I had been existing rather than living. We didn't even own a radio for our home. As soon as I hit town I drove to an appliance store I knew on East Main and bought the biggest table model Philco radio/phonograph combination I could fit into the backseat of the Lincoln. By that time I was exhausted, and a good part of it was a delayed reaction to the previous evening at the cockfight. I decided to spend the night in Dallas and drive the rest of the way home in the morning. I registered at the Adolphus and had a steak dinner in the dining room. Afterward I bought a bottle of White Horse at a liquor store a couple of doors down from the hotel, and then called room service for soda and ice. I had a couple of drinks and then phoned Della and told her to expect me home sometime the next day.

The next morning I rose early and ate breakfast in the coffee shop. As soon as the stores opened I went to Neiman Marcus and bought Della a three-quarter-length cinnamon mink like one I'd seen her admiring in a Memphis furrier's shop earlier in the year. A few minutes later I was on the road once again.

When I pulled into the drive about one o'clock that afternoon, I was surprised to see Della's car in the garage. I managed to get the Philco hauled into the living room by myself. She was in our bedroom, sitting Indian fashion in the middle of the bed wearing a loose pair of white shorts and a yellow blouse. In her lap she held the shoe box in which she kept snapshots of her daughter. Her eyes were full of tears when she looked up at me. "I'm sorry," she said. "I didn't expect you home this early."

"Sorry for what?" I asked.

She didn't answer. Instead she held up a small framed oval picture taken just a few weeks before the accident. The little girl was as blond as her mother, with big eyes and a pug nose. Her name had been Suzanne and she'd been killed by a drunk driver not long after her fourth birthday. Della pointed silently to the picture like a child showing off a crayon drawing to her father.

"I know you probably think I shouldn't do this," she said, and started to put the pictures back in the box. "But these snapshots and my memories are all that's left of her, and if my memories fade she'll be all gone."

I leaned over and took her hands. "I think nothing of the sort. You do this as often as you need to." I bent down to give her a kiss on the forehead and smoothed her hair for a moment. I knew that at least part of her anguish was that her baby had been a cesarean birth and there could be no more children for her.

Slipping quietly from the room, I closed the door behind me. I managed to get the radio hooked up without electrocuting myself, then tuned it to soft music from a station in Fort Worth. A few minutes later I had a pot of coffee brewing in the kitchen. I had just finished my second cup and lain down out on the sofa when Della came into the room.

"Want me to get you some coffee?" I asked.

She shook her head and came over to the sofa. It was long and heavy and almost deep enough for two people to lie side by side. Stretching out, she draped herself half on the cushions and half on me with her head on my chest. "You're not getting much of a homecoming," she said. "I'm sorry."

"It's fine, and stop saying you're sorry," I told her gently.

"I like the radio," she said. "It sounds wonderful."

I snuggled her up against me and petted her hair. She buried her head in my chest and began to cry softly. "I may not be such a bargain," she said through muted sobs.

"Hush," I said, and squeezed her tight. I let her cry herself out and we both dozed off and slept for almost an hour.

Later that night, after she'd gone to bed, I was puttering around the kitchen making myself some bacon and eggs when the phone rang. I heard Simon Van Horn's voice as soon as I lifted the receiver. "I just want you to know that I didn't have anything to do with what happened in the parking lot up there at Tulsa," he said.

"Why, nothing happened to me in the parking lot," I replied casually. "Mr. Little and I just drove home, but I did hear that a couple of Mr. Robillard's friends got roughed up out there."

There was a long pause before the voice spoke again. "I see. Well, I hope you understand that I have enough problems of my own without buying in to somebody else's."

"That's a fine attitude, Mr. Van Horn. I try to live that way myself."

There was a second pause before I heard the gentle click

as the connection was broken. I ate my supper and read the paper for a while. Before I went to bed I sneaked Della's mink coat into the hall closet with the intention of giving it to her in a happier moment. But she found it before I had the chance.

TWENTY-EIGHT

The attack at the cockfight had given me a new respect for the lengths Robillard was willing to go to when riled. And since I intended to rile him even more than I already had, I decided a little protection was in order. There were two pawnshops in town. At the smaller I found a Colt Pocket Auto much like Little's. I also bought a kidskin shoulder holster at a local saddle shop. A phone call to Colonel Garrison resulted in his contacting the local district judge, a thin, acerbic, sixtyish man named Colin Striker who was part of the Manlow Rhodes faction in town. The next day Judge Striker quietly issued me a permit to carry a pistol.

When the next Friday rolled around, Della and I were once again reduced to one car. A bad head gasket put the new Ford wagon into the shop for a few days. It was under warranty, but we were left with only the Lincoln for the weekend. That evening Della dropped me off as usual at the Weilbach, and went on her merry way back home with a stack of books from the library. The first hand had just been dealt with four players sitting in when I came in the room. I stood and watched for a few moments amid the

low murmur of voices and the occasional soft rustle of
money at the table.

Poker is the stuff of legends, though its real history is as
alluring as any of the folklore that surrounds it. A primitive
version of the game was first known in Italy during the Re-
naissance, and some form of it was brought to this conti-
nent by Italian immigrants who came to New Orleans not
long after the War of 1812. From there it spread via the
Mississippi River, which became the mother vein of American poker. The first modern version played on this conti-
nent was the game of draw, and the earliest record of it
dates back to 1829. That mention is a notation in a traveling Englishman's diary that recounts the popularity of the
game on Mississippi River boats a full three decades before the Civil War. Draw retained its ascendancy throughout the nineteenth century, and it was the game of choice in
the days of the old West. It was two pair in a hand of draw
poker—aces and eights, the famous Dead Man's Hand—
that Wild Bill Hickock was holding when the fatal shot
was fired into his back. Around 1900 five-card stud became popular, and there is no doubt in my mind that it was
invented by professional card players. Draw is still the
best game for novices because it reveals very little about a
player's holdings. The advantage of stud to a professional
is that ultimately he knows four of your cards and sees your
hand as it unfolds. He also sees your reaction to those
cards. While you have the same information about his
hand, his superior card skill and his experience at reading
people put him in a far better position to make use of the
knowledge. All the other card games popular today, games
like Omaha hi-lo, Texas hold 'em and Mexican sweat,

were concocted by skilled card men with an eye to their own advantage.

There are two things the novice needs to remember about professional poker players. In the first place the professional is in the game to win money. This seems like a truism, but beginners often overlook the fact that winning the most money is not the same thing as winning the most pots or the biggest pots. Good poker players know that the player who steadily wins more than his share of the small and medium-sized hands will come out ahead of the player who wins only a couple of big, dramatic hands during the course of a game. Good players must also learn to bet by the odds and control their own urges to plunge and gamble against the percentages. The second thing the novice needs to understand is that the true pro has learned to assess the game with his head rather than with his hormones, and that he can usually resist the normal human urge to see a hand of poker as the Gunfight at the OK Corral. While he may have pride in his ability (or her ability; some women are very fine players), he is not humiliated by temporary setbacks and sees no disgrace in folding when the odds are against him. One other thing I have noticed about professionals is that eventually most of them will lose their edge and start to get sloppy. While three hours of poker played each Friday night can be thrilling for anyone, sitting at the table hour after hour, several days a week for years on end can become fully as boring as running a punch press in a factory or practicing tax law. When a card player reaches that point, he either finds it difficult to maintain his level of concentration or he begins to knowingly make risky bets in order to add spice to his life. The latter had happened to me in the last few years before I sat down at the game at the Weilbach.

In my best days I was in the upper echelon of the second rank of good poker players in this country. What kept me out of the top ranks wasn't any lack of skill or knowledge but the fact that I've always been more of a *gambler* than a professional card player. A true gambler, no matter what his level of skill at the table, loves risk and seeks it out for its accompanying thrills. In contrast, the professional card player hopes to minimize risk at all times, and prefers to live a life no more exciting than that of the CPA who does your taxes. Since coming to the Weilbach I had done consistently well, but this was more a testimony to my skill than to my temperament. Other than a couple of exceptions like Wilburn Rasco, I was simply a far better card player than the other men in the game. But my tendency to plunge was a positive advantage to me in confronting Clifton Robillard. All I had to do was keep my head above water financially and go head-to-head with him as often as possible in order to unnerve and rattle him.

Robillard was already at the table when I arrived that Friday night, and his eyes were wary and guarded as I walked in the room. I had decided to maintain my pretense that the attack in the parking lot had never happened. Once he saw that I wasn't going to bite him, he relaxed and even preened a little. News of the bet at the cockfight had spread quickly, and he quickly made a good-natured show of paying me. The man had swallowed his initial humiliation and was now basking in the renown of losing the town's biggest wager in recent memory.

After I'd taken my money and shaken hands all around,

I gave the porter a hundred dollars for my part of the rent. I also threw a second hundred into the jenny. Zip Zimmerman had the deal and he called a hand of seven-card stud. I pitched in the ante and we began. I was a few hundred down an hour and a half later when Robillard relaxed and became talkative once again. I'd just taken him for about $500 when he folded after the third card in a hand of five-card stud. Besides his statuesque brunette, there were two other young women present in the suite that night, both obvious call girls. They'd come up with Simon Van Horn, who was another consummate womanizer despite having a wife and a couple of children back home in Fillmore. One of the other players had already taken the younger of these girls into a bedroom for an hour's interlude.

"You don't ever seem to sample the talents of any of these fine-looking girls," Robillard said to me.

"No sir, I don't. I don't believe in mixing my pleasures, and I come up here to play cards."

"Speaking of women, that little blonde you are keeping certainly is fine looking."

I gave Robillard an easy smile, and said, "Della's not a kept woman. If anybody's kept in the arrangement, it's me. She was the one who got us into the oil business."

"Is that a fact?" he asked.

"It is indeed, and even though Deltex Petroleum is half mine on paper, she's the brains behind the whole thing."

"Brains or no, I bet she's a hot little number in the bedroom," he said. "A fine-looking girl like that . . ."

I gave him another smile, this one more patronizing than amused. "Mr. Robillard, do you know what separates human beings from the lower animals?"

"Why, I never gave it much thought, to tell you the truth. I leave that kind of thing to you college boys."

I nodded and began to shuffle the cards. "Then let me enlighten you on the subject. Some scientists think it's our use of language. Religious people believe that we have souls and animals don't. Philosophers claim that we are aware of the nature of death while horses and cats and so forth aren't, and that this knowledge colors all our actions. Personally, I'm convinced that the main distinction is that we humans have a sense of privacy about our sexual lives that's lacking in animals. We copulate behind closed doors while monkeys and dogs and chickens go at it anytime and anyplace the urge hits, regardless of who or what is watching. And I imagine that if they could talk, they would discuss it with the same lack of discretion and taste."

He said nothing more on the subject that evening, but his face reddened, and I could tell that my comments had stung him hard. He reddened even more a few minutes later when I dealt myself a third ten showing against his pair of queens, and it was several hours before he tried to needle me again.

The cards were cold that night. Finally along about midnight he and I went head-on in a hand of seven-card stud in which I lost seventeen hundred dollars. It wasn't a plunge. I played the odds the same way any good player would have played them, and simply lost the hand to better cards. But it made Robillard voluble and a little curious. "I believe you talk less than any man I ever played with," he remarked.

"The less you say, the less you give away," I told him with an easy smile.

He laughed an honest laugh. "I can't argue with you

there, but I like to have fun, and talking is part of the fun to me."

Needling and humiliating people is part of the fun to you, I thought, but I didn't say so. Instead, I took the cards and passed the deal to my left. "Oh, I have plenty of fun at the table," I said. "It just doesn't take a lot of talk to give it to me."

On the next hand Zip Zimmerman drew one of his freak combinations, but ran everybody out by betting too aggressively. The game took a break and the other players rose from their seats, leaving Robillard and me at the table.

"Have you always been a professional gambler?" he asked.

"I've never really been a full-time pro, Mr. Robillard. But I understand what you mean, and the answer is no."

"What else have you done?"

"Well, after college and law school I put in four years in the navy, then in the late '30s I worked for the State Department for a while."

"Really?" he asked with interest. "What did you do at State?"

"My title was assistant to the attaché for cultural affairs, but the truth is that I was little more than a glorified translator at our embassy in Berlin."

"Germany?" he asked with surprise. "You served in Germany?"

I nodded and gave him a cryptic smile.

"And you speak the German language?"

"Oh yes. Fluently. As a matter of fact I accompanied Ambassador Wilson to the famous dinner party where Hermann

Göring gave Charles Lindbergh that medal. It was called the Service Cross of the German Eagle. Pompous-sounding thing, wasn't it? And later on I played poker with Göring."

He couldn't keep himself from asking the next question. No one ever can who hears the story. "Was he any good?"

"Terrible," I said with a laugh. "But he thought he was an absolute master at the game. You see, he never played with anybody but his own subalterns, and they always let him win. I imagine they were afraid not to, but I wasn't afraid, and I trimmed him good. I must admit that he lost with good grace, though he jokingly accused me of being a Jew because I played so carefully. You see, it was part of the Nazi race theory that each race would play cards a certain way, and play the violin in a certain fashion, and I suppose even fornicate in some racially determined manner. And Göring believed it to the hilt. Or at least he claimed to. Utter nonsense, of course. A Jewish friend of mine in the navy was such a reckless player that he made Zimmerman look like the soul of prudence."

"Are you?" he asked.

"What? Jewish? Hardly. Scots-Irish and Cajun in equal proportions."

He liked that. Now he could start needling me with the coon-ass jokes. But I didn't care. I intended to have the last laugh. I'd planted a little seed with my story about Göring, and the next time we met I intended to tell him about my meeting with the Butcher of Prague.

I broke off and went to bed at 4:00 A.M., then slept until noon, and then went down to the restaurant for lunch. I had just returned to the suite when the porter told me that Della had called while I was out. I dialed our number and got her on the third ring.

"Why don't you tear yourself away early tonight?" she asked.

"Sure. Something special?"

"I'm always something special, you dunce," she said with a velvety laugh. "Be in front of the hotel at exactly nine this evening." I heard the soft click of the connection being broken as she gently placed the receiver back on the cradle.

The game went on through that afternoon without heating up. I managed to slowly recoup my losses from Friday night, and by six that evening I was even a few hundred dollars ahead. I'd bluffed Simon Van Horn out of a good pot with a pair of nines showing and nothing in the hole, and a short time later I had the satisfaction of plunging heavily and seeing Robillard fold a hand that he should have stayed with. The odds had been in his favor, even if the cards weren't, before he lost his nerve and flipped his cards over after looking at his stake with a little frown of concern. I knew then that my information had been correct, and that he was in a cash bind despite his millions.

A little before nine I pocketed my winnings and said good-bye. I was waiting at the curb when Della pulled up in front of the Weilbach in the Lincoln. The top was down and she was wearing her mink.

"So you found it," I said as I climbed into the car. "I intended to surprise you."

"I knew you did, but I thought I would just turn the tables and surprise you instead."

"Isn't it a little hot tonight to be wearing a fur coat?"

"Not if you don't have anything on under it," she said perkily.

"I don't believe you," I told her with a grin.

By then we were only a block from the hotel and Saturday night traffic was fairly heavy. She reached down and undid two buttons, then flipped the coat open. There she sat at the wheel of that big car, wearing nothing but a pair of kidskin pumps, her cute little rimless glasses and the mink.

Much later that evening we sat in the kitchen finishing off a midnight supper of lamb chops, scalloped potatoes and Champagne. Della was in her black silk robe and I wore a pair of ragged old pajamas.

"And now dessert," she said, and rose from the table to retrieve a bowl of sugared strawberries and a canister of whipped cream from the refrigerator. A home-baked pound cake emerged from the cabinet, and a moment later she was building me a strawberry shortcake. Meanwhile, I opened a second bottle of Champagne and filled both our glasses.

"I'm tired of going to work every morning," she said as she sat back down.

"Then let Mona handle the office for a while."

She shook her head. "No, I want out from under the whole thing. She and Andy would like to buy the abstract company from us."

"It's your call, sweetheart," I said. "As far as I'm concerned you can give it to them."

"I thought about that, but I decided not to. They feel too obligated to us already. If we make it a business deal, we can all stay friends in the future."

"I'll sign whatever you want me to. But isn't the abstract game going to play out after the whole field gets leased up?"

She looked at me with an amused smile. "You really don't know much about the oil business, do you?"

I smiled across at her and slowly shook my head. "No, I don't. Never claimed to, either."

"Well, the truth is that it's just going to get even better as these holdings start to get into production and begin to split and divide as operators make assignments to borrow against their royalties. The company will set those two kids up for years to come. Besides, I've lent them a little money along the way, and they've been able to pick up a few leases of their own."

"So sell it to them. Just show me where to sign."

Thus ended Della's short foray into the business world. In a period of four months she'd secured both our futures, and I've always wondered what she could have done with an MBA. Probably she'd have spent fifty years as a midechelon executive for a big Manhattan company, and then retired with a gold pin and a sheaf of windy testimonials.

TWENTY-NINE

The next Tuesday Little and I met with Tobe Perkins in a beer joint on the north side of Fort Worth. Perkins was a solid, calm-looking man with brushy gray hair and steady eyes. We held our little conference in a booth at the rear of the place, far from the half dozen rowdy cowboys clustered at the bar.

"You talked to Little, I suppose?" I asked.

"Yeah . . ."

"And you trust him, don't you?"

"Sure I do. But I don't know you, and I don't know if I trust you or not."

"You're sitting here talking about a heist with me," I pointed out. "Why are you doing that if you don't trust me?"

He smiled. "Sometimes you have to take a few chances if you're ever going to get any work in this business. You know, just feel things out. But talking about it and doing it are two different things, and what you have in mind seems a little strange to my way of thinking."

"How so?"

"Well, I've never had a job steered by a guy who didn't want any of the take. That's the first thing that makes me think there might be something wrong. And secondly, you don't talk or act like any criminal I've ever known in my life."

"What If I told you I'm not really a criminal?" I asked.

"Then what are you?"

The waitress appeared and we all ordered Falstaff. When she was gone I said, "I'm an oil man and a lawyer. I served honorably in the United States Navy where I tried cases with the Judge Advocate General's Office."

Perkins turned to stare at the old man for a moment. "This business don't make no sense at all, Little," he said.

"How does fifty grand above what you get from the job itself sound?" I asked. "Does that make better sense?"

I had his attention. "No, but it's sure got an interesting ring to it," he said with a reluctant smile. "What do I have to do for it?"

"You have to stool on a guy—"

"Never," he said empathically.

"I'm not talking about anybody you've ever run with, any of your partners or anything like that. You don't even know this guy, but I guarantee he's got it coming."

"What is this?" he asked. "It sounds like some kind of personal vendetta deal to me."

"Oh, you're right about that," I said. "It's a vendetta, but it's not personal. Or if it is, there's a lot more than just my own feelings at stake here. So how about it?"

"I dunno," he said, shaking his head dubiously.

I could tell he was reluctant. Most criminals will snitch

under the right circumstances. But not all. There are a few, an elite upper echelon, who really are thieves with honor. Or at least there were back in those days.

"Think about it," I said. "You'll never get another chance for this kind of money backed up by somebody with the resources to make things go easy on you if you're caught. You've never pulled a job under those conditions in your life, and you know it."

"Tell me about this guy," he said, rubbing his chin in thought.

I smiled. I was getting close to hooking him and we both knew it. "Tobe, are you patriotic?" I asked.

"Huh?" The waitress came in the door with our beer. When she left, he took a long pull at his bottle, and said, "I don't get it. I'm talking about a hijacking and you're acting like you're trying to sell me war bonds or something. . . . What is this?"

"Just answer the question, please," I said gently. "Do you love your country?"

He shrugged. "Yeah, as much as the next guy, I guess. I mean, everything I got is here. All my family, my friends. I fought in the First World War. Got wounded, too. But what's that got to do with? . . ." He turned to Little. "Is this guy nuts?" he asked.

"Not in any way that adversely affects our business," the old man said with a grin. "Just hear him out."

"Okay," Perkins said with a puzzled shrug. "Fire away. I'm all ears."

"Tobe, my good man," I began. "I'm going to tell you all about a gentleman who's uniquely lacking in the civic virtues. So much so, in fact, that . . ."

An hour later Little and I stood on the sidewalk outside the little tavern watching Perkins drive away.

"Think he'll go for it?" I asked.

"He already has," the old man said. "Never fear."

When I got home that night I told Della I needed some money.

"Sure, how much?"

"A hundred and fifty thousand dollars. In large bills."

She gazed at me impassively through her glasses for a moment, then asked, "What's going on? Is somebody selling Indiana and giving a cash discount?"

"Seriously . . . Can you sneak it out of our various accounts a little at a time over the next few weeks?"

"It depends on how many weeks you're talking about," she said.

"We have until late November."

"It can be done, but you need to realize there's really no way to cover something like this up."

"That's okay. I'm not trying to cover anything up. I just don't want the withdrawals to cause any talk. Make them random both as to times and amounts."

"Okay. Are you going to tell me what this is all about?"

"Later," I said. "Afterwards you get to know everything."

THIRTY

The following Saturday Little called me and said that
Perkins had agreed to do the job, and that he wanted to
meet me that coming Tuesday at a place called the City
Grill in Sweetwater, a small town about two hours to the
north. I was on time and so was Perkins. It was well before
the lunch hour, and the place was almost deserted. Perkins
knew the owner, and the man let us use a small private dining room. We both asked for coffee.

"Glad to have you aboard," I said.

"I hope I'm glad to be here," he said with a twisted grin.
"I've never been mixed up in anything like this. I've always
been more ordinary. I won't even begin to ask you who all
is involved with this thing. . . ."

"That's good, because I can't tell you. I can say that my
associates were informed of your service in the first war,
and they appreciate it and respect you for it."

He looked like he didn't know how to respond. Finally he
managed, "Thanks," and reached up to scratch his head.

"When do you want to look things over?" I asked.

"That's already been done," he replied.

"You didn't go down there yourself, did you?" I asked. "I mean if you're going to testify later we don't want anybody to remember seeing you—"

He held up his hand to silence me. Then he smiled. "Relax. My wife came down with me to case the job for us. She's asleep back at the hotel right now."

"Your wife?" I asked, dumfounded.

His smile got bigger. "She works in an architect's office up in Kansas City, and she's damn near got a photographic memory. I trust her more than I trust myself on casing a job. A woman's attention to detail and all that . . ."

I shook my head in wonder. "That's a new one on me."

"She drew me a quick floor plan, and let me tell you, that whole damn place is a crackerbox deal."

"Okay," I said. "It sounds good. You go in at eleven-thirty on the night of the twenty-ninth. Now, the timing of this is very important. . . ."

"How come?"

I gave him a serene smile. "Because if everything goes right the cops are going to be busy elsewhere."

"I don't get it," he said.

"Don't worry. You don't have to get it. You'll find out all about it later. It's just a profitable little diversion I have planned, and it should make your job that much safer. Now, back to your end . . . You should be in and out in an hour . . . right?"

"That's about it," he replied. "Maybe a little quicker than that."

"Afterward you come directly here to Sweetwater and check into the Alamo Plaza Tourist Court—"

"Wait a minute," he said. "Why not check in earlier that afternoon before the job to save time?"

"Good thinking," I said. "So come back to your room and wait. At four o'clock, two guys will come to the door." I reached in my inside coat pocket and pulled out an envelope. "Here are their pictures so you'll know it's them," I told him. "They'll have the exchange money, and from the time they knock on that door you're home free."

"Not really," he said. "I've still got to get that money back to Kansas City. A man's always vulnerable on the road with the take from a robbery."

"No, it's going to be different this time," I said with a grin. "You let your partner take your car and go his own route back north. Then you and my men go in their car, and they'll take you and the money on back to Kansas City."

"Okay . . ." he said dubiously.

"Now, as soon as you get in your room at the motel I want you to separate off about ninety-two or ninety-three thousand dollars and put it in a separate satchel. That's the money you're going to leave behind in the room. Be sure to leave the money just the way you got it. It'll be replaced with what I'm sending with the guys who are coming up. You can count it if you want, but—"

"Shit, your men will have me in a position to kill me and take it all. Why expect them to cheat me for only part of it? This is either going to work or it's not. I'm either going to walk away from it or I'm not. I figure it's worth the risk."

I nodded in understanding. "Please try to feel as secure as you can. The amount of money we're talking about here is negligible to me since I got involved in the oil business, so I have no reason to be setting you up."

"I really don't think you do, either," he said.

"The ninety-odd thousand will have to be left in the room," I said. "You *do* understand that, right?"

"Oh, sure," he replied. "It will be."

"Okay. You'll all leave the room around breakfasttime. The guys I'm sending will know when it's time to go. You just do what they tell you to do, and everything will fall into place."

"Okay," he said. "Just one other point about this business of testifying later on . . . How would you like a second witness?"

"That depends," I said. "How good would he be?"

"As good as me, and he could back up my story."

"Tell me about him," I said.

He gave a dismissive shrug. "Nothing to tell. He's my partner on the job, Charlie Needam. I've known him all my life, and we've pulled some pretty big jobs together. He won't stool on anybody he works with, but this is different and he'll go for it. He's smart, he can hold it together on the stand. But it'll cost you another fifty thousand."

I thought quickly. A second witness was infinitely better than just one. If he could pull it off. But I didn't know if Tobe could pull it off either, though I had no reason to think he couldn't. For all I knew, he might be the greatest actor since Barrymore. Or he might be a bumbling fool on the stand. It was just a chance I had to take. "Sure," I said. "You each get the first half after you talk to Crowder, then the other half after the trial."

"Fine. You won't be disappointed in the guy. See, I ain't

done a job since I got out of the pen ten years ago. I mean I been hewing the straight and narrow right down the line. Charlie ain't been quite so clean, but he ain't got no arrests in the last few years either. So . . ."

"So on paper you both look pretty good as witnesses."

"Right."

"Okay, the two of you go over the story I cooked up and make sure you've got it down right. Don't make every little point agree, though—"

He grinned and held up his hand to silence me. "Please. Me and Charlie know how to run out a story."

A few minutes later we walked out to our cars and shook hands in the bright sunlight. "The only thing that still worries me," he said, "is that long trip back home with the money. That's when you're always the most vulnerable."

"I told you that you can relax from the moment my two men get to the door. Believe it."

He shook his head in doubt. "I don't see how."

I smiled at him and put my hand on his shoulder to give it a reassuring squeeze. "Because the guys you're going to be traveling with will have documents identifying them as high-level employees of the United States government."

"Aw, man . . . That's real dangerous," he said. "Using bogus government IDs is hard to pull off."

"Tobe, these papers aren't bogus," I said, looking him right in the eye. "They'll be the real thing, and so will the guys carrying them."

THIRTY-ONE

August turned into September and soon October was upon us and the leaves began to turn. The days were still warm, but the occasional cool front blew in and put a bite into the night air. In the middle of the month the drought broke, and for two weeks it rained every day. The Donner Basin became a quagmire, and the new residential districts that had sprung up on the edges of town were little better. Few of their streets had been paved, and some of them became nearly impassable. The deluge transformed Nanny Goat Gully into a surreal nightmare world where each sunset brought legions of drunken roughnecks to slop and whore and fight in its ten acres of knee-deep mud. Had it not been for the Rangers' horses, law and order would have ceased to exist there.

On September fourth the pipeline from Odessa was completed and the wells began going online. For three months the Texas & Pacific Railroad had been running several tank trains out of town each week, and we had received a few royalty checks, but with the coming of the pipeline our income shot up to a point that the numbers ceased to have any meaning to me. Della hired an accountant and we began paying the IRS quarterly. Meanwhile, she was looking for places to invest outside the oil industry.

During those months we made two trips to Dallas so she could spend some of the money on winter clothes. Then one night during the last week in October a phone call came from Chicken Little. "We need to get together," I heard him say as soon as I picked up the receiver.

"Sure," I said. "When and where?"

We agreed to meet that coming Wednesday at the Fan Tan Club on Greenville Avenue in Dallas, a joint that had long been a hangout for hijackers, cardsharps and pimps. Back during the war business had taken me there several times, and I'd always found the clientele amusing. Della and I drove up on Tuesday afternoon and took a small suite at the Adolphus. That evening we had a light dinner, and then danced the night away to Harry James and his band at the Mayflower Ballroom.

When I awoke late the next morning Della was already out shopping. I had an early lunch at a Greek café a few doors down the street, and then whiled away the time until my meeting. When I arrived at the Fan Tan I found Little in a booth near the rear, a pint of whiskey in a brown paper sack near his elbow. In those days sale of liquor by the drink was forbidden in Texas, and taverns could only offer their customers beer. Private clubs like the Cottonwood Country Club were exempted from the law, something that caused a fair amount of resentment since working stiffs couldn't afford private club memberships. Anyone who wanted to drink the hard stuff in his favorite bar had to "brown bag it" and bring his own. This meant you had to order what was called a setup, which in most cases was nothing more than a glass of ice and some soda. A setup often cost as much as a civilized mixed drink would have in a place where one could be legally sold.

I sat down across from the old man and ordered a bottle of Falstaff and a glass of ice. "What's on your mind?" I asked.

"I've been studying on this matter, and I think we need to bring in another man. For our project, I mean."

I was surprised by the change in plans at this late date, but I could see no reason to object. "Do you have somebody lined up?" I asked.

"Yes, I do," he said, his fedora bobbing up and down as he nodded. "The boy has just come back home to Oklahoma. Like I told you, I didn't have too much to choose from and that's why I brought in Willie. But this kid is as solid as they come. His name's Lum Shamblin. He's Otis Shamblin's middle son. You remember me mentioning Otis, don't you?"

"Sure. You say he's steady?"

"As a rock. He fought in Europe in the last war and won a bunch of medals. Great big fellow, and tough as a stump, too. I was considering adding somebody anyway when he come to me. He was in a terrible tight for money, so I went ahead and advanced him five thousand to get him out of his bind, but he knows you have the final say. If you veto him, then the five thousand will be just between me and him."

I thought it over for a few seconds, then nodded. "It's a sound idea. We probably should have planned on three men from the beginning."

"That's my notion too. It's been kinda nagging at the

back of my mind all along that we were going too light. I'll stay downstairs with the car. That's the one thing that had been worrying me. . . . Leaving that car down there without somebody in it."

"I trust your judgment on this, Little. That's why I came to you in the first place. But it means a smaller split for you and Willie."

"Like I told you, I never was a hog about money. Hell, I'd do this for nothing and be proud of it."

"Is Willie okay with the change?" I asked.

"Yeah. He knows it's a good move. And he understands that since this oil boom come in the take is going to be a lot bigger than we expected in the beginning. Besides, I think he's in this as much for the fun as for the money anyway, no matter how much he bitches about being broke."

I couldn't help but grin. "I'm aware that he's a little peculiar."

"So when do we do it?" he asked.

"The last Saturday in November," I said.

"What date is that?" Little asked.

"The twenty-ninth."

"Good. Annie's birthday comes on the twenty-fifth, and it wouldn't do for me to miss that. But we need to make sure Robillard's going to be there."

"He's always there. Or at least he has been since late spring. I'm not worried about it. Besides, I'm going to ruffle his feathers enough the weekend before that he wouldn't miss the opportunity for revenge no matter what."

"Now about Tobe . . . Were you going to meet with him again beforehand?"

"I hadn't planned on it," I said. "We could if he wants to,

but everything is going to be set. There's going to be some diversion for the cops that night. That's already planned out."

"Good. I don't think he'll be wanting another meeting. He knows his business, and he don't need no supervision."

The waitress was back with my beer and a small glass of ice along with an empty shot glass and a bottle of 7UP for Little. He handed her three dollars and examined his glass carefully in the club's dim light. Taking out his handkerchief, he gave it a through and careful wiping down. "Don't that beat all?" he asked. "You have to pay a dollar for a nickel sody water just so you can sit here and drink your own whiskey out of a dirty glass. This damn joint must be run by criminals."

That night Della and I had a bad dinner and saw an even worse comedian at a gaudy, overpriced place called the Singapore Supper Club. The Singapore had opened earlier that year and become fashionable in the months since, though I couldn't see why. We left in the middle of the comedian's act and caught Harry James's last set at the Mayflower. The next morning we got a late start home. When the valet brought the car around to the front of the hotel, I tossed the keys to Della and told her to drive. My legs were worn out from dancing and the rest of me was worn out from other things. For some reason Dallas always made that woman as wild as a young mare.

THIRTY-TWO

The next Friday I began to hammer away at Robillard once again. At this point it was no longer crucial to my plans, but since we discovered Lisa the Leak I'd come to enjoy being a thorn in his side.

He'd brought a new girl to the suite that evening, this one a blonde. She was a tall number with long legs and a pair of perky breasts beneath a low-cut white cocktail dress. Her skin was flawless, and her face was a perfect cameo marred only by a smug, cat-in-the-cream smirk and a pair of blue eyes that were void of either character or intelligence. As soon as she arrived, she made a spectacle of herself by loudly insisting that the porter mix her up something she called a Teeny-Tune, a concoction that turned out to be a sort of reverse martini made with five parts of vermouth to one of gin. While Robillard gambled, she lolled around on the sofa like an overindulged poodle, drinking her Teeny-Tunes and flipping through the stack of fashion magazines she'd brought with her.

There had been a change in the way the game was played. Back in the heady days before the Depression, the management of the Weilbach had commissioned a Chicago manufacturer of poker chips to make a custom set of chips stamped with the hotel's name. These chips had recently emerged from the office safe, and one of the hotel's book-keepers had been hired as the banker. It was his job to sell the chips to players from a special valise that had been built at the same time the chips were minted. The valise also had a ranked compartment like a bank teller's drawer into which a player's money went when he bought into the game. Not only did using chips instead of currency make the play more convenient but it centralized much of the cash in the room into one location.

The game ground on. Toward midnight Robillard gave the blonde some money and told her to get herself a room for the night. After extracting a promise from him that he'd follow shortly, she left in a blizzard of chatter, taking her magazines and a large shaker of Teeny-Tunes along with her. I was not sorry to see her go. At 1:00 A.M. the game re-cessed for a few minutes. I quickly ate a sandwich and had just returned to the table with a cup of coffee when I heard Robillard call for a bourbon on the rocks. A few seconds later he took his place opposite me, drink in hand.

"Been back to the cockfights?" he asked.

I shook my head. "Not my meat."

"Strictly a card man, huh?"

"That's about the size of it. And speaking of cards, I've just been sitting here thinking about something you and I were talking about a while back. Do you remember me telling you that I'd played with Hermann Göring at one time?"

He gave me a slight nod. "Yeah . . ."

"Well, I thought you might find it interesting that I knew several other Nazi bigwigs. Did you ever hear of a fellow called the Butcher of Prague?" I asked.

"Can't say that I have," he answered casually.

"He was a fellow named Reinhard Heydrich."

"I see," he said, and took a sip of his bourbon. His hand was steady and his eyes never left my face. "I don't recall the name, but I never took too much interest in all that business."

"Heydrich was a fascinating man," I continued, ignoring his apparent uninterest in the subject. "I don't know that I ever encountered a more remote individual."

"Who're you talking about?" I heard Wilburn Rasco's voice boom out behind me. He'd just returned to the table with a drink and a cigar.

"Reinhard Heydrich," I replied. "I played cards with him once."

"You knew Heydrich?" he asked with surprise.

"Yes sir, I did. I worked for the State Department in the late '30s, and was stationed in Berlin for a couple of years."

"I didn't know that."

I gave him friendly smile. "No reason you should have. But speaking of Heydrich, some people say that if Germany had won the war, he would have been Hitler's successor. After spending an evening with him I'm inclined to agree. He was the most ruthless man I've ever met. He built up a thing called the SD, which was an intelligence unit within the SS, a sort of secret police inside the secret police, and he had something on everybody, including Himmler, and maybe even Hitler himself. Later on he was entrusted with setting up the system for transporting and exterminating the Jews."

"How on earth did you happen to meet a fellow like that?" Rasco asked.

"Through a mutual acquaintance. Somewhere along the way Heydrich discovered poker, and he'd become fascinated with the game. For a while in the late '30s he played every chance he got. Since I had a reputation in diplomatic circles as a good card player back in those days, I was invited to his home for dinner and a quiet game afterward with him and a couple of his top assistants."

"So you were actually in his house?" Rasco asked.

"Yes, and the man was a very congenial host. He was in his thirties then, tall and slim and blond. The perfect Nazi physical type. He was married to a semiaristocrat named Lina Von Osten, and as one might expect she was a good match for him. Tall, slim, blond. Large breasts, small brain. And she was a fanatical Nazi."

"Our young friend claims to have led an interesting life, does he not?" Robillard asked, a measure of skepticism in his voice. By this time Howard Northcutt and Simon Van Horn had returned to the table. "Why, he even says that he once played cards with Hermann Göring."

I gave him an easy, indulgent smile. "That's right, I did. But Göring wasn't in Heydrich's league, either as a card player or as a man. You see, Göring was little more than a self-indulgent opportunist, and with him brutality was an offhand, casual sort of thing. But Heydrich was a different matter. And he had a hidden purpose in inviting me to his home that evening, just as he had a hidden purpose in almost everything he did."

"Oh, really?" Van Horn asked, intrigued.

Robillard laughed a velvety laugh. "Oh, hell, Simon . . . He's pulling your leg. Don't you know that?"

"What makes you think so, Mr. Robillard?" I asked, my voice casual.

"I have a hard time seeing a man who once hobnobbed with all kinds of important Nazis showing up at an Oklahoma cockfight with an old yokel like Herbert Little."

I treated him to a cryptic smile. Picking up the cards, I gave them a quick Scarne shuffle, then cut them smoothly with one hand a couple of times and set them on the table in front of him. "I'm a man of many parts, my friend. And I believe it's your deal."

"You said that Heydrich had some hidden purpose in inviting you to his house," Van Horn said. "What was it?"

"You see, I was considered something of a rogue in the department. Gambling and all that sort of thing. Such people usually need more money than they have, and this led him to believe that it might be possible to recruit me into a sabotage network he was setting up here in this country."

"You mean they were active over here even before the war started?" Northcutt asked in surprise.

"Oh, certainly. Heydrich had begun making contacts as early as 1936. Hitler never intended to fight the United States, but Heydrich knew the time would come when they would have no choice. His main interest was sabotage. The Nazis were very active in Texas and Louisiana, primarily because of the petroleum industry and all the chemical plants up and down the Gulf Coast. He had grand notions of blowing them all up. He also hoped to put the Port of Houston out of the game by sinking a half dozen big vessels in the ship channel."

"How close did they come to doing it?" Northcutt asked.

"I've been told that they came closer than anyone likes to admit."

"And Heydrich tried to recruit you that night?" Van Horn asked.

"Not that night, and he didn't make the offer himself, of course. He just sized me up, and then a week later a minor German industrialist who'd been present at the game approached me."

"Why you?"

I laughed. "Rest assured that I wasn't the only one they had their eyes on, and I don't flatter myself into thinking I was all that important to them. They were after anybody they could get who might prove useful."

"I don't suppose you let yourself be recruited," Rasco said with an uneasy laugh.

"Hardly," I said. "I have a lot of faults but treason's not one of them."

After another hour Robillard left the game. I played on until dawn and then fell into bed in one of the rooms. I came alive once again in the early afternoon and went down to have some late breakfast. Passing up the hotel restaurant, I walked four blocks up the street to a barbecue joint and had a double order of pork ribs. When I returned to the Weilbach I went into the barbershop for a shave and a trim.

A few minutes later I was back in the Plainsman Suite and ready to play. Five men sat at the table, including Robillard. Miss Teeny-Tunes and her fashion magazines were nowhere to be seen, but two women Van Horn had brought up the night before were still lounging around, one of them dressed only in her slip. Each weekend that passed, there was more money on the table and more sleaze in the air, and I didn't mind a bit. The reporters would have a ball with it.

When I left the room earlier I'd scooped up my chips and put them in my coat pockets. Now I piled them on the table, and said, "Deal me in, please."

By nine o'clock that evening I had hammered Robillard into the ground three more times and he was ready to cut my throat. The pots weren't particularly large, but in each case he thought he had me beaten. On the last hand I turned over the fifth diamond against three queens and saw murder in his eyes. He carefully raked his chips off the table into his hat. "I'm cashing in for today," he said.

"Hate to see you leave," I told him with an easy smile.

"I've been thinking," he said. "Why don't you and I go head-on for a while next weekend? I'd really like to find out which of us is the best player."

If there was any doubt on that subject left in his mind by this time, then he was a fool. But I didn't say so. "I see two problems with that, Mr. Robillard. In the first place I won't be here next weekend. And secondly some of these gentlemen might think it's rude of us to cut off on our own."

"That's no worry," Zimmerman said, his voice a deep rumble. "It's been done before."

"Very well," I said. "But we'll have to make it the following weekend."

"What's the date?" Robillard asked.

"The weekend of the twenty-ninth. Are you planning to be here?"

"I'll be here with bells on," he said. "You can count on it."

It wasn't necessary to my plans for the two of us to be playing alone that Saturday night, but it didn't hurt anything either. So I agreed. "Fine with me."

He extended his hand and we shook. With any luck at all I'd only have to shake hands with him one more time.

THIRTY-THREE

That Monday I got a call from one of my Washington friends. He was coming through town the next day on the morning train and had decided to take a few hours layover so the two of us could visit. I picked him up at the depot and we drove to the Weilbach for breakfast.

Bascomb Barfield IV was my senior by seven years. When I was an undergraduate at Harvard he'd been in the law school, working his way through as a clerk in the federal courthouse in Boston. Because he came from an old South Carolina family that had produced one governor and two generals, everyone assumed he was wealthy, an impression he'd never quite been able to correct. I knew better. The truth was that while the Barfields had once owned over fifty thousand acres of prime rice land, three generations of alcoholic gamblers had depleted the family fortune to the point that his father finally shot himself in despair of his crumbling finances before my friend was out of the University of South Carolina. Fearful of his heredity, Bascomb neither gambled nor drank. After Harvard, we'd served together in the navy, where we'd both tried cases in the Judge

Advocate General's Office. Then I'd lost track of him for a few years until we both turned up in the OSS during the war. He'd been my immediate superior, a man naturally prone to worrying in a business where tension and anxiety were the common currency of everyday life. Though a brilliant fellow, his appearance was not at all impressive. Short, stumpy, and muscular, he had a bald, domed bullet of a head and a round, care-filled face that held a pair of tired brown eyes.

"So . . . I hear you've become quite the oil baron," he said after the waitress had filled our cups and left with our orders.

"I had some free time on my hands," I said defensively.

"Relax," he said. "I'm not complaining, and your oil speculation has just made your cover that much more credible."

"Then what's this visit all about?" I asked with a grin. "Just a social call? After all, I could have gotten the exchange money to you by bonded courier."

He sipped at his coffee for a few seconds, then put down his cup and sighed. "I had to go to San Antonio anyway, so I decided to come by and tell you that this new scheme of yours is better than what we had planned at first."

"You honestly think so?" I asked.

"No doubt about it. I mean, after all, this country is a democracy. It's always better not to kill when you don't have to. Every time you do something like that, you weaken the fabric."

"I agree," I said.

He sighed tiredly once again. "I also wanted to ask you face-to-face if you're certain sure you want to go through with this thing."

"Of course I do," I said, more than a little surprised by his question. "What gives you the idea I'd want to pull out now?"

"I believe I'd chuck it if I were in your position."

"Why?"

He shrugged and picked up his cup. "Your life's taken a different turn. Look at what you're risking. All this money you've made, and you've got a good thing going with a really fine woman. You're a lucky man there."

"Thanks," I said. "But why did you think I might want to quit now?"

"I really didn't, but it's important that you understand that we're not the damned Gestapo. We don't expect people to do things against their better judgment."

"I know that. But just who are you talking about when you say 'we'? I mean, when this venture was hatched it involved just a few of us old buddies from the OSS, but now . . ." I looked at him sharply across the table. "By any chance are you involved with the new outfit that Congress just chartered?"

He shook his head. "Absolutely not. We're just some of Wild Bill's boys cleaning up leftover details. And you're one those boys, as you well know."

"Do you have any plans to join the new agency?" I asked.

"Oh, hell no! I've had enough of this business. In six months I'll be back in Charleston practicing law."

"I don't blame you," I said. "I've gotten my fill of it myself."

"So it's next weekend, right?"

I nodded.

"Any reason why he might not be there?" he asked with a frown of mild worry.

"He's missed a couple of weekends since I've been playing. Business, he claimed, and I imagine he was telling the truth since he's got some pretty far-flung interests these days. But I expect him to make the extra effort this time because he wants to nail me pretty badly."

I went on to tell him about the girls who had been coming to the game, and the twenty-five thousand I'd won from Robillard at the cockfight. "Young women, huh?" he asked with a cold smile.

"Oh yes. Young enough that he ought to know better."

"You've really done a fine job," he said as the waitress set our food on the table. "It's all falling into place."

An hour and a half later we were back at the depot. "I almost forgot," he said just before he stepped onto the train. He quickly jotted down a name and number on the back of one of his business cards and gave it to me. "A reporter in Dallas," he told me. "Get in contact with him when the time comes. He's on the team."

"Another one of Wild Bill's?" I asked.

"Not exactly, but his heart's in the right place, and he knows what to do."

I handed him the satchel containing a hundred thousand dollars of the money Della had slipped out of our accounts. "Just be sure those two guys are at the Alamo Plaza on time," I said. "The success of the whole thing hinges on them being there."

He regarded me bleakly. "You've been out here in the amateur world too long if you think you need to remind me of something like that."

"You're right," I said. "Sorry."

He hefted the satchel. "This money will be paid back, but it may take a year or so. . . ."

"Doesn't it always with the government?" I asked.

We shook hands and the door to the coach closed behind him. I never saw Bascomb Barfield again. In less than six months he'd be dead of a heart attack, brought on by over-work and stress. The madness of the late war had claimed yet another victim.

That Friday I went back down to the Texas & Pacific station and picked up five pounds of fresh gulf shrimp I'd ordered sent in on ice. The next morning I went out to a local meat market and bought a large prime sirloin, and at my favorite liquor store I found three bottles of prewar Taittinger. That evening I put a stack of records on the Philco, and as soon as the shrimp were boiled and rechilled and the steak grilled I brought the food in from the kitchen and spread it out on the coffee table. We sat on the floor and ate a leisurely supper washed down with glass after glass of cold Champagne. Then we rose and danced for a while. A slow, moody Artie Shaw number finished and Andy Kirk's arrangement of "Big Jim Blues" dropped onto the turntable. I began to gradually remove Della's clothes as I guided her around the room. When she was naked I lowered her to the sofa and we began to make unhurried, gentle love. Afterward I cradled her in my arms and held her close.

"It's almost time, isn't it?" she asked.

"Yeah," I whispered. "Next Saturday night."

"What do you want me to do?"

"Stay here by the phone and wait to see if I call. Little will phone you a few minutes before ten. If you haven't heard from me, then you tell him that everything is okay."

"Is that all?"

"That's it. And there's one thing I want you to know. When this is all over, I'll tell you the whole story and answer all your questions. But as it stands now, the less you know the less chance you have of being pulled into it if something goes wrong. Do you trust me?"

"Of course I trust you," she said, and rose from the sofa. She went into the bedroom and came back with our robes. Once she'd slipped into the black silk, she filled both our glasses with Champagne, then sat down beside me on the sofa. She picked up one of the shrimp and dipped it in the cocktail sauce and began to nibble.

"Something else on your mind?" I asked.

She slipped her glasses back on and gave me a critical look. "There's always something on my mind, but I'm not going to bother you with it now with this business about to come up."

"Whatever it is, I want to know."

"You're sure?"

"Positive."

"When this is all over can we move someplace else?" she asked plaintively. "I hate West Texas."

I laughed and gathered her into my arms, shrimp and all. "Is that all? I thought you were at least going to tell me that you're leaving me."

"Leaving you? Why would I leave you?"

"I'm an old man, Della."

"Don't worry. I'll catch up with you in a few years."

"Where do you want to move?" I asked.

"Anywhere we can find real trees. Oaks and pines and elms. Forests and shade. How about East Texas? You grew up there. Would you like to go back?"

"I'd love to, but I thought that if we stayed together you would want to go back to Tennessee."

"No," she said. "There's nothing there for me. And you're not getting rid of me unless you run me off."

"Della, running you off is the last thing on my mind."

"Then East Texas sounds good. After the first of the year we'll get in the car and just drive and drive until we find someplace we like. . . . How about it?"

"Splendid," I said, and began to nuzzle at her neck.

"Again?" she asked. "I think you're the kind of old man I like."

The Monday before the game I ran into Simon Van Horn in the lobby of Manlow Rhodes's bank. We shook hands, and I said, "Say, I've been meaning to come see you."

"Really? What about?"

I put my goofiest grin on my face. "Could I guess that like myself you have a small investment in the local constabulary?"

"I think that's a safe assumption," he replied with one of his cold smiles. "It seems to be the cheapest insurance one can buy these days."

"And have you been getting good service on this investment?"

"I believe I have," he replied. "Why?"

"Well, I was thinking that perhaps it would be both

neighborly and prudent to send them a little holiday cheer this weekend in gratitude for the attention they haven't been giving us. I mean with this head-on match between me and Clifton, plus it will probably be the biggest game of the year . . ."

"You're right," he said. " 'Don't bind the mouths of those that tread the grain,' as the Bible says."

"You know, Mr. Little is fond of that verse," I said.

"Chicken Little's no fool," he said. "But what did you have in mind for the cops?"

"I thought I'd have a couple of cases of good whiskey delivered to the police station and a couple to the sheriff's office. Since I don't want to seem like I'm hogging all the glory, I thought I might put your name on the card too."

"That's fine with me," he said. "Let me know how much and I'll get half the tab. But why don't you just say it's from 'The Weilbachers.' I think they'll get the message."

"That's a superb idea," I replied.

"Thanks," he said. "And with Will Scoggins at the game that night his deputies might actually get some of the whiskey for themselves. If he was there when it came he'd take it all home for himself."

"Scoggins? At the game?" I asked. "What brought this on?"

"Gossip, I suppose. All this business about you and Clifton."

We shook hands and he left. A few moments later Rhodes's secretary called me into his office.

"I hear that quite a match is coming up this weekend at the hotel," he said as we shook hands. "I hope no hard feelings come of it."

"Don't worry, sir," I replied. "We're just a bunch of lighthearted fellows having a little fun."

An hour later I was at home and on the phone to Chicken Little. Later that afternoon I paid a premium price to a local courier service with an impeccable reputation to deliver a case each of scotch and bourbon to the police station and the same to the sheriff's office. The deliveries were to be made at eight o'clock the evening of the game, and the card had specifically reminded the recipients to see to it that the boys on patrol got their share. There was nothing more I could do; from here on out it was in the hands of fate.

THIRTY-FOUR

Early in the afternoon of the twenty-ninth a blue norther howled in off the Panhandle plains and the temperature dropped thirty-one degrees in nineteen minutes. Large flakes of snow whirled and eddied through the air as we drove to the hotel. Della sat at the wheel wrapped snugly in her mink with the car's heater turned on high. When I kissed her good-bye and stepped out onto the pavement I was hit by a north wind that felt like razors against my face. I stood shivering on the sidewalk and watched with a mixture of sadness and elation as the little Ford disappeared into traffic. When I could see its tail lights no more, I turned and pushed my way through the revolving door. As soon as I stepped into the Plainsman Suite and looked at the card table, I felt a wave of revulsion rise in me, and I knew in that instant that for the first time in my life I was tired of poker. And I understood something about the nature of the game I'd never seen before: it was the commonplace become unbearable, the mundane raised to a fever pitch and turned into a lifelong obsession. I knew then as I stood there amid the familiar rustle of cards and clatter of chips that no matter what else happened that night, the game would no longer have its old allure for me.

Will Scoggins was already there and dressed to the nines in a three-piece suit of charcoal gray. He'd had the sense to take off his hat—something he hadn't done in my office the day he'd arrested me—and his hog-leg .44 was nowhere to be seen. There wasn't a bulge under his arm either, which caused me to think that if he was armed he carried no more than a little ladies' pocket automatic in one of his pockets. Probably pear handled and nickel plated, too. He gave me a polite nod and a wary handshake, but I was as courteous to him as I was to everyone else.

Robillard was playing when I came in the room. When he finished the hand he rose from his chair and approached me with a false smile on his face. "Time for our little match, it seems," he said, his eyes never leaving mine.

"Yes, it's time," I replied with more cheer than I felt.

The management had sent up a bridge table for us. Made of heavy oak, it was covered with felt like the poker table, though it was somewhat smaller. It sat to one side of the room, behind the sofa, flanked by two comfortable-looking chairs.

"Why don't you break open a pack of cards," I told him. "I want to get a drink."

He nodded and walked over to the table. I bought ten thousand dollars' worth of chips, then did something I'd never done before while gambling. I asked the porter to mix me a scotch and soda. A stack of clean ashtrays sat on the bar beside the glasses and I took one. At the table I unwrapped one of my Coronas and carefully touched a wooden kitchen match to its end.

"Table stakes, dealer's choice, pot limit . . . How does that sound to you?" Robillard asked.

"Why don't we just play five-card stud, Mr. Robillard? That's all either of us ever deals anyway."

He nodded. "That suits me fine." He noticed my scotch. "I don't believe I've ever seen you drink up here before," he commented as he fanned the cards out on the table. "Or smoke, either."

"This is a night of firsts, Mr. Robillard. And lasts."

I drew a three to his jack and he had the deal. As he shuffled the cards he said, "Lasts? Why, don't let me run you out of the game, young man."

I smiled at him calmly. "Hardly. Besides, I seem to be the one who's a little ahead overall."

"Yes, so it seems. But we'll just have to do something about that, won't we?" he said, and promptly relieved me of $1,600 with a natural straight against three aces.

That night it was not necessary for me to win. I merely had to stay in the game and kill time. But my natural sense of competitiveness and my need to embellish pushed me to play aggressively and slam him whenever I could. Twice I bet heavily with large pairs showing before the fourth card and forced him to fold when he was working on a flush. I was a few hundred dollars ahead sometime after nine o'clock when we both rose from the table to stretch our legs and freshen our drinks. I made myself a second scotch, this one stronger than the first. As I turned away from the bar I felt a hand on my elbow. "How's it going?" Wilburn Rasco asked.

"Well enough. I'm a little ahead at the moment."

"I never liked these one-on-one matches, and I wish they

weren't allowed." He sighed. "But back in the '20s old man Weilbach's son started them, and they've been a tradition ever since. Every now and then a couple of fellows will square off, but it almost always leads to hard feelings. Don't take it too seriously."

"I won't," I said, regretting that he was there. He was the one regular player in the game that I had come to truly respect. He stood to lose financially that night, and he would doubtlessly suffer considerable embarrassment from the publicity. But there was nothing that could be done about it.

Back at the table Robillard and I played for a while without really talking, neither of us drawing the cards to engage the other in an interesting hand. The porter came by, and I asked him to replenish my drink. As soon as he returned Robillard picked up the cards and gave them a few quick shuffles, then laid them on the table for me to cut. I ignored the deck and took a sip from my scotch. "You know, it's an odd coincidence that we were talking about Germany the other night," I said. "Not long afterward somebody told me that you had been there, but I didn't believe it because you never mentioned it while we were on the subject."

His body stiffened for a moment, then relaxed. "Actually, I was in Germany for just a few days back in 1936," he said smoothly. "With a delegation from the American Bankers' Association."

"And how long have you been a banker?" I asked smoothly.

"I've been chairman of the board at Mercantile Bank for two decades, and back then I was forced to take over its day-to-day operation for a few years. Just as I was again about six months ago."

"So you're running the bank now?" I asked.

"Only until after the first of the year. We hope to have a new president hired by then."

"Why did the banking association send a delegation to Germany?"

"In those days the German banking system was quite different from ours. Their banks were strictly commercial banks, and almost all of them were located in the larger cities. Their government was interested in the possibility of setting up a number of banks in smaller towns to do consumer lending, and they wanted to get some ideas from us American bankers."

"I see," I said, and looked down at my wristwatch. It was a few minutes before ten. "When we talked before I didn't tell you the whole story about Heydrich. At the time the offer was made to me I wanted to take it."

"Really? But I thought you said—"

"Oh, I had no intention of becoming a turncoat. What I really wanted was to infiltrate the German sabotage network here in this country. My superiors at the State Department vetoed the idea, of course, and I've always thought it was a great opportunity lost. But later on I had a chance to do a little work in that area, and it was amazing the things I learned."

"I'm sure," he replied dryly.

I reached down and cut the cards and pushed them across to him. "Yes, those were heady days," I said. My voice sounded dreamy and detached in my own ears, as though it was coming from someone else, or from a radio speaker far away. I took a long pull from my scotch and unwrapped another cigar before I continued. "Mosley's fascists were marching in England, and over here we had William Dudley Pelly and his Silver Shirts and the German-American Bund. Charles Lindbergh and the America First Committee were riding high, determined to keep us out of the war that everybody knew was coming, and all of them were being financed directly by the German intelligence apparatus."

"Is that right?"

I nodded and chattered on. "Oh yes. They had a very elaborate system. The money came from Argentina and other South American countries, and was funneled directly to banks right here in the States. In almost every case they were state banks that were free of federal regulation and scrutiny, banks where it was easier for substantial sums of money to materialize and then disappear once again, leaving few traces behind."

"Fascinating," he murmured in his silky voice. At that moment he knew that I knew, but he thought there was nothing I could do about it.

"Yes, isn't it?" I asked with a smile as smooth as his voice. I reached over and cut the deck and the game went on.

It was not the famous Dead Man's Hand that was showing when the two men burst into the room just after ten. Instead, after the third card was dealt each of us held a pair of nines on top, and I had just raised my eyes to smile ironically across at Robillard when the door swung violently open. The first thing I saw was the off-duty deputy who'd been posted outside to guard the door. He came flying headfirst into the room propelled by a hard kick in the rump. The next thing I noticed was a sawed-off pump shotgun, and it was pointed directly at my head.

They were both big men, but one was much larger than the other. Both were dressed in overcoats, Shriners' fezzes, and Santa Claus masks, and both knew their business. The first order of that business was to cow and intimidate everyone present through the immediate and unexpected application of violence. As soon as they were in the room the larger of the two clubbed the deputy nearly senseless with the butt of his shotgun. Then he turned and gave the porter a casual backhand slap that put him on the floor beside the guard. Reaching down to pull the guard's gun from its holster, he said, "Don't neither one of you hired hands give me no trouble. They don't pay you enough to die for them." Then he pointed the muzzle of his shotgun right at Will Scoggins's chest and said, "Hi, Sheriff! You're not packing heat tonight, are you?"

Scoggins hesitated. Manlow Rhodes had been right about the man being a coward; I believe he was the most frightened person in the room. He'd gone deathly pale and it wouldn't have surprised me if he'd fainted.

"I said are you packing?" the big man repeated.

Scoggins managed a nod. The big man jerked his head at his companion, who quickly stepped over to give the sheriff a quick frisk. He reached his hand in Scoggins's coat pocket and pulled out a small automatic.

Then the big man turned to look at Robillard and me. "On your feet, you two," he growled.

Apparently I didn't move fast enough for him. He jerked

me the rest of the way up by the collar of my coat, then gave me a good belt in the mouth that split my bottom lip and chipped a front tooth. I started to raise my hand to my face and he said, "Keep still. You're not hurt bad."

By this time his partner had closed the door and jerked the phone cord out of the wall. Then he leveled a silenced automatic pistol at the men sitting at the poker table. The larger intruder quickly checked the bedrooms and emerged from the last one dragging a half-naked and screeching blonde by the hair. He slapped her twice and threw her on the sofa between Miss Teeny-Tunes and a dark-haired girl who was there for the first time that evening. "Shut up or I'll cut your goddamned throat," he growled at her.

He pushed Robillard and me roughly over to the other end of the room beside the poker table. "Any of the rest of you got a gun?" he asked. "Better tell me now because if I find one later I'll kill whoever's holding it."

I nodded and pulled my coat open where he could see my Colt. The rest shook their heads. He pulled the little auto from its holster, then went over to the valise and pulled out the two drawers of chips and slung them aside. I guessed at the time that there was probably about a hundred thousand dollars in the deep cash drawer, but he wanted more. He pointed to the valise, and said, "Wallets and money clips in this suitcase. Right now, one at a time. Turn your pants pockets inside out. If I don't see enough money go in here, I may decide to search everybody, and I'll kill any man I find holding out."

We filed by one at a time and dropped our cash into the yawning black mouth of the case.

"Any more?" the larger man asked.

We all shook our heads.

"All right," the big man said. "Listen and listen careful. We're gonna take one man with us as a hostage just to keep you worthless bastards honest. Don't nobody go out that door for one hour. And don't try to fix the phone and call nobody. If an hour passes and we haven't been bothered by the cops, we'll turn the hostage loose on the road. But if the red lights hit us before then, he's going to die. Period. Remember . . . One hour."

He motioned to his partner with a jerk of the head. "Get somebody."

The smaller hood came over and poked me with his pistol. "Grab your coat, asshole," he growled.

While I quickly pulled on my overcoat, the big man said to Scoggins, "Don't get any ideas about jumping the gun on the time. If you do you'll be killing this man."

"The sheriff is going to sit here like a good boy," Wilburn Rasco said, his voice steady and seemingly free of fear.

"Damn right he will," Van Horn said.

The larger man clipped a heavy cord that hung around his neck to an eyelet in the shotgun's stock. Then he slid the shotgun under his overcoat and let it dangle there. Buttoning the coat over the gun, he said to me, "Mr. Man, we're gonna walk out of here like we own the damn place. We're going down the stairs and through the back door, and if you make one peep you may as well order your coffin because you're gonna be dead. Do you understand?"

I gave him a jerky nod, and the smaller robber prodded me toward the door. Just before we left the big hood turned back to the room, and said, "You better do what we say or your friend is deader than hell." Then he picked up the valise and opened the door.

"You'll get your hour," Simon Van Horn said. "I promise you that."

"We better," he hissed, and then we were gone.

THIRTY-FIVE

Out in the corridor the big man pulled a fourth Santa mask and a folded-up fez from his pocket. I quickly pulled both on, and we headed for the stairs at the end of the hall. Suddenly a door opened and a middle-aged couple emerged. "Wheeee . . ." the smaller robber said.

"Evening, folks," the big man said to the couple, slurring his words. That was all they would remember: three half-drunk Shriners, probably on the prowl for women.

We descended by way of the service stairs. Once we were on the ground floor, we went quickly down a short utility corridor and emerged into an alley where a gray 1941 Pontiac sedan waited, its engine idling softly. The driver wore a wide-brimmed fedora pulled low over his face, and the collar of his overcoat had been turned up so that his features were invisible. The man with the shotgun pushed me into the backseat, then climbed in beside me while his companion took the place beside the driver. The Pontiac eased down the alley and pulled carefully out into the street. Once the car was moving we removed our masks.

The snow had stopped and the roads were clear. We drove

slowly and obeyed all the traffic laws. After a few blocks the downtown area fell behind and we turned off Roosevelt into a residential neighborhood. Beyond the residential area came a district of warehouses and cotton gins where the streetlights were few and far between. Another mile farther and the Pontiac turned off the paved street and onto a rutted dirt lane that was cloaked in darkness. After two blocks we pulled up in front of an old metal-sided garage.

The front passenger leaped out to open the garage's door, and a few seconds later the car glided almost soundlessly into the building. Above our heads a single small bulb cast a dim glow that did little to dispel the gloom. Three cars stood parked along the back wall, a Chevrolet, an Oldsmobile coupe and a new black Ford sedan.

"Well, that went pretty slick," the driver said, turning around to grin at me. "I hope you weren't scared."

"Not really, Little," I told him.

"Sorry about that lick I gave you," the big man said, sticking out his hand to shake with me. "I hit you a lot harder than I intended to. I was a little keyed up, if you understand what I mean."

"Forget it," I said. "We needed to make it look real."

"We can get together and be sociable later," Icepick Willie said. "Let's get a move on now."

The valise emerged from the trunk of the Pontiac. Quickly the stolen wallets and money clips were stripped of their cash and thrown aside. We took the money and placed it in a waterproof sack that had been originally made for the U.S. Army for a purpose not too different from the one it was to be used for that night. The cash drawer from the valise was then emptied into the sack, and on top of that went a fourteen-pound weight made of high carbon steel. All the air was then squeezed from the sack, and its special seal was fastened. Finally, it was placed into an identical sack, and it too was sealed. Then the whole thing was tossed into the trunk of the Ford. The shotgun and the Colt pistol used during the robbery went into the backseat of the Pontiac along with the valise and the Santa masks. All three men had worn gloves throughout the evening, and all three guns were untraceable.

A few seconds later the garage door opened once again and three cars emerged. The Ford and the Chevrolet waited while the Oldsmobile coupe stopped long enough for its occupant to shut and lock the door. Before he climbed back into his car he threw the keys to the door far out into the weed-choked field behind the garage.

I knew that the men in the Oldsmobile and the Chevrolet would go in different directions and end up spending the night in different tourist courts, each of which was many miles away. In the morning they would be on their way back to their homes in different states.

Little drove as carefully as he had while behind the wheel of the Pontiac earlier in the evening. Our route took us back through the center of town and past the Weilbach Hotel, where I noted that everything appeared perfectly normal. Once beyond the city limits, we proceeded seventeen miles northward, and then turned off the main highway onto a county road. After three miles the little Ford swung onto a rutted gravel lane that ran a few hundred yards out into the mesquite thickets. At its end sat an abandoned farmhouse, its cracked and broken windows casting jagged reflections of the car's headlights. We pulled around behind the house and stopped beside a stone well curb. Quickly Little sprang from the seat and retrieved the sack of money from the trunk. Using a key he'd had for months, he unlocked the lid on top of the well and swung it open. A few moments later I heard a splash as the sack hit the water. The key followed the sack into the well, and then he carefully slipped the locking arm of the padlock back into its hasp and clicked it shut.

Soon we were back at the main highway with nothing in the car to connect him in any way to the robbery. When he stopped, I opened the door and stepped out onto the shoulder of the road.

"I sure hate to leave you way out here all alone," he said, "but it can't be helped."

"Don't worry," I said. "I'll catch a ride. "Just get rolling and be careful."

"Ain't I always?"

I shut the door and stood watching as his taillights gradually disappeared into the icy darkness. It only took me about ten minutes to catch a ride with a friendly trucker who was heading toward town. "Jesus," he said. "What's a guy dressed like you doing all the way out here in the middle of the night?"

"I got robbed," I said with a rueful laugh.

"Damn! Did they take your car?"

"No. A few friends and I were having a friendly little poker game at the hotel back in town when two big guys swarmed us. They took me as a hostage to keep the others from calling the cops for an hour."

"You're talking about that game at the Wielbach, aren't you?"

"Yeah. You know about it?"

"Hell, everybody in this part of Texas knows about it. It's been going on for years up there. I bet they were serious hijackers with the kind of money that game brings in," he said.

"My friend, you have no idea how serious these guys were."

"Here," he said, and reached behind the seat. After groping around for a few seconds he hauled out a bottle of whiskey. "I bet you could use a snort," he said.

"I bet you're right." I replied, and looked at the bottle. It was White Horse. "My brand," I said. "This must be my lucky day."

"Oh, it's your lucky day all right, but that whiskey ain't got nothing to do with it. Your luck was when they let you walk away instead of putting a bullet in your brain.

"You're right," I said with a laugh. "No doubt about it."

"Where to?" he asked. "I'll drop you off anyplace you need to go."

"The hotel," I said. "I guess it's time to face the music."

THIRTY-SIX

When Ollie Marne finally brought me home at almost 4:00 A.M. Della was still awake. "Are you all right?" she asked as I entered the bedroom.

"Yes," I said, and gathered her into my arms. "But I'm bone weary."

"Could you eat something? I've been so nervous that I haven't had a bite since breakfast."

"Sure," I replied.

She quickly whipped up bacon, eggs, and toast, and broke out the last bottle of Taittinger. While the bacon was frying we each had a stout belt of scotch over ice.

"It's not completely over yet," I told her. "The worst is behind us, but I promised to tell you—"

"Not tonight," she said. "And not ever if you don't want to. But tonight we just eat and try to get some sleep."

We polished off the last bottle of Champagne with our food, and soon we were in bed with neither of us feeling any pain. There were no fun and games that night. Instead we drifted quickly and quietly off to sleep spooned together. I held her small body pressed close to my chest. As I buried

my face in her hair, I breathed in the rich smell of her per-
fumed shampoo, and I thought for the first time since late
1942 that all might really be well with the world. And it
was. For a little while, at least.

Della was already up the next morning when the phone
rang just before noon, but I was still in bed. It was Marne.
I stumbled into the living room and picked up the receiver.
"We need to talk," he said, a tightness in his voice. "Have
you had your morning coffee yet?"

"No," I answered.

"Then why don't me and you get together at Bartlett's
Drugstore down on Roosevelt Avenue for a cup? We can
visit there."

Fifteen minutes later I found him waiting for me at the
counter. "Come on," he said, and led me to a small back
room that held only a table and a half dozen chairs. "This
is where us poor folks play our poker. Old man Bartlett lets
me use it when I need to talk to somebody private."

The waitress stuck her head in the door. We both ordered coffee and I asked for a hamburger.

"The Mercantile State Bank got burgled last night," he
announced without small talk or fanfare. "About the same
time your poker game was getting hijacked."

"No kidding? I asked calmly. "What happened?"

"They came in the back and torched the vault."

"How did they get in?" I asked, honestly curious.

He laughed. "They just threw a big hydraulic jack across
the door and jacked the door facing apart. That was after
they tricked out the alarm, of course."

"But the vault," I said. "I heard they had a new vault put in a few years ago."

"They did. It was fireproof, but not much for security. It was an old design, a time-lock deal. They just cut through the steel with an acetylene torch and knocked one pin out of the way with a sledgehammer and a big drift punch. Nothing to it if you know your business, and these guys obviously did. They got almost three hundred grand."

"That's unfortunate, but I don't bank there, so—"

"Me either," he said with one of his braying little laughs. "But it is odd, don't you think?"

I just shrugged indifferently.

He gazed at me for a few moments, his hard, marblelike little eyes full of unasked questions. "Then something else strange happened," he said. "Clifton Robillard had no more than got home this morning when Bob Crowder and two other Rangers rousted him out and took him to the DPS office up in Sweetwater for questioning. The story is that it was on Homer Garrison's orders."

"Is that a fact?" I asked. "Well, they may be talking to a lot of us before this thing is all over."

We sat for a few moments in silence. Finally he leaned forward, and said confidentially, "I got my first royalty check. It was even better than you said it would be."

"That's good, Ollie. I like to think that everybody I touch gets what they deserve."

"I don't deserve that money and you know it."

"Sure you do," I said soothingly. "You're a good family man. You work hard in a dead-end job, and you don't get much thanks for it. And even if *you* don't deserve it, that little girl of yours does."

"I'll buy that, but the lease ain't really what I wanted to talk to you about." He stopped speaking, an expression of discomfort and confusion on his face.

"Go ahead, Ollie," I told him. "Say what you need to say."

"This is hard for me to bring up, but after the bank robbery, and after Robillard got hauled off by the Rangers, I got to thinking about something you said one time about killing pillars of the community. And you know, there's more than one way to kill a man. I mean, you don't have to actually render him dead to do him in. . . ."

"Surely you don't really think I had anything to do with all this mess?" I asked calmly.

"No, but I'm here to tell you that I don't care if you did. That's between you and me, of course. Robillard is just about the biggest bastard in this town, and as far as I'm concerned he deserves whatever happens to him."

"Then maybe that's the way you ought to handle the investigation, Ollie."

"Huh?" He looked at me with a puzzled expression. "What do you mean?"

The waitress was back in record time with our orders and we fell silent till she left the room. I took a bite of my burger and sipped my coffee. Finally I spoke. "We both know that he's got a piece of all the action down on Buckshot Row, including the prostitution and the gambling. Maybe that's where you ought to start looking."

"But we don't have any proof that he's involved in any of that stuff. I mean, everybody knows he is, but—" he broke off, and shrugged.

"You could find some proof quickly enough if you went and talked to some of those bar owners and whores down on the Row. And maybe if you did a little prowling around in the deed records down at the courthouse." I took another bite of my hamburger and let him think it over for a while.

"It might work," he said.

"It will, but you need to plant the seeds in the mind of the public before the newspapers find out about his connections on their own."

"How do you know they'll even be looking that deep?"

"Ollie, you just watch. The papers are fixing to root through that man's life like hogs through a collard patch. Some reporters from the Dallas papers have already been in town today, haven't they?"

He nodded. "Yeah. Fort Worth and Houston, too. They were on their way just as soon as word got out last night about the robberies. I imagine somebody at the hotel tipped them. Then he or she got a few bucks when they got to town."

"Of course," I said. "How are you handling the poker game with the press?"

Marne laughed and shook his head. "We aren't. Scoggins told them it was a bridge tournament that got hijacked."

"For God's sake," I exclaimed, amazed at the man's audacity. "How did he explain that much money being lost at a bridge game?"

"He didn't. He just let out that it wasn't but a few thousand dollars in all. You know, just about what you would expect a bunch of rich guys to carry on them."

"How much was really taken? Do you have any idea?" I asked.

"About a hundred and sixty grand, as best we can tell."

"Christ . . ." I muttered.

"Big haul, ain't it?" he asked with a bemused smile.

"Yeah," I said with a little laugh and a rueful shake of the head. "But let's get back to Robillard. How do you feel about connecting him with the rackets?"

"I dunno," he replied with a worried frown.

"Ollie, if I give you some inside information I got a week ago, will you not bug me about the source?"

"Yeah, sure . . ."

"Robillard has been embezzling from his own bank."

He looked both amazed and dubious. "But why? I mean, he's worth—"

"Several million dollars," I said, finishing his sentence for him. "But guys like him never have enough money. When this oil strike hit, Simon Van Horn offered to let him go partners with him on some of his deals. But Robillard didn't have the free cash, and he couldn't borrow it. So he simply pilfered it from his own bank."

"How much?" There was amazement in his voice.

"About two hundred thousand dollars. I think he originally intended to pay it back, but I guess he got greedy and started thinking why not just have the bank robbed on a weekend after he'd faked the amount of money in the 'cash-on-hand' account. Then the robbers get, oh, say a hundred or a hundred and fifty grand, but the books show that they got much, much more."

"Are you sure about this?" he asked.

I nodded. "Absolutely sure. He'd been bribing a state banking examiner. The guy was arrested yesterday down in Austin."

I didn't tell him that the arrest was arranged and that the man had expected it. Or that he'd already made a deal for probation in return for his testimony against Robillard. Instead, I let him think it over while I finished off my hamburger.

"I don't mind seeing him tied up with the rackets," he finally said, "but I'm not sure I want to be the man to do it."

"I understand," I said, pushing my plate aside. "If he and the sheriff were as close as I heard they were, then Scoggins may not want you to handle it this way."

"The sheriff has his own damn problems at the moment, and he's not really studying Clifton Robillard one way or another."

"Oh yeah? What kind of problems?"

"The Rangers are back on his ass. That Bob Crowder is like a damn bulldog."

"Ollie, exactly what are they looking for?"

"Just what you'd expect. Payoffs. And they'd like to get him for extortion too, if they could. You name it and they'll use it if it'll nail Will Scoggins."

"Ollie, could you get dragged into this?"

"Nah. For years I've run what he called his 'little bag,' just the kind of nickel-and-dime goodwill offerings you got coming in from merchants to every police department in the country. The big stuff he did on his own because he never trusted nobody else. He was afraid that we'd short him."

"Then here's what you do. . . ." I said, and took out my pen and fished around in my pockets trying to find something to write on.

Marne grinned and handed me one of his business cards. "What's wrong? Did you let some crook get away with your wallet?" he asked.

I wrote the name and phone number Bascomb Barfield had given me on the back of the card and handed it across to him. "This guy is a reporter on the *Dallas Morning News*. You call him and mention my name. Tell him what to look for on Robillard, and then go help him find it. But before you talk to him, call the paper here in town and tell them that you're investigating possible connections Robillard may have had with the local rackets. You must know somebody on the paper."

"Yeah, sure." He gazed at me with a puzzled frown. "Jesus! You've got this all thought out down to the last detail. Just who in the hell are you, anyway?" he asked.

I looked him right in the eyes. "I'm a guy very much like yourself, Ollie," I said. "You're a country boy, right?"

He nodded.

"Well, so am I. And we've both had to wade through our share of slop in this life, have we not?"

"Oh yeah. You're damn right about that."

"And we both have fine, devoted women we were lucky to get, don't we?"

His head bobbed up and down.

"Then that's who I am. Just another Ollie Marne, but one with a high-toned college education and a few years in Europe. Those are about the only differences between us. And Ollie, I've never done anything that you wouldn't have done yourself in the same situation. I'm convinced of that."

"Okay, if you say so . . ." he replied dubiously.

"You're not worried about what's going to happen to Will Scoggins, are you?"

"After the things he's said about Dixie? Don't make me laugh."

"Did I steer you wrong about the oil?" I asked.

He shook his head vigorously. "No."

"Then do this my way. Call your local reporter friend. Besides, what's the worst that could happen to you if it doesn't work out?"

"I could lose a job I don't even need anymore," he said with another one of his braying laughs.

"That's right. And this is the payoff I've got coming for the percentage of the lease that I gave you. After this we're even."

"Okay, I'll do it." We rose to leave, and he said, "But maybe I ought to go talk to Crowder myself."

"Oh, you'll talk to Crowder all right. But don't approach him on your own. Let him come to you."

"But what if he don't?"

"He will. I can guarantee you that. And it won't be long, either." I threw my arm around his shoulders. "I've told you before and I'll tell you again . . . we're the good guys in this deal."

He shook his head vigorously. "Don't say that. Like I said, the good guys are clowns. Let's just be the neutral guys in the middle. . . . Okay?"

I laughed. "Ollie, I really like you. You know, Marcus Aurelius said that only a man who's truly noble in character consistently underestimates his own virtues."

"Marcus who?"

"Aurelius."

"Never heard of the guy."

I grinned and slapped him on the back. "That's okay, Ollie. He lived a long, long time ago."

THIRTY-SEVEN

A little before eight o'clock that morning an anonymous phone call reporting a loud argument brought Sweetwater police to the Alamo Plaza Tourist Courts. The best the officers could later determine, four men had left to go to breakfast, only to return sometime later to see their cabin surrounded by police. They abandoned the place, of course. And in doing so they also abandoned two cheap suitcases full of nondescript clothes, a few bottles of whiskey and a duffel bag containing $94,000 from the robbery of the Mercantile State Bank.

That afternoon the cops brought us all back in and grilled us until late in the evening. There were two Rangers present, and they were more thorough in their interrogation than the local cops. They interviewed us separately and they interviewed us as a group, but nothing changed. At last they grew tired of hearing what they already knew, and told us we were free to go.

It turned out to be a busy week for Bob Crowder. The

next day the Attorney General's Office in Austin announced that Clifton Robillard had been arrested and charged with seventeen counts of embezzlement from a state chartered financial institution. It was Crowder who made the arrest. Twenty-four hours later he drove to Dallas, and then flew on to Kansas City. He was gone three days. The newspapers speculated that the trip was related to the robberies that had occurred the previous weekend.

Shortly after returning to town, he and two Dallas FBI men rearrested Clifton Robillard, who had managed to make bail on the embezzlement counts. This time Robillard was jailed on both state and federal charges of bank robbery and suborning a felony.

The following morning Crowder walked into Will Scoggins's inner sanctum, laid a warrant on his desk and told him that he was under arrest for numerous charges of bribery and extortion. Normally in Texas when peace officers are arrested for nonviolent crimes they are not handcuffed and subjected to the public humiliation of being led away in chains. But such was Crowder's contempt for Scoggins that he disarmed and cuffed him and took him out into the street manacled like a common felon.

The robbery of the bank had already brought a number of big-city reporters to town, and word quickly spread among them that the sheriff was to be transported to Sweetwater in neighboring Nolan County for arraignment. When Crowder and Scoggins arrived at the courthouse there, a crowd of newsmen awaited them. The next day pictures of the sheriff in irons graced the front pages of the state's major daily papers. In the *Dallas Morning News* those pictures ran alongside a story that quoted Detective Ollie Marne as saying his office was investigating possible ties between Clifton Robillard and organized criminal elements in the community. On that same front page a shorter article documented the long-standing personal association between the recently jailed Robillard and the recently jailed sheriff. These stories were quickly picked up by the wire services, and the affair was deemed timely enough that reporters for several out-of-state papers, including the *New Orleans Times,* were dispatched to the area. Within days, documentation of Robillard's Buckshot Row connections began to emerge and appear on front pages all across the Southwest. One of the most interesting developments was proof of his outright ownership of one of the most lucrative of the Row's hot-pillow fleabag hotels.

A tastefully written and almost nostalgic account of the history of the Weilbach and its longtime patrons appeared in the *Dallas Times Herald.* The same week a San Antonio daily noted neither for taste nor nostalgia ran a similar article, only this one was much longer and it dwelt on the darker side of the hotel's past. It did further damage to Robillard's reputation by revealing that the "bridge tournament" the now-disgraced sheriff had spoken of was actually a high-stakes poker game that had been going on for decades. Mention was made of the presence of mistresses and call girls in the suite, and the article dwelt at great and vivid length on the amounts of whiskey consumed and the large sums of money that had flowed across the table. A photo of one of the bedrooms appeared with the article, and its caption read, "Millionaire Cattle Barons Gamble, Tryst in Famous Old Hotel." Meanwhile the West Coast tabloids had pounced on the story. A reporter for one of them, a Los Angeles rag called *Whisper,* found Miss Teeny-Tunes, and the band played on.

THIRTY-EIGHT

"Damn," Della said one morning at the breakfast table a week after the robbery. "If I'd known you were having that much fun I would have come up there myself some night."

"It wasn't all that lurid, I promise you."

"Does this mean the end of the legendary Weilback poker game?" she asked.

I shook my head and laughed indulgently. "Of course not. The city will go on a reform bender for a few months, but this business will all blow over and things will be back to normal before you know it."

"But the town will be rid of Will Scoggins."

"Yes, and Clifton Robillard too," I pointed out.

"He's completely disgraced, isn't he, darling?" she asked. "I mean his reputation is absolutely *ruined*."

"It appears that way," I said.

She was up getting us more coffee a few minutes later when the doorbell rang. "I'll get it," she said, and headed off toward the living room. She was back in a matter of seconds with Ollie Marne in tow.

"Well, look what the cat dragged in," I said.

"Sit down, Ollie," Della said. "Would you like some breakfast?"

"That's nice of you," he replied. "But I've already eaten. I might take a cup of coffee, though, if you still have some."

"What brings you calling this early?" I asked.

"Oh, I had a little news I thought you might find interesting."

"Really? What's that?"

He looked at me with his hard, impassive little eyes and smiled his benign, Shmoo-like smile. "Ever heard of a couple of guys named Tobias Perkins and Charles Needam?"

I shook my head. "No. Should I have?"

"Probably not, but I sure as hell know who they are. They're both old-time bank burglars. Master safecrackers, is what I'm talking about."

"Ahhh . . . I see. And you think they did the bank job."

He shook his head. "Nope."

"Then what?" Della asked.

He burst out laughing. "This is a great story, so don't you two hurry me."

We both grinned. "Take your time, Ollie," I said. "Savor it."

"Don't worry. I will," he said. "Perkins has been straight ever since he got out of the pen about ten years ago. Needam? Well, nobody knows for sure about him the last few years, but apparently he's going straight now. See, both these guys are almost sixty, and they're ready for a little peace and quiet. But according to Perkins, about three months back a guy he knows in the outfit up there in Kansas city wanted to give them five hundred dollars each to come down here and talk to a man about a job. That's all . . . Just talk. No strings attached. Perkins knew what kind of job they were talking about, but for him five hundred bucks is nothing to sneeze at. So down they came and who do you think they meet with once they are here?"

"It must have been Clifton Robillard," I said.

"Right you are. And as you probably have also figured out that he wanted them to crack his bank—"

"But why?" Della asked. "That doesn't make any sense at all."

"Sure it does," Marne said. "It was to cover up his embezzlement."

Her mouth hung open for a few moments, then snapped shut. "I got it!" she said excitedly. "The papers said almost three hundred thousand dollars was taken in the robbery, right? But only ninety-four were found at the tourist court in Sweetwater."

"Correct," Marne said. "And the difference between what the books showed was stolen and the amount of money found at Sweetwater is what he embezzled from his own bank."

"Does this happen often?" she asked.

"It's happened a jillion times in the past, even way on back into frontier days. It's harder to pull off these days, but occasionally some rascal like Clifton has a shot at it."

"How did you find out about this, Ollie?" I asked.

"Hell, every cop in town knows about it. That was what Bob Crowder's trip up to Kansas City was all about. You see, Perkins and Needam got to worrying that somebody had seen them with Robillard, and they were afraid the job would be hung on them even though they'd turned him down. So they called Crowder."

"How about the contact up in Kansas City?" I asked.

"He's dead now, but it was a mob hit. They're in the clear on that too, and Clifton Robillard is finished. They're going to testify in court, and Crowder says they'll be fine witnesses. And why not? Hell, what have they got to gain by lying?"

THIRTY-NINE

It was to be our first Christmas together. The previous year my job had taken me to Washington right before the holidays, and I hadn't returned to Memphis until after New Year's. This year we wanted something special. We took the Ford and drove far out into the country hunting a tree. It took a while, but at last we found a dense, perfectly shaped cedar we could both agree on, and hauled it home in the back of the wagon. That evening I put a stack of Christmas carols on the turntable and we got mildly plastered on rum punch and had a ball decorating the tree. Later we made love on the sofa once more, and then fell asleep, our arms and legs twined together, only to waken much later when the fire had burned down and the room had grown chilly. We stumbled off to our bedroom, giggling at ourselves. The next morning Della departed for Dallas on an overnight trip to do her gift shopping, leaving me alone at the breakfast table with my morning coffee. She had no more than rolled out of the drive when I got three phone calls in rapid succession. The first was Ollie Marne inviting us to a Christmas party at his home. The second was from Manlow Rhodes with a similar invitation, this one a dance at the Cottonwood Country Club. The third was from Chicken Little. "We need to talk," I heard his voice say across the distance.

He had business in Fort Worth the next day. I suggested that we meet at Cattleman's Steakhouse, which had just opened that year. He objected on the grounds that it would be too crowded at noontime. We finally settled on Nana's Café, a hole-in-the-wall joint run by Nana Puckett, a woman I'd known for years. Nana was the widow of a once-famous rodeo star named Clyde Puckett, a tiny, acerbic man who'd been the country's top bull rider until a two-thousand-pound Brahman stomped him to death in Phoenix a decade earlier. Her café was only a block from the Stockyards Coliseum, and I'd been there many times.

Like our meeting at the Fan Tan, Little was already waiting for me when I arrived. After the waitress had taken our orders, the old man looked across the table at me with an expression that made me think of the Grim Reaper. "Lum Shamblin is dead," he said.

"Wha—?"

He shook his head sadly. "I couldn't do nothing to stop it."

"Willie?" I asked.

"No. Willie didn't have a thing to do with it. It was woman trouble. Lum had been seeing a married woman. She wasn't but twenty-two, and her husband was about ten years older. He was also mean as hell, from what everybody says. He'd beat her up a few times, and didn't give her much attention nowhere except in the bedroom, so she took to seeing Lum on the side. Then last Friday night her husband give her a really good shellacking, and Lum was able to talk her into leaving and going with him. The husband drove a bread truck for that big bakery there in Tulsa, which meant he left home about four every morning and was gone most of the day. They'd been careful, but he must have suspicioned something. The next Tuesday she and Lum were packing up her things about ten in the morning when he come home unexpected, and shot and killed both of them with a twelve-gauge shotgun."

"It sounds pitiful, and I'm sorry to hear it," I said.

"It was pitiful, and it's left us with problems."

"How so?"

"Lum's momma is old and sick and I think she ought to get his cut, but Willie's raising sand for a three-way split now that Lum is dead. He says the old lady didn't take any of the risk and she's not entitled to any of the money."

"Hell, let her have my share," I said. "Then everybody will be happy."

He shook his head. "No. I don't work that way. That ain't the way we started out to do it, and be damned if I'm going to stray from our appointed course. And there's one other hitch. Willie don't want to wait till after Christmas to get the money."

"But that's what we all agreed on, Little. I was going to bring it up to Tulsa right after the holidays."

"Yeah, I know. But it seems like agreements don't mean too much to him no more. If I'd knowed he was going to be such an aggravation I wouldn't have brought him in on this business in the first place."

"It's not your fault," I said. "I checked him out myself, and from what I heard he's solid."

"Oh, he is," Little said. "During the job itself you couldn't want nobody better, but he's got to where he's a damn squirrel the rest of the time. See, my whole reason for putting the money in the well in the first place is that the heat's always the worst the first couple of days. It's been my policy to get rid of everything that can tie me to a job as soon as possible. Then you can go back in a week or a month or even a year if you have to, and pick it up. But he didn't like doing that from the start."

"It was the smart way to do it. With the bank job they could have had roadblocks all over the county, and there we would have been. They would have searched an out-of-state car for certain."

"Yeah, and this was my last job, no doubt about it, and I wasn't about to take chances. Hell, if it wasn't for the principle of the thing, I'd tell him where the money is and let him go get it. I've got more than enough for me and Annie to live on from here on out. But I be damned if I'm going to let him strong-arm me this late in life. Besides, there's something else about him that's worrying me."

"Yeah?"

He nodded. "It's a story I heard a little while back, and I believe it, because the old boy that told me about it don't lie. Anyhow, he said that about three years ago Willie done a little five-year-old girl."

"You've got to be joking. . . ."

"I wish I was," he said, shaking his head sadly.

"But why?"

"Money. Pretty big money. A bunch of bootleggers wanted to scare the hell out of a guy, a jeweler in Little Rock that was gonna testify against one of them in a murder case.

He had four kids and this was supposed to show him what would happen to all of them if he didn't keep his mouth shut."

"Who was behind it? The Kansas City outfit?"

"Oh, hell no. The Dagos won't mess with nobody's family, and especially not with their kids. It was a bunch of white trash peckerwoods out of the Mississippi Delta."

"And Willie did it for sure?"

"Yeah, he done it all right enough."

"Then we can't let him have all the money now," I said. "We'd just look weak, and there's no telling what he might come back on us with later on."

The waitress came with our food, and we ate our meal in near silence. Finally the old man looked across the table at me with a sad expression on his face. "I hate for something like this to come up," he said. "And I hate that I put you in this position. Fifteen or so years ago, back when I first met Willie, he was a lot different. I don't know what happened to him, but in them days he wouldn't have done nothing like that little girl. Like I said, he just got to where he liked killing too much."

"Forget it," I said. "We've been friends too long for you to think you have to apologize when you've done your best."

"Son, I'm awful glad you feel that way."

"Then what do you think we ought do? . . ." I asked.

"Well, I guess we could just tell him to go to hell," Little said. "Then you bring it on up to Tulsa after the holidays like we planned."

I shook my head. "No. Let's compromise with him. There's really no reason not to go ahead and get the money and split it up before Christmas. That's apparently the only thing that will shut him up."

"If you're sure you want to do it like that. It could be dangerous. Willie don't like you, and he may have ideas."

"I'm aware of that, and I think we ought to be prepared," I said.

He smiled a grim smile and nodded. "Don't worry. We will be."

"Good. Why don't the two of you meet me in front of that newsstand on Roosevelt at five o'clock on the evening of the twenty-third."

"We'll be there," he said. "And by the way . . . Tobe wanted me to tell you that the take from that job was almost three hundred thousand."

"I know you must have wondered about the money found in Sweetwater," I said. "I'll give you the whole story when we come up after Christmas," I said.

"You can if you want to. It's none of my business, and I wouldn't have mentioned it except that he asked me to. He also wanted you to know it was a pleasure doing business with you."

"Tell him the pleasure was all mine."

A short while later we stood and shook hands, and then I watched Chicken Little leave the café, a trim, erect old man in his neat gray suit and snappy fedora.

FORTY

As Little and I had agreed, they picked me up in front of the newsstand on Roosevelt Avenue at five on the evening of the twenty-third. They were in the old man's black Ford two-door sedan with Willie at the wheel and Little in the front passenger seat. I was lost in my thoughts when Willie broke the silence. "Hey! You got a big Christmas planned?" he asked. I looked up to see his muddy eyes dancing beneath the bill of his seedy cap as he gazed into the rearview mirror.

"Not really," I replied. "I'm not big on celebrations."

"That's a shame," he said. "What are you going to do with your share of the money?"

"I don't know. Buy some oil leases, I guess."

"Oh, ho!! Going into business, huh? Not me. I'm gonna have fun with mine."

"Just how does a man like you have fun, Willie?" I asked.

He'd been watching me in the mirror when suddenly the right tires began throwing up gravel as he let the car drift onto the shoulder of the road. He quickly whipped the wheel and the Ford swerved back up on the highway.

"Shut up and drive the damn car," Little said. "You go to fooling around and you're liable to get us all killed."

"I just want to have a conversation here," Willie said angrily. "You know, a little exchange of opinions."

"We don't need no conversation," Little replied.

Willie was quiet until we reached the place where we turned off onto the county road. Then I heard that private little laugh of his, and it sounded like it came from an empty room. "You asked what I do for fun," he said. "Well, I like to watch."

"Watch what?" I asked in spite of myself.

"Whatever's going on. I'm a big watcher."

"You shouldn't need much money for that," I observed.

He gave me a throaty chuckle this time, and once again I could see his eyes darting around in the mirror. "It depends on what you wanna watch and where you go to watch it. The more classy your tastes are, the more it costs."

"Willie, just be quiet and pay attention to the road," Little told him. "You keep this up and you'll have a wreck, I tell you."

"I happen to think some good talk spices up a drive in the country," Willie said, glaring over at the old man. "That's all."

"We can do without the spice right now," Little replied.

Willie fell silent for a few seconds, then began humming some melody off-key while he patted the wheel in slow time to the music. Finally I recognized the tune as "Nearer My God to Thee," and I felt like laughing.

"Is that your favorite hymn?" I asked.

"Yeah!" he said, his eyes reappearing in the mirror. "Ain't it great?" He lapsed back into silence for a couple of minutes, then resumed his humming. The little Ford sped along toward the setting sun through a bleak and frozen land. The scrub oaks in the creek bottoms were bare and lifeless and the pastures had been grazed down to the quick. We passed through a field that must have held a thousand acres of ranked cotton stubble that hadn't gotten over a foot high before the drought hit. Off to one side of the road I caught a glimpse of a coyote shivering on the crest of a low bluff, its coarse, ratty fur ruffled by the icy wind. Ahead, the dull orange orb of the sun looked cold and depleted as if the dead earth had sucked the very life from it. Darkness would be falling soon, and with it would come the end of the day.

"You don't talk much, big guy," Willie said at last. "You're as bad as Chicken Little here."

"What's there to talk about?" I asked.

Willie chuckled once again.

"Here's the turnoff, Willie," Little said. "You almost missed it fooling around. You need to keep your mind on business and look where you're driving."

We pulled up behind the old house just as the sun began to drop below the horizon. Willie killed the engine and we climbed from the car.

"Get the keys and open the trunk," Little told him.

Once the trunk lid was up, Willie stepped back away from the vehicle. "Go on and get the magnet out," Little said, exasperation beginning to creep into his voice. "Do I have to tell you everything?"

"I guess I'm thinking about other things," Willie said as he leaned over into the yawning trunk of the Ford. He jerked and tugged at something back in its far recesses for a few moments, then straightened up. "Damn it! It's stuck in there."

"What?" Little asked.

"It's too damn strong. It's stuck to the floor of the car."

"If it wasn't strong it wouldn't pull that sack and that fourteen-pound weight out of the bottom of the well," Little explained patiently. "Can't you understand nothing?"

"Move over and let me get it," I told Willie. As I turned my back to him the hair on the nape of my neck tried to stand up on end. Near the rear of the compartment sat a large industrial magnet. An eyelet had been affixed to a semicircular handle that was cast into its top. A short length of heavy chain that ended in a coil of half-inch rope was fastened to the eyelet with a spring-loaded clasp. I reached in and easily jerked the magnet loose with one hand, then hauled it and the coil of rope out of the trunk.

"Goddamn!" Icepick Willie said with a shiver. "Let's get moving and get that money out of that damned well. It's cold out here."

"Don't take the Lord's name in vain, Willie," Little admonished. "I've told you that kind of talk don't do a man no good at all."

"Shit," Willie said to nobody in particular. He looked off at the horizon, his face drawn up like a sullen child's. "I hate cold weather."

"You got the key?" Little asked me.

"No," I replied after feeling around in my pockets.

"Shit!" Willie blurted once again, wheeling around to glare at me. "If this ain't turning into a hell of a mess. First the magnet gets stuck, and now we got no key. I don't see why we didn't bring a bunch of damned Chinamen along to really clabber things up."

"Settle down and don't pitch a fit, Willie," Little told him. "Just get the tire iron out of the trunk and we'll bust the lock open."

Willie bumbled around behind the Ford until he finally managed to unfasten the tire iron from the clamp that held it to the jack. Once he'd pulled it from the trunk, he trotted over to the well and slipped its tip under the hasp. Then he put his shoulder under the end of the iron and heaved upward. The screws that held the hasp to the wood gave way with a loud creak and the well was open.

"See how easy that was?" Little asked.

"Shit," Willie announced once again.

"Why don't you go fish that sack out?" Little asked me quietly. "His mind is somewhere else, and he's liable to drop the whole business in the well, magnet and all, and then we really will be in a fix."

I held the magnet over the side of the curb and began to uncoil the rope. The well was only about thirty feet deep and it didn't take long for the magnet to hit the water. It took me a couple of minutes of probing around, picking the magnet up and moving it until at last I came close enough to the steel disc inside the bag. Finally I felt a tug at the rope as the disc and the magnet made contact. Slowly I began drawing up the rope. Finally the bag came up and I dropped it on the ground. By putting my foot on the sack I was able to tug the magnet loose and then unseal the first bag. I pulled out the second bag and threw it over at Little's feet.

"Hot damn!" Willie said, rubbing his hands together gleefully. "Let's split it up."

"Not out here," Little told him. "We'll go up to Sweetwater and get a room in a tourist court where it's nice and warm, and then we'll count it out and divide it."

"I don't like that idea," Willie said with a sly grin and slipped his hands into his coat pockets.

"Well, I like it," Little said. "And that's the way we're going to do it. There's something else we may as well air out while we're on the subject. Lum's momma is going to get his cut, and there ain't no use arguing about it."

"Oh, ho ho," Willie chuckled. "I got a better plan. How about we do a one-way split? Then we won't need to do no counting."

Little's face was grim beneath the edge of his fedora. "Now, why don't it surprise me that you'd come up with a notion like that?" he asked rhetorically.

Willie glanced at me and winked. I shook my head, and said, "Better back away from it, Willie."

"And you better zip it shut, city boy," he growled as he pulled a .45 automatic smoothly from his overcoat pocket and pointed it at us. His big, blurry face held a happy grin and his swampy eyes danced. "The first time we met, I told you payday was gonna come someday."

"I'm sorry it's come to this, Willie," Chicken Little said. "I could overlook some of the other stuff you done, much as I hate it. But I got no use for a man that turns on his own partners. There ain't no place for him in this world. Maybe not in the next one, neither."

"Well, who in the hell are you to be so high and mighty,

Chicken Little? You ain't nothing but a damned old Okie
moonshiner."

"Maybe not, but my word's good."

"It ain't gonna be for much longer," Wille said. He
pointed the gun at Little and pulled the trigger only to
have the hammer fall against the firing pin with a dull
click. He looked down at the .45 for a moment as though
he'd never seen it before, then quickly jerked the slide back
and fed a fresh cartridge into the chamber. Aiming at me
this time, he squeezed the trigger a second time with no
better results. "You gave me a damn gun that don't work!"
he bellowed.

"The gun works fine, Willie," the old man said, and
pulled his own old Colt Pocket Auto from his shoulder holster. A silencer appeared in his left hand and he began to
screw it carefully onto the Colt's barrel. "I just took the
powder out of them cartridges about a week ago. That's
one of them little things I keep trying to tell you about. You
don't never pay no attention to the little things."

Willie crouched there beside the old abandoned house in
the falling darkness while he worked the pistol's action and
squeezed the trigger again and again, aiming first at Little
and then at me, back and forth, until the gun was empty. He
stared at it for a moment with an expression of sick bewil-
derment on his face, then raised his head to glare at us with
eyes that were growing wide with fear. An icy wind had
been blowing earlier, but it had lain with the sunset, and
now a deathly stillness reigned. In the west a band of fading
crimson marked the place where the sun had dropped below the horizon, and beneath it the cold, desolate land was

passing quickly into night. For a few moments the whole earth seemed to hang suspended in silence, and then I heard Little's voice, low and apologetic. "I know it's a hell of a note, but we ain't got a shovel."

"That's okay," I said. "We'll just throw the body down the well."

FORTY-ONE

When I came into the house I found Della reading on the living room sofa. She laid her book aside, and when she saw her eyes widened. "What happened?" she asked. "And where on earth have you been? I was worried to death."

"Later," I said. "I'll tell you later."

I went in the kitchen and filled a glass with ice cubes, then poured a generous measure of scotch over them. After I tool a long pull of the drink, I refilled the glass from the bottle, and then went back through the living room on my way to the bedroom. Della followed me, a look of confusion on her face.

"What's wrong?" she asked.

"Nothing now," I replied, and began stripping off my clothes. "Everything's fine now."

"Do you need anything?" she asked.

"Yeah. I'm going to take a quick shower." I threw the bag on the bed.

"Okay," she muttered, an expressions of pure confusion on her face.

I went into the bathroom and shut the door. It only took

me about ten minutes, but hot water had never felt better. Once I'd toweled dry and brushed my teeth, I threw on my bathrobe and drained the last of my drink. Della was in her black robe, and she'd been into the scotch herself.

"Now I feel much better," I said with a warm smile as I picked up the bag. "Finish your drink," I told her.

She downed the last of the scotch, and then came that delightful little wriggle she always used when she dropped the robe to the floor. I gave her a long, tender kiss and then picked her up and dropped her in the middle of the bed.

Neither of us had eaten since early that morning. Once more Della cooked bacon and eggs and we had a late-night supper on the coffee table in the living room. When I finished the last bite, I stretched out on the sofa. "I guess it's time to tell you the whole story," I said.

"If you want," she replied. "I've never said that you have to."

"I do want to," I said, and then went on to relate how Clifton Robillard, who in 1936 was little more than a deadbeat hanger-on with the American Bankers Association's delegation to Germany, had been approached by one of Reinhard Heydrich's agents, and how he'd given this agent a favorable response and then been taken to a private meeting with Heydrich himself two days later.

"Eventually he became Heydrich's paymaster for the whole southwestern United States," I said. "He helped the Nazis transfer and route millions of dollars into this country and into the pockets of German agents. In doing so, he was responsible for the death of a half dozen good men, including one of our own."

"What happened to him?"

"He was tortured to death by Heydrich's agents."

She grimaced. "Then Robillard was a Nazi," she said.

I shook my head. "No, he was just an opportunist. Men like him really don't have any politics beyond personal profit. I'm sure he wasn't the only one they had their eyes on, but the Germans had good intelligence in this country, and they'd done their research well. They knew that he'd lost the bulk of his fortune in the Crash of '29, and that he was willing to do just about anything to get it back."

"You must have found out about all this while you were with the OSS," Della said. "But I've read that it only operated abroad."

"We were supposed to only operate abroad, but that distinction sometimes got blurred. Heydrich was dead by then, assassinated by Czech partisans who'd been trained and sent in by the British. But his sabotage organization was still very much alive."

"I thought that the FBI was responsible for catching spies and all that sort of thing," she said.

I laughed softly. "So did they, but we operated domestically, too. Very carefully, you may be sure, but we were active inside the country. We were better at it than they were. At least up until 1944 we were, and by that time Heydrich's organization was out of business. You see, a counterintelligence outfit needs a good network of informants, and the Bureau has never been strong in that respect. That's how I came to meet Col. Homer Garrison. Bill Donovan knew him from way back, and he was able to help us quite a bit. He had about fifty Rangers plus two hundred Highway Patrolmen. Many of those men had come from city police departments, and they all had their old informants to fall back on. Plus, about twenty retired Rangers were working as company detectives and security chiefs and what-not for oil companies and chemical firms down on the coast. We got a lot of good information through Garrison's men."

"What did you do with these German agents when you caught them?"

"We didn't really catch them because we didn't have any power to arrest anybody. Most of them we turned them over to the FBI. Ironic, isn't it? But you need to realize that the Bureau has a lot of good field agents, even if Hoover is an ass. We fingered one gang down in Louisiana for the Secret Service. They were a part of a Nazi scheme to undermine the economy financially by flooding the country with counterfeit money."

"But why didn't the government just prosecute Robillard?" she asked. "The man was a traitor, after all."

"Yes, and a very smart one. About the time that Heydrich's organization collapsed in 1943, Mercantile Bank had a new fireproof storage room built for all its records. Amazingly, they'd just transferred their current notes and mortgages and so forth into this vault when a fire broke out one night in the old record room. All the bank's records going back to the turn of the century were destroyed, including the information it would have taken to convict Robillard. So from that point on, the government simply didn't have the evidence necessary to be sure of a conviction, and for political reasons the attorney general felt that they couldn't risk an acquittal. And there were other considerations. Robillard was a political ally of Governor Stevenson, who was openly opposed to Roosevelt and the New Deal. If the Justice Department had gone after Robillard and the case had fallen apart in court, it would have looked like the president was trying to embarrass a critic, and destroying a man's reputation to do it. And now I want another drink."

I started to rise from the sofa, but she stopped me. "I'll get us both one."

She was soon back with two large glasses of scotch and soda. She set both drinks on the coffee table and resumed her place on the floor. "This is an awful lot to digest," she said.

"I know. But you can see why we couldn't let a man like him get away scot-free. Originally we'd intended to have him taken hostage instead of me when the poker game was robbed, and then Little was going to kill him and leave him in that building where the robbery car was found. But when Colonel Garrison called me and told me about the embezzlement I got the idea of having the bank burgled and framing him for it instead. I found the idea of him rotting away in federal prison for the rest of his life considerably more appealing than a quick bullet in the brain, to tell you the truth."

"But if he would have gone to prison for the embezzlement anyway, then why bother? . . ." she began.

"On state embezzlement charges he could have proven that he'd made restitution and been out in seven years. In fact, he might have even gotten probation, considering that he'd once been a state senator."

"But if it was a state chartered bank I don't see how the federal government can—"

"Don't you read the papers?" I asked with a grin.

"The papers? What have the newspapers got to do with it?"

"They've carried several stories in the last few months about Mercantile Bank applying to join Federal Deposit Insurance System. Federal insurance went into effect back on the fifteenth of November, making robbery of the bank a federal offense. Which is why I had to wait so long to pull this off. And it's also why Robillard was cash poor back when I won that big bet from him at the cockfight. He was using his oil royalties to replace the money he'd pilfered, and he was trying to get it all shoveled back in before the bank fell under federal scrutiny."

"But why did he join the federal system if he'd been embezzling?" she asked.

"Robillard doesn't own the bank, Della. He's just the largest stockholder. And the board overrode his objections and voted to join."

"But I still don't see how he can be convicted of bank robbery," she said.

"It's simple. Perkins and Needam will testify that he tried to engage them to rob the bank just a couple of months before the bank was actually robbed. It's a logical assumption that he went to somebody else when they turned him down."

"It may be logical," she objected, "but proving it in court is another matter."

I couldn't help but smile at her indulgently. "Della, all the time you hear people talk about proving stuff in court, but you really don't have to prove anything. All you have to do is convince a jury."

She opened her mouth as if to say something, then snapped it shut and we were silent for a couple of minutes. Finally she asked, "Was this a government operation?"

I sighed and shrugged. "Sometimes there aren't any clear yes-and-no answers to a question like that. It started out as a scheme dreamed up by me and a couple of guys I worked with during the war, one of them a friend from college I'd later served with in the navy. It was financed with government money, and nobody in the government who knew about it objected to what we were doing, so I really don't know the answer to your question."

"You must feel very satisfied that it all came off so well," she said.

"What makes me feel most satisfied is that he really had paid the money back to the bank. But like Ollie Marne said, the embezzlement gives him the strongest motive in the world for the robbery. Add that to the discrepancy between what the books showed as cash-on-hand and what was actually recovered . . ." I stopped and smiled at her. "Beautiful, isn't it?"

"But why did he embezzle the money in the first place? After all, he really is a wealthy man."

"Yes, but he was heavily in debt when the Coby Smith well came in, and his lines of credit were about tapped out. So when Van Horn offered to let him go in on some oil deals, he just swiped the money he needed to invest from his own bank with every intention of paying it back as soon as he could. The burglars actually got almost three hundred thousand that night, but—"

"But everybody assumed," she said, finishing my thought for me, "that the ninety-four thousand found up at Sweetwater was the whole haul from the robbery."

"Right."

"But didn't it seem a little careless for the robbers to be going off to breakfast and leaving the money in the cabin?"

"Maybe, but criminals do dumb things like that all the time," I replied. "That's why the prisons are full. Besides, the anonymous call to the police said they were drunk and arguing, and who knows what drunks will do?"

"Neat," she said.

"And in addition to all Robillard's other legal problems, Ollie Marne told me yesterday that the IRS is looking into his finances."

We finished our drinks and set our glasses on the coffee table. I stretched back out on the sofa, and she lay down beside me, her head on my chest.

"Della?" I asked after we'd lain there a few minutes.

"Hmmmm?" she said without looking up.

"I love you."

She raised her head and propped her chin on my breast bone, then regarded me thoughtfully. "It's about time you told me," she said softly, and lay back down on my chest.

FORTY-TWO

On the morning of Christmas Eve I found myself in a typically male predicament: I hadn't yet shopped for Della. I was afraid I would have to make a daylong trip to Dallas, but I found what I wanted only a block from the Weilbach. The next morning we unwrapped our gifts. She had bought me several things—too much in fact, while I had only bought her one gift. It was what she wanted but would never have mentioned. Three carats, pure white, surrounded by smaller stones and set in gold. "Which finger do I wear it on?" she asked.

"I was hoping you'd be willing to put it on the third finger of your left hand."

She slipped the ring on her ring finger and kissed me and that was all we said on the subject.

Della was a good cook, one who believed in the traditional holiday turkey with dressing and all the trimmings. She was in the kitchen most of the morning, and we spent the rest of the day in a pleasant, overfed lethargy. After the New Year came we drove northward to Oklahoma and spent three days with Little and Annie. Each morning we rose to a big country breakfast, and in the evenings we sat by the fireplace in the living room and drank corn whiskey and listened to the radio. One evening we heard a live broadcast of Bob Wills and the Texas Playboys, returned after many years' absence to play at Cain's Ballroom in Tulsa.

When we started to leave I tried to get Little to take my share of the money and split it with Lum Shamblin's mother, but he refused. "That would be straying from my appointed course," he explained. "And I done did that once in my life to my own regret."

"What if you were to just give her my whole share?" I asked. "I've got a feeling that I don't need to keep any of this money. A strong feeling."

"I can do that," he said with a nod, giving me a quizzical look. "You ain't getting superstitious on me, are you?"

"Let's say I'm convinced that keeping it would be straying from my appointed course."

That was something he could understand. He nodded and shook my hand. "She'll get every penny," he promised.

"I know she will," I replied, and climbed behind the wheel.

We bought a house near the park in Tyler and joined the country club and settled into the comfortable life of the small-town wealthy. I rented an office downtown in the Peoples' Bank Building and pretended to practice law. Della had a cubbyhole there where she managed our investments. In the early '50s she plunged heavily into IBM and we grew even richer.

During those years we traveled all over the world and made a trip to Europe almost every fall. Occasionally we went back out to West Texas. The town changed over the years, and not all the changes were for the better. The Weilbach went broke in the late '50s and stood boarded up for years. Eventually the local historical society got title to the place and the last I heard they were trying to raise money to convert it into a combination museum and flea market. Whatever its fate, it will never again be the glittering place it was in the days of the Donner Basin Boom.

Except for Andy and Mona Wolfe, most of the people we knew from those days are dead now. Sheriff Will Scoggins's case was moved to Sweetwater on a change of venue. He hired a flamboyant El Paso criminal lawyer named Durwood Kean, and went to trial in the late spring not long after we left town. Kean mounted a spirited defense, but no one who watched the trial had any doubt what the jury's verdict would be. Scoggins would be going away for a very long time. The final arguments ended on a Friday afternoon, but the judge decided to wait until Monday to charge the jury and send them out for their deliberations.

It was Scoggins's last weekend of freedom, and he and everybody else knew it. In those days Texas prisons didn't segregate convicted cops in their own units as they do today. They were thrown in with the general population, something that was tantamount to a death sentence in his case. Early Saturday morning he sent his wife to her sister's house for the weekend. That evening he sat in his den brooding and drinking Seagram's Seven straight from the bottle. When the bottle was almost empty, he took his long-barreled Smith & Wesson from its holster, put it to his right temple and blew what few brains he had all over the room. Ollie Marne, who knew Scoggins's history well, later told me that if you consider that by pulling that trigger he rid the county of one of its biggest thieves, you soon realize it was the only time in his long career that he fired a shot in the line of duty.

Chicken Little lived twelve more years, and Della and I visited him and Annie almost every spring. At last, at age eighty-two, his heart simply quit beating as he sat on his front porch one afternoon in early summer. Annie found him slumped there in his chair, an empty toddy mug in his hand, and the best she could determine, he'd died about the same time the sun set over the Cimarron River. She only survived him by three years, and they're buried side by side in a little churchyard cemetery in the Cookson Hills not a mile from where he was born. Manlow Rhodes thrived for two more decades and managed the bank up until the day he went in the hospital to die of pancreatic cancer. I was a pallbearer at all three of their funerals.

Zip Zimmerman and his redheaded mistress were killed in a car wreck just a couple of years after we left town. Wilburn Rasco and Howard Northcutt both died of natural causes before a decade had passed, and Captain Bob Crowder was felled by heart attack in 1972 after a long and distinguished career with the Rangers. And I heard just last month that Simon Van Horn was still alive in Fillmore, but that he'd become something of a recluse, old and rich beyond imagining.

As I'd once told Ollie Marne, the 2 percent interest in the Havel lease never made him wealthy, but it made him comfortable and independent, and it sent his little girl to the University of Texas. After we left town, Ollie quit the Sheriff's Department and banged around the house for a few months, getting in his wife's way every time she turned a corner. Neither a reader nor a homebody, he was at loose ends. Finally he asked for his old job back. About five years after we left town he was killed in a shootout with a pair of robbers in the lobby of the Farmers and Merchants National Bank. Manlow Rhodes told me that he took a bullet he didn't have to take, and thereby saved a customer's life. I hope Ollie had time to laugh at himself before he died. He always did say the good guys were clowns.

After several months of legal wrangling, Clifton Robillard finally pled guilty to embezzlement in state court, maintaining all the while that he had returned every penny of the money in the weeks before the robbery. No doubt he was telling the truth, but the fact that only $94,000 had been found in the room at the Alamo Plaza made his contention appear ludicrous. The judge, unimpressed by his attorney's appeal for mercy, gave him twenty-five years. The newspapers reported that he wept when he heard the sentence.

But his troubles were far from over. The federal prosecutor had him hauled out to El Paso on a bench warrant where he faced charges of bank robbery, conspiracy to commit bank robbery, and suborning a felony in violation of the federal penal code.

Tobe Perkins and Charlie Needam earned their money; on the stand they proved to be credible witnesses, and the jury bought their story. Robillard was found guilty on all three counts, which resulted in a total sentence of thirty years. Since federal law supercedes state law, the federal time would be served first.

Bob Crowder rode along with the two deputy U.S. Marshals who took him to prison. Years later he told me about that trip. It was a cold day in December of 1948, and the sky was gray as iron. A light sleet started falling just as they crossed the Kansas state line, icing up the roads and slowing traffic to the point that the last thirty miles took better than an hour to cover. Crowder said that the prisoner gasped when he saw the great walls of the Leavenworth Prison looming dark and grim on the horizon. The guard at the entry examined their papers, then picked up his telephone. A few seconds later the gates swung open to give Clifton Robillard his first glimpse of the harsh, pitiless world in which he would spend his final years on this earth.